Riley Craig was born in Scotland and lives there with her partner and their many pets now. The animals made their presence known during the hours it took in the creation of this work by resting on her lap or by her feet. Growing up, she developed a fascination with the horror and thriller genre, a love which continues to this day. *The Outcast* is her first book.

I would like to dedicate this book to the two women in my life who supported me throughout the process of writing my first novel.

To Zoe and Emily XX

# Riley Craig

## THE OUTCAST

# AUSTIN MACAULEY PUBLISHERS

LONDON * CAMBRIDGE * NEW YORK * SHARJAH

A CIP catalogue record for this title is available from the British Library.

ISBN 9781037110306 (Paperback)
ISBN 9781037110313 (ePub e-book)

www.austinmacauley.com

First Published 2025
Austin Macauley Publishers Ltd®
1 Canada Square
Canary Wharf
London
E14 5AA

I would like to thank everyone at Austin Macauley Publishers for their dedicated work in making this book become a reality for me. And for their trust in a first-time author.

# Chapter One

Up in the tower, the bell was finishing its cycle. It was twelve o'clock and outside, the December morning light was dimming. A swirl of red etched itself against the paling blue sky, breaking through a line of clouds. Down below in the chilled and hollow air of the bell chamber, Charlie Rose's head swayed painfully, almost in sync to the unfeeling rhythm. The notes grew louder with each chime, striking hard with a precise aim.

Between the bellow of rings eight and nine, his focus was stolen by blurred images and he thrashed to see what was flashing across his mind. A foreign feeling took hold of him. He was lying down, not on his soft warm bed back home but hard steel with an almost clinical feel to it. Shifting shadows surrounded him in the clouded air.

Circling.

Stalking.

Preying.

And then, nothing. He was alone in the darkness, not even the beastly shadows remained.

Struggling to maintain his grip on the rope, he fought off the urge to surrender to the vision, pushing it away. Burying it within himself. The blurs faded and his mind settled, but the ringing of the bells continued with their onslaught. His fingers curled tighter, causing the rope to dig into his palms. By the time the air had calmed and the bell grew still, first blood had been drawn.

With the sound of footsteps approaching and his fragile body now shaking, he hurriedly stuck both hands into the pockets of his freshly ironed pants and swished them around to wipe away the evidence. One more stain on his church clothes and he would be spanked till his ass was raw. An extra-large bauble would hang on the Christmas tree this year.

He told himself he was safe. His parents wouldn't go so far as to actually look inside the pockets.

*Surely.*
*Definitely.*
*Maybe.*

The door creaked open and more than a moment passed before a man, with a body that mirrored his age, appeared. Light came down the tower's shaft and shone harshly on his weathered face. A lifetime spent in the dark lure of the pulpit had corrupted his features, once fresh and fruitful but now only a landscape of scarred craters and ruined trenches remained.

"Ah, Charlie, that was a very good first try. You have good strong arms for a boy your age. I shall inform your parents of my intention to make this a permanent position. Would you like that?" Father Adam Stringer asked, his diminished eyes trying to catch Charlie's but failing.

"W-w-we-well, I'm n—"

"Excellent, m'boy; you'll make a fine bell-ringer," Father Stringer interrupted without pausing for breath. "You can make your official debut this coming Sunday. If your excitement can wait three days, I know your mother, in particular, shall rejoice at the news."

"I dare say she has worried about your direction in life, with good reason too, I might add. But in serving the church, you shall follow the path of the Almighty and be welcomed into the graceful arms of the eternal one in this life and the next." A toothless smile broke across his crusted mouth. "Now, I gather that your family are traveling for the holidays, is that correct?"

"Y-yes, we le-eave on Monday. For my aunt E-e-eve's." He struggled to get the words out, his ears still ringing.

"Ah yes, I remember Eve well. Fine woman. Loyal to the church all her life, as is your mother, and I hope, as you will be too."

"Y-y-yes, F-f-father," he answered politely but failing to put any real motivation behind the words.

His parents had been dragging him to church since before he could remember and he had never liked it. Everything about the place made his stomach queasy and his mind hazy.

The windowpanes that shuddered even in a light breeze, the ceiling that seemed to stretch on forever as if reaching up to the heavens themselves, the clammy smell of the masses as they herded themselves in like cattle, and most of all, the feeling of fear and shame that rose within him as he was forced to listen to Father Stringer's raving sermons. Now, he could add the bell chamber as a reason to give the place a wide berth. Sadly, a berth that would never come to pass, it seemed.

The idea of being a bell-ringer seemed cool when his mother had first asked, suggested, pushed, forced; but now that initial reaction had dulled, giving way to a jittery panic. Thinking about subjecting his senses to that kind of attack every Sunday made his chest swell and deflate in a sweated loop.

"Come Charlie, your parents are out in the main hall; let's go give them the splendid news. Thanks to you, your family will now be able to sit front and centre on Sundays. You'll have the best view in the house. This is an honourable position, m'boy, one not so easily squandered.

"Now then, you lead the way; my balance isn't what it used to be, I'm afraid, so I'll just rest this here."

They exited the chamber together, Charlie slowing his normal pace as Father Stringer placed one arm around him. He could feel every rigid, cloying bone as they imprinted themselves on his shoulder. The hard, bitter nails grazed curiously around the silky flesh of his collarbone. Old sins cast long shadows and Charlie was dwarfed under his.

His parents were by the main door at the far end of the room, standing apart. Heaven and earth could have comfortably slotted in the gap they were creating. Charlie was beginning to notice they had a real knack for distance. His mother, Mary, rocked on the spot with a rabid eagerness dawning behind her eyes when she saw the jovial pair approaching.

His father, Michael, stood placidly ajar with arms crossed just below the ribs. From his cheeks, Charlie could tell he was running his tongue around the inside of his mouth. That was never a good sign. Even in church, they had brought their troubles with them; but then again, isn't that the whole point of church? Charlie mused. You can't unburden yourself if you leave your troubles at home.

"Your son has done a fine job. We are both pleased to announce he shall be my new bell-ringer."

"Oh, thank you, Father. I cannot tell you what this news means to us," Mary quipped excitedly with a nodding gesture to her husband, who simply let his shoulders rise and dip at the news.

She had donned a pair of beige half-moon glasses that always slid down the bridge of her nose. She only readjusted them whenever she had some reprimanding to do. She may cast a meek shadow but she was intimidating nonetheless when the mood struck her, spitting with her unmistakable hiss.

After a widening-eye look from Mary, Mike too thanked Father Stringer. He was a gardener who could count on one hand the amount of new business he had received over the years. He never involved Mary in his business affairs and he was too lazy to spend time speculating on ideas that would bring in additional customers. Very few of his thoughts were purely his own but the ones that were, resounded with a selfish bell.

"Think nothing of it. The previous boy I had for the job was becoming too lacklustre about the whole affair. No, what I need is a boy with a special something about him. Isn't that right, Charlie?"

"I g-g-uess so," Charlie answered, squashing his fear beneath his need for approval. A tug of war where the odds were always stacked against him. Standing beneath Father Stringer's ghostly figure, he could still feel the rope burn against his soft skin.

They headed outside into the crisp afternoon glow, a storm was reported to be speeding in their direction but in that moment, a calm sky was all that stretched above them. Charlie held in a groan as Father Stringer finally relented the pressure and released him into the free air. His shoulders cracked and something shifted beneath the surface of his juvenile bones.

"So, now that he has passed the audition, so to speak, Sunday will be his first official performance. And then, I gather I am losing him until after the New Year has broken?"

"Yes, my sister has asked us to spend the holidays with them and help out with the new baby. This will be her third," Mary said as Mike and Charlie seized the opportunity and headed for the gate.

"Dad, c-c-can I go o-o-ver to Nick's af-fter lunch?"

"I suppose so, I doubt your mother would object to it today. You becoming Father Stringer's new favourite should keep her happy for a while," he answered, silently hoping that *for a while* meant *forever*. "Just remember to change out of your church clothes first."

# Chapter Two

—

With a stomach full of cold instant mash and re-heated chicken nuggets, Charlie made his way over to Nick's house, swinging his arms wildly as if they were two jet planes soaring through the air in a madcap dogfight. He didn't understand how planes could have a dogfight but it was fun to pretend to be them; so, who was he too judge?

It was obvious to everyone who met his sweet soul that Charlie Rose was a fairly naïve little boy of twelve. Simple was the word that Violet Finch from across the road had spread around town when she, rooted in her worn-out position behind her equally worn-out curtains, saw him building a nest made out of discarded cigarette butts for a smooshed beetle he found by a drain cover at the end of his driveway.

This quickly got back to his mother who, after turning a shade of red known only among the juiciest apples, had taken Charlie aside, struggling to look into his eyes and very calmly told him:

"Don't you ever do anything like that again! Did you not hear me the last time I pulled you aside after your hijinks humiliated me? Jeez, Charlie. Work with me here. I am trying my best to create an image for this family and you're going around acting like you're blind to that. Is that what you are, Charlie? Deaf, dumb and blind?"

Charlie had fallen asleep that night with a tear-stained face and thinking of the beetle who, thanks to Mother knows best, now resided at the bottom of the trashcan (*where all vermin belong*) in the back garden. He told himself the tears were for Mr Beetle (or Miss, he had never gotten that close an inspection), but even he didn't believe that story. Almost always, he cried for himself.

Charlie arrived at Nick's house and found him already in the garden by the foot of the treehouse. Nick and his older brother had spent two very long afternoons building the *damn* thing one summer when Todd was home from college.

During the holidays, the treehouse was Todd's domain. He would always brag to his pre-teen brother about the scores of lucky ladies who had followed him home; though Nick seldom saw more than Todd's own shadow accompany him through the swing latch and into the *love nest,* but his brother stood firm.

Nick shuddered at the type of girl who was turned on by rickety ladders, rugs stained with orange juice (courtesy of Charlie) and an atmosphere tainted by bird crap.

While Todd was away, the treehouse became the clubhouse of the forgotten geeks or the golden trio: Charlie, Nick and their friend, Denny. It was the number one place to be, at least in their circle, to while away a lazy afternoon and it was just good fortune that Denny's dad owned Legacy Comics downtown.

There were always spare copies of everything from superheroes to Jugheads laying around his house that he could pinch when the trio had exhausted all of their allowance in the actual, melon-coloured store.

Charlie's mum had forbidden comics, his one true love, in the house after a protective, motherly peruse one Sunday after an inspiring sermon from Father Stringer. Mary Rose was unshakable in her judgement of anything she deemed unsavoury and being the devout church bug that she was, there was a great many things on that list.

She found nothing fit for the soul within those graphic pages and so, on the trash heap they went. Every single issue. The tattered Beanos with their splintering staples and faded colours as well as the crisp yet-to-be-read issues of Earth's Mightiest Heroes.

Garfield was his favourite comic of them all but now, his only chance to find out the happenings of that fat cat was to borrow Denny's copy. His adored collection now nestled uncomfortably alongside various bugs and crawlies in the trashcan. Spider-Man was in excellent company.

Charlie's idea of a happy afternoon was devouring the latest, previously un-rifled, issue in Denny's comic collection and inhaling the fresh ink. For those joy-filled days, they could forget themselves and become fully immersed in the worlds and characters rippling between their fingers. Charlie's only chance of ever being the hero.

In just over a day, the clubhouse would revert back to the rocking shack Todd imagined it to be and so, the next few hours would be Charlie's last chance of bliss before the dreaded trip to his aunt's. Nick supplied the locale, Denny supplied the goods and Charlie supplied the—umm—well, Charlie was Charlie and that was good enough for Nick and Denny. Plus, he was always good for the odd laugh, even if it was at his own expense.

The clubhouse of the forgotten geeks could have been mistaken for one of those ancient monasteries whose bald, stumpy monks are bound by an oath of silence; as some days, the only sound coming from within the rough and rugged den was the ruffling of pages as they sped through the latest issue of whatever had taken their fancy that week. And, of course, the occasional 'Yow' as the paper from those delicate works of art sliced into their less than delicate fingers.

"So, you're really going to be spending more time in church? Gross, man. Why would you wanna do a thing like that?"

"My m-mum is m-making me."

"Oh yeah, I forgot you said she goes a bit nutty for all that religious crap," Nick said as he opened the hatch of his treehouse and lumbered inside. Charlie followed, giggling at the swearing. "Denny will be here in a few. So, you won't have to read that Garfield comic for like the hundredth time."

Nick laughed as he playfully slapped his head when he saw Charlie's reaction. Of course, he would want to read it for a hundredth time. And a hundred more after that. Happily.

It was another ten minutes before the third and final member of the clubhouse arrived, panting from climbing the ladder with a full rucksack. He gave the customary four knocks to gain entry and entered to see Charlie holding open the latch for him, and Nick casually sprawled across a novelty chair shaped like a baseball glove.

"Alright, losers? What's today's word?"

"Fuck. Come back tomorrow for the You."

"Hilarious, I think I've only heard that joke, hmmm, let me see—oh that's right, a bazillion times," Denny said, plonking himself down on a polka-dot bean-bag chair. Charlie buried his face in his hands to keep from spraying the two of them in saliva.

"Actual news for you, Charlie's mum is making him ring Stringer's bell," Nick said, fighting off the laughter. A fight he was prepared to lose.

"Oh right, your mum is a damn squirrel, Charlie. You would think if she was such a fanatic, she would want to ring his bell herself," Denny replied before joining Nick in his defeat.

"Hey, c-come on, g-guys, what's the joke?" Charlie asked, looking between the two hyenas and starting to nervously chuckle along with them.

15

"Nothing, we'll tell you when you're older," answered Nick smugly. Being a whole three months older than innocent Charlie gave him a bloated sense of pride. He gave him a knowing wink before turning his attention to the bulge in Denny's sack.

"Rucksack looks full to the brim today, ole sport. I hope it's full of goodies, and by goodies, I, of course, mean boobies."

"Of course you do. You always do, Nick, but you can cool your jets, Casanova. It's just comics today."

"Alr-r-ight, I h-hope there's s-s-some Marvel ones," cried Charlie.

"Ha-ha that's why we love you, Charlie. Sorry, Nicky boy but my dad's started locking the desk drawer where he keeps the good stuff."

"Speak for yourself, man, but I ain't loving him. I ain't no Stringer," Nick started, causing them both to dry heave with laughter again. Once again, Charlie missed the beat and failed to catch up. "And I can't imagine why he would lock it now. It's not as if he caught you wrist-deep in his prized issue of *Filthy Femmes* last month. Oh wait—"

"Yeah, yeah, laugh it up, but I don't see you supplying any of the goods."

"I supply the pair of you with the street cred. Shame you guys didn't inherit the cool gene like me, but that's why I take pity on you. Otherwise, you would just be a couple of guys geeking out over Captain Underpants."

"I'm okay wi-i-th that," Charlie said, reaching for a can of soda that was brimming with the sweet nectar of forbidden sugar. The bubbles frazzled his tongue and he jerked his hand. They all watched in horror as the can dropped in slow motion and within seconds, Charlie's beloved fat cat was soaked.

Sadly, one of Garfield's many hilarious traits was not the ability to withstand a sticky drenching. Cats do not like water at the best of times but now he, Odie and the rest of the gang were completely washed out.

"Aw fuck's sake, Charlie, we get that you can't keep your words from shaking, you know we could be like everyone else and rip you for it, but we don't; well, not that much, but c'mon, how hard is it to simply keep hold of something? Aww jeez, you spilled some of it on my brand new Snoopy and Friends. Dumbass!"

Denny spoke with a growing annoyance, his voice drying out and Charlie turned blue with shame, shrinking into himself further and further the longer Denny stood over him. This was not the first instance of Charlie spilling and he suspected it would not be last. It was just his nature.

It was not his fault that he had slippery fingers; thick ones too, he was beginning to notice but that did not stop Denny from laying into him. Nick remained silent throughout, his head buried in a comic, with just the occasional peek above the page.

Charlie left the clubhouse soon after and as he descended the ladder, he could hear Nick and Denny gearing up for an almighty duel to the death with broken sticks in place of lightsabers. Despite coming away feeling like a wannabe-Smurf, he still thought it was one heck of a day. Comics and carbonated drinks.

*Two sins in one day!*

His mother would scold him from here till next Tuesday as his dad always said, though Charlie never quite understood what that meant. Rule one of the clubhouse was no girls allowed (at least during term time.) That was just standard and happily accepted by the three founders.

Even though they were inching their way to the age where the idea of a girl did not totally repulse them anymore, the worn-out paper variety could satisfy their needs for now. No way was an actual real-life girl making her way past the threshold; mainly because, if an actual girl did enter their domain, the trio would surely crumble into a spotty adolescent mess of hormones, squeaked voices (and stuttered, in Charlie's case) and uncool clothes.

Denny added a new rule before Charlie left; the only Charlie-allowed entry on new comic day was Charlie Brown. Ambling home, he couldn't help but feel a little more forgotten than his fellow geeks. Shunned and cast out from his haven left Charlie to adopt a mask that was expertly moulded to his blue face.

A mask of shame; one that caused his knuckles to tense and his mind to slowly sink into a pit so dark, he wasn't even aware that he had fallen.

# Chapter Three

Charlie awoke late on Saturday morning; neither parent had made a point of waking him sooner. They both valued the quiet and calm too much. He rolled over and felt a wet patch soiling his snowmen pyjamas. The first time in over seven years, but the smell was just as strong and stung his eyes; it was the painful memories of towering eyebrows, swollen necks and sour words that caused him to cry.

*Help* played on repeat inside his mind. A soft voice squeaking in the darkness. He didn't know how to use a washing machine. He wasn't allowed near anything technical with flashing buttons and futuristic beeps. The toaster was the most sophisticated piece of equipment he was allowed to touch.

Panic rushed through him and he could feel his chest tightening. He sprang out of bed, paced the room in dread but stopped almost as fast as he had begun, scared that his rattling footsteps on the hardwood floors (he wasn't trusted with carpets since an incident with a mug of hot chocolate) would alert one of his parents.

He also wasn't allowed hot chocolate after that miserable day. Why his parents thought it necessary to punish his stomach as well as his feet, he still didn't understand.

"Charlie? If you're up, then you better hurry up and get down here if you want any breakfast. It's almost ten-thirty and this kitchen isn't open all day. We can't all just lie around in bed all day. Some of us actually have a life with things to do," cried his mother from downstairs. "And stop dashing about up there. If you mark those floors, I'll stop your allowance till next Christmas. Just you see if I don't."

The panic gripping his chest descended toward his stomach and he could swear that he heard his insides hurling about. Breakfast was fast becoming the last thing on his mind. Before he could react, he heard footsteps shuffling about

18

outside his bedroom door and he thought he was going to faint when he saw the knob turning.

"Charlie, did you not hear your mother? Come down n—" his father began, poking his head round the door before his nose came under attack and he saw the stained sheets on the bed. Charlie's whole body strained on cue, ready for the wrath, but when he looked up, his dad was only shaking his head. "I don't have time to deal with this. I'm meeting the guys at the boat in like twenty minutes."

Charlie relaxed an inch at his father's soft tone. But what came next was not a comforting hug, a reassuring pat on the head or anything that was remotely calming. His father said six words, now with a flat quality, that took Charlie's fear and doubled it. Math was his worst subject at school but even he knew that was a really high number.

"Your mother can deal with you."

His dad made a swift retreat and Charlie heard his clunky, yellow boots on the stairs. His mind, swimming in a sea that was as thick with dread as his bedsheets were with piss, blocked out the hushed voices of his fatigued parents. At least, they still had one thing in common, he said to himself as he heard the front door slam shut and then the sound of his mother's heels clicking their way toward him; they were both tired of their only child.

Adoption agencies may rigorously vet potential new parents, knowing that not everyone was fit to care for a child; however, nature, sadly, had no such standards.

In the doorway, he saw the silhouette of a disgruntled woman, ripe with fury over this latest incident. There was nothing motherly about her presence and from the way she bounded into the bedroom, it was clear that she possessed a temper that matched the fire of her voice.

Charlie, cowering and desperate to cover his ears, was rooted to the spot out of familiar fear, and recognized the steam emanating from her mouth. His mother had clearly been taking notes from Father Stringer.

After the scolding, Charlie had assumed the position and braced himself. His body was prepared for the punishment but the first whack always took his quivering nerves by surprise; a small part of him still believing his mother may spare him from her fury and show mercy, but she was not the type of woman to abandon her natural instincts.

The pain bolted all the way from the impact zone right up to the tip of his ears. The hairs on the back of his neck, previously standing rigid with fright, now swayed in the ripples. His body was always sore after a reprimand but there was something different about this time. Something new ached inside his fragile frame and his skin was now tender to the touch.

As she departed the room, leaving him crying where he stood, and with the sheets now bundled in her arms (held out far in front of her), she informed him that breakfast was now forfeit. *Good*, he thought. He had lost his appetite.

Charlie collapsed to the floor in a huddled mess. So far, the start of the Christmas break had been a real bummer and as he rubbed his reddening behind, he knew just how that felt. This was only the beginning and he doubted if it would get any better.

He stayed curled up on the bedroom floor and refused to look over at the clock on his bedside cabinet. Digital and in the shape of a half-completed Death Star. Despite there being no actual ticking, he could feel its uncomfortable melody as the morning died. Time pulsed inside his head, the shame growing with each passing minute.

Around one in the afternoon, his stomach let out a growl that he was too helpless to ignore. Feeding the beast inside was more important than avoiding the one downstairs.

"Ah, there you are. I wondered when you would show your face after your little episode this morning," his mother spoke calmly but her words still pierced through his skin and shook his bones. "If you're hungry, there's a sandwich in the fridge for you. Your father is, supposedly, bringing back fish for tonight, so do not fill up on snacks."

She rolled her eyes on the word 'supposedly'. She had been let down too often to let herself believe that Michael would deliver on his promises.

Charlie hurried over to the fridge and dug out the cheese and ham sandwich that awaited him, poured himself a glass of apple juice and sat down at the table. His mother was opposite him, reading one of her magazines (church approved) and thinking about how best to hide the cracks from her sister on their upcoming trip.

Charlie ate fast, not just to appease the ravenous beast that lived in his stomach (*Oh Great One, please accept this offering of ham and cheese),* but also so he could scoot out of the kitchen and return to the foetal position upstairs.

As the last morsel of crumbs passed his lips, he thought that perhaps if he had been up earlier and not pissed the bed, and his parents had been in a better mood (that thought in particular laughed in his face), then maybe his father would have asked him to join him on the fishing trip today. He would have said yes before the words had even finished forming in his father's mouth.

He had only ever been out on the water with his dad and some of his dad's friends once and despite the fact that it had been a wasted disaster of a day, he wanted to do it all over again, because this time, it might end differently. He had begged and begged to come along on their outing a few months ago, desperately hoping to catch a shark or something exciting that he could take to show-and-tell on Monday morning at school.

Some unbelievable rarity that would trounce Susie Costello's antique vase, the one that she just happened to bring in every week. A grin, increasingly smug, was always shot in his direction as she took her plump self to the front of the classroom. Every week.

His dad agreed to let him join the trip, partly out of wanting to put a stop to his needy little tantrum and partly out of amusement at his son's idiocy. Normally, his mum would protest at the idea of their son being around a bunch of slobbering fools (one was bad enough in her opinion), but on that occasion, she said nothing as they headed out the door. She too wanted peace. A moment would do but she would gladly take a whole day's worth.

All the grown-ups on the boat had howled with laughter when Charlie, at his father's pushing (literal and otherwise), told them why he was so insistent on coming aboard. Shattering little Charlie's dreams came all too easy to Michael Rose.

"No f-f-fair. I wanted a sh-s-shark. Like th-the one in that m-m-movie we saw l-last month."

"Listen Charlie, this little boat wouldn't put up much of a fight against a shark like that. We would end up at the bottom of the ocean, and then, not only would you get to see all the fishes you want, you'd be swimming with the damn things. Now, stop making a fuss over nothing," his dad said, exasperated. It had been a long day and the beer supply was wearing thin.

His dad liked to drink beer while out with his friends; pretty much any other time, come to think of it and he let Charlie try a sip that day. The moment it touched his son's lips and his spotty face contorted in disgust, Mike turned from a mere howler into a full-blown hyena. The rest of the pack quickly followed suit.

Charlie looked around his would-be crewmates of chuckling fools as the smallest drop of the brownish liquid flowed out of the can and danced along his adolescent tongue before sliding its way down his throat, inflaming as it went.

The adults all seemed to enjoy the onslaught of gags and slurs it plagued upon them but to Charlie, it was foul and sharp and made his teeth feel weird. His head went swishy and his stomach made him relive the awful experience he had once had on a rollercoaster when a fair came to town.

The constant sway of the boat against the pushing waves did little to ease his sloshing discomfort. He had been visibly seasick from the moment his first foot touched down on shaky hull but now, it felt like the sick was about to make an appearance. And it did, as did another chorus from the wannabe hyenas. A harmony of humiliation, all at the expense of the twelve-year-old boy who just wanted some father-son time.

"Here, take this," his dad said, tossing him a grease-stained cloth. "Clean yourself up and don't tell your mother that you had beer. That's the last thing I need."

Charlie did not like beer and you could take that to the bank. Nick had taught him that phrase, but he wasn't allowed to have a bank account, so he didn't fully know how to react, so he just chuckled along blindly, or *chuckie-d* along as Denny liked to say.

He also did not know why the grown-ups had laughed at him but one thing he was aware of was that, as they made their way back to shore as the sun started to fade beyond the horizon and a dark sky drew in, he was sad to be the butt of everyone's jokes.

Hours of humiliation and not even one shark or sturgeon to show for it. Zero. Zilch. *Only some measly salmon and that was hardly going to impress his class chums,* he thought, disappointment now spreading soberly across his face. They sold salmon at the local mart downtown, not that they could afford to shop there anymore.

Super Savers, it was called but Charlie felt it would have to change its name to Super Duper Savers before it felt the shuffled feet of the Rose clan cross its meshed entrance again.

Charlie sat on his bare mattress, remembering that day on the boat and despite how sad it had made him feel by the end, he still looked on it with some fondness. He would happily suffer a little blue if it meant he got time with his dad. He was always closer to his dad than his mum. Only in theory though, as it seemed both parents wanted only distance from him.

# Chapter Four

Charlie was kitted out in a tight, ironed suit that constricted his movement above the ribcage. Just perfect for the arduous task of bell ringing, he thought as he had struggled into it with the unhelpful push and prod of his mother. If the sleeves tore mid-chime, then at least he wouldn't have to spend the holidays with his relatives, he would be too busy learning how not to choke on dirt six feet underground.

Mary wore her best Sunday clothes; a floral dress with neutral colours that was hemmed below the knee. Everything squirreled away under the dying roses. Mike only had one suit and so, it was simultaneously his best and worst. Mary always felt a nagging irk crawl over her face whenever she opened their shared closet and saw it idly hanging there. Listless.

"Don't be so bloody stupid. I'm a gardener, Mary, for Christ's sake. Why would a gardener need more than one suit? Why would they need one AT ALL?" He continually asked when the topic arose. Every Sunday morning, the pestering would come. Like clockwork. Begging for an argument. He tried and failed not to bite back.

"For church, Michael. For church. And I have asked you countless times never to take the Lord's name in vain. Not in this house and certainly not with Charlie within earshot. Church is no place to be sloppy. He is always watching us and so, we don our finery to show our faith. Our commitment."

"It's all a fucking show," he had whispered with his back now turned as he readied himself in the suit he was married in, *And most likely, the suit he will be buried in too,* he thought.

The Rose family entered the churchyard at nine-thirty on the dot and Father Stringer was eagerly awaiting the young bud's arrival, beckoning them over to the side door, which led directly into his study.

"You all look splendid. I'm thankful the weather is holding out. It would be a shame for those suits to be washed out; although it looks like yours already has been, Michael."

"It has seen better days, but it still fits and in this climate, we cannot square away the cost of a new one."

"Yes quite. You, on the other hand, Charlie, look very well groomed!" Father Stringer exclaimed, extending an arm.

The study was tightly packed, the four of them could barely squeeze in. It was clearly more suited to a one-to-one session. There was all manner of papers overflowing from the one filing cabinet in the corner, spilling onto a rug emblazoned with a shining pillar and, unsurprisingly, the Almighty himself.

With a south-facing window, there was not even a spark of sunlight yet and so that shine was more of a dull fade at this time of day. Come midday, it would be blinding.

"A cluttered workspace leaves the mind clear. Those are words that my predecessor lived by and when he passed on, I unsuspectingly inherited his little motto as well as this glorious community. And glad to have done so. I believe a clear mind to be a free mind. Free of sin, free of temptation and free of desire," he said and seated himself on the velvet-lined chair beneath the window.

Michael fought to keep a scoff from escaping while Mary lapped up every word that fell from Father Stringer's mouth; though at his age, it would be more of an aching stumble. Charlie remained silent, letting his eyes follow the dust freely dancing above the desk.

They spoke casually for about ten minutes, mostly about how the church was the answer to everything. Father Stringer rooted around in one of the drawers in his desk, retrieved some notes and stashed them in his cloak before he ushered them out the door.

"Well, I think the time has come. If you two would like to take your seats out in the main hall and Charlie, you can follow me. It's show time."

Charlie returned to the bell chamber and was immediately hit with the same uncomfortable feeling that had overwhelmed him on Friday. He was not going to enjoy this. Not one bit, but he knew how to grit his teeth, so he figured he would survive it. Something he picked up from his father but didn't allow himself to believe it would actually work. Distrust seemed to be his inheritance.

"Right, five minutes to go, so I shall leave this rope in your fine, young hands. Now remember, bell ringing is an art and you, m'boy, are my artist." His hand found its way onto Charlie's shoulder. A sundry of wrinkles overlapped on themselves before falling into the same smooth spot on Charlie as the other day. "Any fool could just ring the bell, but I am trusting you with this special job because I know you will do a terrific job."

Father Stringer knelt down so he was on the same level as his new recruit, his ancient bones creaking in the flat air. "I am a servant of the Lord, Charlie. You understand what that means?"

"Yes," Charlie replied, his voice retreating into himself.

"I am a messenger and so, through my work, I can deliver HIS blessed word. Devoting yourself, mind, body and soul, to the church is a high honour but not one that I can undertake alone. When the Almighty shines his light upon one of my flock, it is my solemn duty to bring them into the fold and ensure their eternal service."

Charlie could feel himself stiffen under the weight of the words that were being carefully wrapped around his juvenile ears.

"I have been watching you for some time now, m'boy, studying your development, and in all my years, I have never seen someone shine as bright as you. You practically burn under HIS spotlight. The will of the Almighty has placed you at my feet, and only I can help you flourish."

Father Stringer slowly caressed Charlie's writhing skin before withdrawing. "Now, I believe that is enough for now and you have a job to do. I like to have a little mystery and so, the details of your artistry shall remain a secret. Just between you and the bell. We all have a little secret or two in us."

He clapped his hands together and departed. Charlie, now alone, found himself heaving but never quite able to catch his breath; he was never any good at catching things. Sports day always sucked. All the air in the chamber had been stolen by Stringer's bitter, unsettling words.

He felt a chill tingling down his spine and swore he was being surrounded by the same grim-laden shadows from the other day. They inched closer toward him as his feet shuffled nearer to the tattered, hanging rope in the centre of the chamber.

He glanced back but when he looked, all he could see was his own shadow plastered against the concrete floor. Small and unthreatening. Hardly the stuff of nightmares. The clock on the wall adjacent to the door ticked and a hand landed on the delicately styled '10'. A miniature bell sprang forth from the centre point.

Showtime.

He gave a small tug on the rope, so far so good. No blurriness, no visions. Just the grating sound of the bell as it resonated through the chamber. He continued with his pull, hoping and praying to be left in peace. At least, he was in the right place for that. Two weeks far away from Stringer's grip was all he wanted for Christmas now. The one time he would get what he wanted.

He was able to breeze through the lower chimes without his mind straying into murky waters and in his disbelief, he was able to blot out the ringing. As number ten approached, his hands sweated and slipped an inch. The sores from his *audition* now scraped over an old knot and he waited for a pain that, thankfully, never came.

Done and dusted. Charlie released the rope to its carefree swinging and took a step back, admiring how he had gotten through it unscathed. Maybe his dad's trick did work after all. He exited the chamber and chuckled over how he now had a secret between him and the bell.

Miracles do happen.

Charlie entered the grand hall and saw the aisles were being quickly swarmed by a crowd of cawing patrons. He found his parents in the front row and once seated, with his feet barely touching the cold, stone floor, his mother glowed at her newfound privilege.

She asked how the bell ringing went and after answering courteously (his mouth rallying off everything she wanted to hear), she nagged him not to squander the opportunity and how badly they needed this break. He didn't understand that, but Charlie thought it funny how she practically recited a part of Stringer's advice from Friday word for word. His dad paid no interest to their conversation and showed no interest in his son's new role.

A few minutes passed, now in silence, and Father Stringer strode into the room. The scattering of conversation died on impact and now, the only sound that echoed around the hall was the faintness of his cloak that hung an inch too low as it was dragged up the steps of the pulpit.

Once in position, he removed the notes, now crumpled from a bad fold, from his cloak and looked down on the crowd. He allowed himself a smile, this time baring his teeth. From the angle, no one in the congregation could see the yellowing stains that were taking hold. No one, except the loyalists in the front row. And Michael. And Charlie.

"Welcome, one and all. It is my deepest joy to see such a great number of you here today. Our number, however, has curiously trebled from last week," he began quite innocently, adjusting and straightening out the papers in front of him, but while his face remained unmoved, his voice was just beginning to brew. It, unlike the rest of him, showed no signs of slowing down. Standing strong against the storm as old age set in and battered his body.

His voice was his weapon. One which he kept in excellent condition, polishing it weekly. Inside the pulpit was where he shone. Inside the pulpit, he could command attention. The crowd below hanging on his every word. Or rather the word of the Almighty, he was merely the messenger.

Stringer dutifully accepted this sacred role and executed it with his own unique brand of venom. He could incite action against the unholy, purge the impure, and weed out the hesitant and the unfaithful among his flock. His town was being overrun by heathens with sinners ambling about unimpeded.

A few words from the safety of the pulpit and soon, the sinners would meet their end and the town's wholesome air would be restored. Conscious thought would be destroyed. There would only be the way and the word of the Almighty.

"I am, however, disheartened that the majority of you are not here out of a pure, clean worship, but rather for the selfish need to falsely claim to be believers. Faith is not a half-hearted concept or a part-time pursuit. Turning only to the church when in need of HIS guidance but where are you when the church needs you?

"When your problems go away, so does your interest in the Lord. You are here now only to rid the dirt from your heathen souls before the dawning of a new year." His voice cracked, strangling through the air with every word awakening from deep within.

Charlie cowered in his seat, shrinking lower and lower into himself but the fury penetrated him, his eardrums trembling through the rising sweat. The storm settled over a huddled mass in the back rows, who were lazily crunching an unimaginative assortment of smuggled snacks and scoffing at the silly old man in fancy dress.

"I have no doubt that once you depart my sanctum today, I shall not see your treacherous faces until the next religious holiday that your modern media has abused. You will take the Lord's name in vain with your boosted ego and soil the good work we faithful men, women and children do in HIS stead." His fingers arched tauntingly as he spoke and the eyes narrowed, honing in on those he sought to expel.

Charlie did not like his new front row seats. This show scared him. He much preferred the shows he used to watch on television back before they had to sell it to pay off some of his dad's bills. "Debts," he had heard his mother call them. He could rely on those shows not to scare him.

People on the TV were just acting, pretending. The same could not be said for Father Stringer. There was not even a hint of pretence in his voice. Charlie, though shaking, believed every word that slithered out of the Father's mouth.

The sermons had never felt this intense from their old placement, squarely in the middle of the church hall. He had certainly seen the passion in which Father Stringer spoke, but his old sermons felt ordinary, almost predictable.

First, he would mull over the week's, usually dreary, events before moving on to ramble intently about how the outside world was changing and starting to become more accepting of sinful behaviours, then he would finish on how we must all stay true and faithful if we were to overcome these challenges.

"Do not tolerate that which cannot be forgiven, my children," was a classic line that Father Stringer relied too heavily upon in his advancing years.

Perhaps all those drab sermons would have felt this forceful if he had been ringing Father Stringer's bell from an early age, but he doubted it. This one was different. It was a bad kind of different. He could feel the hate rising among the loyal flock.

Charlie squirmed in his seat, his naturally avoiding line of sight now focusing on a cracked dip in the floor to the right of the ancient organ in the corner and tried to blot out the remainder of the lecture. Trying and failing. And trying again.

Father Stringer was spitting fire today and Charlie did not want to get burned. Only the most faithful would feel the warm glow of his embrace. The rest would simply roast. Their encounter in the bell chamber had allowed Charlie to see Father Stringer in a new light; one that was as darkly lit as the recesses of his own now frantic mind.

The sermon concluded after a long hour of conspiring vengeance and the sheep departed. Charlie rose to follow, his feet scurrying to beat the crowd out the door to put a lot of distance between him and the Father, but was abruptly halted in place by his mother. Of course, she would want to stay; she was doing everything in her power to become his shadow. Charlie was disheartened but not surprised.

"Father, allow me to congratulate you. That is surely the most riveting, engaging and exquisitely thought-out sermons our family has ever witnessed," she spoke with a beaming smile and a hunger that had been heartily satisfied.

"A heated sermon, I shall admit but heat is the only thing a sinner should feel. The Almighty calls on me to dispel any seeds that will grow against his beautiful vision. Unfortunately, false faith will see the end of us all and I will not stand by and let it infect our holy garden. Those crooked saplings must be stopped. Cut down root and stem. Otherwise, we shall be overrun with heathens for none shall grow in a garden left to rot."

Mary, speechless, could only nod in wondrous agreement. Mike, desperately looking around for anything that could be used to sever his ears, was trying to inch him and Charlie closer to the exit. They were now the only ones left in the church, even the organ player had made a swift getaway.

"I shall let you and your family depart now, Mary. No doubt some last-minute packing needs your attention. Do pass on my regards to your sister tomorrow. It was a sad day to lose her from my garden but I would have failed in my duty had I not recommended her for that position. She is very well placed there."

Michael, subtly stroking the door, swallowed a gulp.

*I've seen the state of your garden. You don't know a damn thing. Damn old fool. Mary needs to find herself a new hobby. This decrepit is no good for her sanity. Or mine. God only knows what effect he is having on Charlie.*

"Yes, I miss her terribly, but she will be overjoyed to know you still think of her. I know that she has kept up with her faith, but I fear her local church leader lacks your devotion."

"Sadly, that is often the way nowadays but do enjoy your trip and I shall be looking forward to your return. In the meantime, however, I shall be with you—in spirit. And Charlie," he shouted over toward the door, his voice booming around the empty room. "I have a few notes on your performance today, but it can wait, for now. There will be plenty of time to get into a rhythm that pleases us both when you're back."

Father Stringer followed them out into the churchyard, waving them off in the only way someone with crippling arthritis can. He produced another full frontal smile, causing all three of them to collectively turn their backs and walk away.

As Charlie settled in to sleep that night, his little mind refused to grant him any peace. He shook and fidgeted to free himself right up until he was able to drop off to sleep where a grim fate was waiting for him. A fate, brimming with fire and stalking his shadow from behind a sickly, yellow stain.

# Chapter Five

The next day began with a delayed start as Mike and Mary found themselves squaring off against each other before they set about loading up the car. The car, faded blue with a teal tint to the rear, displayed scuffs of speckled red by the wheel shaft from an incident involving Mary and an unfortunately placed cyclist. All of the driving duties were now in Mike's domain. Mary would never admit such a notion, but her nerves had been shredded as efficiently as the bicycle's tires at the moment of impact, and even from the passenger seat, a feeling of terror would sweep across her.

She would evolve from a normal, upstanding woman into a screeching mess, quaking at every tight bend and sped mile. A compassionate husband would take his beloved's tremors into consideration and smooth out his style of driving, but whether he was behind the wheel or on the sofa, Michael Rose was not a thoughtful man.

With the departure now imminent, she channelled those panicked feelings and jittering nerves into something constructive, something she could understand, control even. Anger. Toward the one person who could, and would, flaunt his driving prowess in her powerless face.

Charlie stayed in his room until the voices downstairs died, as he knew they eventually would. They always did.

"Charlie, it's time to leave. We have already wasted enough time," said his mother with desperation unknowingly creeping its way into her throat.

"C-coming."

They hauled their luggage into the car, climbed in after it and took one final look at their home before departing. Mary's knees gave a shudder as the engine burst into life.

"We are never going to miss this storm now, Michael. They said on the radio that it's likely to be the worst one in years, certainly since Charlie was born. And thanks to you, we will be caught up right in the thick of it."

Michael, like so many times before, said nothing. He simply danced his tongue around his teeth and when it couldn't find any new unexplored cavities, set about creating a few of its own. It was going to be a long road and his patience was already dangerously worn through.

*The road heading out of the town was unnaturally quiet, no doubt because every other family had the sense to leave at a sensible time,* Mary thought to herself. Who knew when they would reach Eve's now? Not until nightfall at the earliest.

*Or not at all,* was whispered softly into her ear by the foreign notes of fear.

They passed an empty, mud-drenched field where Mike had taken Charlie to his first drive-in movie that the local community hub had organized. It had been such an unprecedented hit that it now showed old films twice a month. Any movie before 1980 was old as far as Charlie was concerned, though this jokey comment failed to slap a smile on his dad's face.

All it did was drive him to open his second can of beer during the showing of *The Odd Couple.* Charlie noted that out on the peaceful stillness of the water was not the only place where his dad liked to drown his liver in alcohol. It seemed anywhere Charlie was, a can of beer was not far behind. He was just young enough to still believe in coincidences.

The field was rented out to the community every other Saturday for the film fanatics in town and it was no surprise to Mike that his darling wife did not count herself among that group. She, despite Charlie's lingering requests, never entertained such a ridiculous idea. A woman in her social circle had a reputation to protect. At all costs.

Image was everything but she failed to avoid its unholy presence completely as she had happened upon an upcoming film's poster once in one of the town circulars. One that now sadly displayed advertisements of an obscene nature rather than actual wholesome news.

She had gone straight round to see Father Stringer. The clicking of her heels on the wet stone path was like the sound of a thousand hornets as they whipped into a fury. The heathenistic takeover of the community space had quickly become a hot topic among her Sunday ensemble, even on the weeks where there no films on show.

The film schedule may have been staggered, but the outrage it caused remained firm. Mary could only imagine the horror of her young son being enveloped by the big screen bimbo and, despite her protests to protect little

Charlie's innocent soul from the sinful world around them, her husband, Michael, disagreed.

They disagreed on a lot of things of late. Horrid, awful flicks, she called them but he, and Charlie, couldn't get enough of them. The recklessness those movies displayed was only part of Mary's reasoning for her contempt; the other being that they often had women bearing bosoms, shabbily contained, she might add, which were large enough to nurse the whole parking lot rabble but from the shaking static as the first reel had burst onto the screen almost six years ago, Charlie had been enchanted by the glorious wonder of it all.

It was a win-win situation for both of them; Charlie got quality time with his dad and Mike got to spend time with his son in a situation where it would be impolite to their fellow guests in the car (all zero of them) for Charlie to open his mouth.

Mike made a point of explaining theatre etiquette very quickly, and very sharply, to Charlie on their first outing. Regardless of the setting, a film is a film and so that means hush.

Since they had had to sell the TV to pay off some debts, though Charlie was sure he overheard his mother occasionally mutter under her breath at the breakfast table that she was still paying for it (must have been a pretty big bill if a whole TV didn't cover it, he thought), the twice monthly drive-in was now Charlie's only means of escape into a new and exciting world.

Lord knows his own was fraught with disappointment and oftentimes, despair. Although he was sad to lose the television, he certainly did not miss the time his mum caught him watching a program mere inches between him and the set. If he had blinked, the lone ranger was sure to have felt a slight tickle down their cheek as his eyelashes gently brushed against the glitching screen.

"That'll make you go blind," his mum had always said but he didn't understand that. All he knew was that television was cool and it was fun to feel his eyes turn hazy and his brain turn fuzzy with the dancing lights and swirling colours.

*Dad must have agreed,* he thought, as when Mom glared at him and gestured for support, he simply shrugged. The shrug was a weed, a marriage killer and in their household, it was rampant.

His dad was a man of simple taste, hence his marriage to the lovely Mrs Rose, and was the type of man who, except for the habitual arguments with his wife, wouldn't say boo to a goose. Charlie learned that phrase from Nick one day when the clubhouse took on the form of Noah's Ark before a sudden command switch turned it to a space cruiser.

He wasn't entirely sure why someone would spook a goose, but he got the gist of the phrase. Or gizz, he said one time as a joke at Thanksgiving, drawing a snigger from his cousin who was two years younger than him. His glee had ended before it began when he felt the cold, sharp hand of his aunt graze along the back of his head.

A bruise developed almost as quickly as his meal was forfeited but it lay unnoticed beneath his curls of red hair. Like a tree in a forest, it was hiding in plain sight.

He liked drive-in movies because they were thrilling. Seeing those well-to-do heroes projected against the blackness of a clear night's sky and feeling the cool air breeze in through an open window of his dad's car gave him a feeling of peace. The notion of peace, especially in the presence of a parent, was alien to him, but on those nights, it was if he was being hugged for the first time in a long time.

As much as he loved a good movie when the time came around the downside, besides the scolding look from his mother as they headed out the door each time, was the state of his dad's car.

Charlie was forced to sit on itchy, black leather that had been long ago stained with a mixture of ketchup and mayo. He learned in an instant one night that he was no fan of mayonnaise and he certainly did not like it on his hotdog. Without thinking, he spat it out into his little square napkin but missed and it splattered the seat as he climbed into the car. He got a good smackarooni on his left side for that one, causing his stubby fingers to flex a beat of their own accord.

The greasy guy at the hotdog stand was pimply and liked to scratch his *bee-hind* with his tongs whenever a posh family drove by. Charlie and his dad were safe from such an abominable sight, his mum, on the other hand, may not have been so lucky.

If only hotdog Doug, or hot-Doug as none of his friends called him despite his constant insistence, hadn't been out of mustard, then he would have happily chomped down that juicy dog in one—two—three bites, no problem. Well, maybe a killer of a stomach-ache to follow but he was positive that would still have been better than a crimson cheek and ringing ear.

He wasn't allowed hotdogs at drive-in movies anymore. If he was hungry, he had to satisfy himself with some stale and sticky mints he found under his seat from journeys forever ago.

They headed out of town and the storm overhead was beginning to grow, circling overhead like a swarm of ravenous vultures preying on the weak and vulnerable below. A feuding family would make an easy picking.

# Chapter Six

As they climbed another bend on what was fast becoming a gravel slip-and-slide, Mary was sure it would be one push on the gas too many and they would career off the edge, plummeting into a fireball in the valley below. Like the over-the-top spectacle crashes featured in those movies she, quite rightly, detested.

"Slow DOWN!" She cried from the front passenger seat. What started as a low hiss evolved into a howling screech, her grip on the seatbelt tightening in tandem with her racing heart.

Her shrill voice pierced directly into her beloved husband's ear, causing the matted, greying hairs within to sway and quiver with the vibrations and a chill as cold as the falling snow to creep its way down his spine. Charlie began to notice this was not uncommon on their family trips of late.

Mike grunted a few defeated hums and relented the pressure on the gas pedal. He liked to think he was too car savvy to push it too far, especially with the weather worsening. They had been on the road for almost an hour and the car was now freckled with a dusty white as snow beat down from the darkening sky. The clouds overhead shuddered in the chill.

The car was a real beauty in its prime or so Mike was led to believe by the desperate dealer as it was already approaching the rowdy teens by the time Mike laid his eyes upon it. He had gotten it for (almost) a steal from the local dealership not long after the big boss shot himself in the head, bang centre in the showroom (spraying a run-down Honda Civic in the process) to escape his money troubles, or his wife, some in town had speculated at the time. Mike had chuckled a beat too long when he heard that theory.

This trip was the first real chance he had gotten to really break the car in but with the storm stalking their path, its limits were drastically shrinking. There was a slim chance that this trip would be a dream family vacation, wholly because if anyone saw within, then they would see the Rose clan were no one's vision of an ideal family. It was becoming more and more likely that this particular dream was really more of a nightmare.

As a family, they got so little time together, though neither parent would raise a complaint at that fact, but it did not slot in well to the pretence of a happy family if the cracks started to show to the outside world. Image was everything and one sure-fire remedy was a generous coating of a family holiday.

A summer vacation was always a dead-end conversation as Mike simply refused to turn down any work that came his way. The summer was what he called his 'golden time' as a lot of people would be having fancy barbeques and inviting their boss round to angle their way in for a promotion, and no boss would be bowled over with succulent steak and refreshing lemonade (hand-squeezed that very day by Mrs Obvious) if the ass kisser of an employee let his garden go to rot. Or so Mike continually harked back.

There was simply no place for unruly branches hanging over the fresh patio, darkening the chiselled marble or rotten weeds spreading their ill will upon the unsuspecting geraniums. That was where Mike came in. It was a perfect system because there was a perpetual supply of people who valued the rewards to be found between those two scratchy cheeks.

It kept him just ahead of the storm, just enough, so who was he to judge. It also kept him away from Mary for large parts of the day, so he was doubly happy. She was a whole other kind of storm. No snow, just ice.

In the winter, however, he was more than okay with letting the business slide and there were times when that slide became more of a sheer drop. Despite enjoying the freedom of working outdoors, he was, above all else, selfish. There was no way he was going to freeze his balls off just to add an extra five inches to some decking.

He had a different kind of five inches he would be more inclined to give the bored, sex-starved housewives of the suburbs. He could be a tool in her fantasy and she could drool over the size of his tiller. It was harmless, it was fun. Two things which Mary Rose most certainly was not.

When Mary brought up the idea of visiting Eve over the winter break, in her delightfully demanding nature, he consented. Not out of enthusiasm, if that was even a thing anymore, but more out of a weary obedience.

He didn't like an irate Mary at the best of times; hell, there were even times he didn't like her full stop (more and more recently it occurred to him), but an irate Mary in the middle of a harsh winter was not something to be trifled with.

He wasn't prepared to have his balls freeze off over winter, nor was he too keen on them being ripped off either.

Being under the same roof as the two Smythe sisters, with their sheer unyielding faith, was a recipe for disaster (one far worse than one of Mary's bland, undercooked concoctions), but it would provide the perfect opportunity to put on a united front for all the eagle-eyed gossip whores in town.

Escaping the drudgery of everyday life and slapping some more paper over the cracks at the same time. Everybody's happy, at least for the time being, plus it might do Mary a bit of good to remove herself from Father Stringer's skeletal clutch, even just for a short while.

The freckled snow on the exterior had now developed into a full-blown blanket rash.

# Chapter Seven

The road had levelled out, the mountainous climb now lay behind them, but the snow drift persisted with its fury. The car grew tired, struggling under the weight of the snow as it worked its way through the grooves of the beaten-up tires. Mike had meant to get them checked days ago but nothing he could about it now. He saw no point in arguing over spilled milk but something inside him told him to brace just in case. Even spilled milk had a habit of turning sour in his house.

Soon, the tires would concede to the storm. Perhaps he knew nothing about cars after all.

"I'm h-hungry. Is there an-a-anyt-thing to eat?" Charlie pleaded for the fifth time in as many minutes but so far, his pleas had been going unanswered, though not unheard.

"We just passed a sign that said there was a diner up ahead. Its only about ten miles, so you can be quiet till then."

Stopping in at the diner gave Mike the perfect chance to give the tires a once-over and perform the amateur's beloved move. The kick. It would also put the nuisance in the backseat on standby.

They entered the diner and were immediately struck by wafts of layered steam that escaped from the kitchen through a hole in the wall in short bursts, drifting its way around the establishment before dancing under their now watery eyes and flushing their face. The steam finally settled and they took their seats in a tattered, fake leather booth.

Charlie had wanted one of the milkshakes on offer on the reverse of the menu, which just happened to be the size of a pillowcase and had the uncomfortable feel of time-worn felt. Chocolate would have been his first choice, but he would have settled for banana and still come away with a satisfied tum.

However, thanks to Mummy dearest who sat opposite, with her arms folded and a grim look stretching from ear to ear, he had to settle for neither. A most dissatisfied tum it turned out. It was to be diet soda or still water. Stuck between a rock and boring place, Charlie chose the former.

He ordered a half-portion of cheese fries and his drink from Mindy, their waitress, who had a sauce-smeared nametag pinned just below her collarbone. She reminded him of Susie from his class, only more grown-up and with longer, blonder hair. Oh, and fully developed boobs. Can't forget about those. Charlie certainly wouldn't, especially the way she nestled her pen, tip side up, between them when she was done taking their order.

He was sure to tell Nick and Denny about Miss Mindy at the next club meeting when he returned home from the trip in the New Year, or then again, maybe he wouldn't. Maybe he would keep schtum about this beauty and that way, she would exist only in his mind. He liked his friends, dearly, but he suddenly got the feeling that they were both takers and Charlie did not want to share her.

He knew there many things that he did not know. Wrapping his head around that dizzying fact made him, well, dizzy, but when he awoke one morning at the start of December and found himself standing slightly off-balance as he sprung out of bed, he looked down and saw his dingle (Nick called his a dick, but Charlie preferred dingle, it just sounded funnier) poking its way out from under his Captain America underpants.

It throbbed with an expectant ache. On that morning where there was a chill in the air and frost on the grass, Captain America wore two helmets. Staring down at the speck of pink and seeing it stare back, almost winking at him, he knew what to do with it.

He didn't know how he knew, must just be instinct, he reckoned, and he would have let loose on himself there and then if not for the pesky shrieks of his mother calling him from the kitchen. Who would think about breakfast at a time like this?

Some other time, he told himself, but he was embarrassed to say he was yet to unload. Maybe out of fear of being caught and shamed, though with its nagging persistence, he felt the time was fast approaching for him to, you know—*crack one off*. That was how Denny had described it to him one day in the treehouse, now a pirate ship with Charlie being forced to walk a plank that wasn't there.

It was the hair flick, showing a tinge of red that streaked its way across her scalp, as she walked away that bowled him over. He wondered if he could sneak away, quite innocently, to the toilets and make it back before his cheese fries arrived.

Quick and slick, he told himself. He had been building up all this needy, nervous energy for about three weeks now, so he was confident in his speed. The light of the finishing line far outshone any fears or doubts he once had.

Pushing his way through a broken oak door marked 'gents', he was met with an unwelcome reality. The air was thick and foul with what he judged to be stale piss leftover from last Christmas and the floor awash with thrown-up house specialties.

Tonight's offering was chicken and Charlie wanted to believe they were using a different chicken to the one whose sauce-dipped strips he now faced in tiny puddles under the cracked sink at far end of the room.

This would simply not do. This vile room was not fit to be the birthplace of his love affair with the fabulous Miss Mindy. She deserved a hillside in summer with the cool breeze carrying scents from a lavender patch as the caramel-kissed skin on her bare buttocks fell beneath a line of white roses.

Only then, after seeing how thoughtful and romantic he could be, would she deem him and his standing-to-attention equipment worthy of the job at hand. He headed inside the far end stall, slipped his trousers and underpants (Flintstones today, how undignified) to just above the knee and went to give an initial tug as he waited to hear, or rather sense, the pop of the starting pistol but it was to no avail.

This horrible, horrible place had infested his fantasy. The roses wilted and the lavender air was now poisoned. How could he seed his sweetheart with the stench of a shit-stained cubicle door bearing down on him?

Despite his eagerness, it would take an age in here, and not to mention the best god-damn nose clips in the business, to release his love within the gorgeous vision that was Miss Mindy. His cheese fries would have congealed before he was able to do a little congealing of his own.

His mood turned sombre as he relinquished his softening wood and returned Fred and Barney to his hips, Dino took centre stage in this cotton show. Charlie retreated back out into the main diner area, his head turning to look at his new love as he walked.

"S-s-soon, my sw-sweet," he mouthed, hoping beyond hope that she would turn and mouth back, 'Soon, my big handsome boy'.

God, he wanted a shower so bad. Needed one. He just had to flesh out his fantasy and feel her soft, supple flesh as their bodies embraced. Conjoining and retracting in a glorious pile of hot sweat till they became one.

One body.

One soul.

One flame.

As Charlie re-joined the pallid booth, soiled with a lashing of sickly syrup, he was pleased to see his parents had been able to fight off any urges to bash in the others' skull with the novelty oversized pepper mill. A rooster of all things with wilted feathers, one tiny hole in the beak and a stopper in the butt for the glamorous job of restocking. If they could survive five-ish minutes alone, then maybe, just maybe, they stood a chance.

Neither parent said a word on his return and were seemingly unable to see the disappointment on his face. To them, that was just his normal face. His mum, in particular, would be most horrified and displeased with her innocent little boy if she were to know what he had been planning to commit in that dank cosmos of whirling filth.

But she remained oblivious. Phew! The last thing Charlie needed was a lecture on respect and dignity, especially with his sweet gal within earshot. Their food arrived soon after and as Charlie chowed down on his fries, his dad rather glumly moved his charred chicken through the split sauce.

Dotted around the thigh bone piece were flecks of black that he hoped was pepper and not dirt or gristle. But in a place like this, he couldn't be sure. Charlie half-thought about warning him about the little chunks of clucky he saw swimming in the restroom but found it all too easy to restrain himself. Could chickens even swim? He wasn't sure.

"Hardly dinner conversation," he imagined his mother saying in her icy, sharp tone, readjusting her half-moons as she did.

Mary had opted for what was described as mushroom soup but what confronted them all was more of a decaying sludge creature from one of those old sci-fi shows, with pocket bubbles for eyes and streaks of curdled cream for veins. Save for a few courteous spoonfuls, the creature lay undisturbed.

The minutes wore on and finally, Mike had given up on waiting a respectable amount of time before slapping his knees, signalling the end had come. He waved Miss Mindy over to pay the bill and in doing so, got more than an eyeful at her bountiful bosom as she perched down to claim her sixty-two cents tip.

*Back off, old man; she's mine.*

Charlie toyed with the rest of his food, prying a singular fry free from the rest of the brigade, and watching the barely melted cheese string itself as it tried to harness the departing soldier and pull it back into the comfort and safety of the company.

Mary, unimpressed with her husband's lustful gaze at the harlot in the red plaid skirt, showing far too much leg for her liking, said she would meet them at the car and braved a visit to the restrooms before the long journey continued. Charlie wondered if the ladies was as unpleasant as the gents. A part of him hoped not, but not a big part if truth be told.

As he and his dad headed out the door and into the parking lot, they remarked how the snow was starting to come down thicker than the soft flurries that had dusted the doorstop of what passed as food in this neck of the woods when they arrived not even a half hour ago.

One step forward and Charlie hesitated. He just had to have a final glimpse at the girl, no, the woman, who had captured his heart and set his imagination ablaze. He was sure to remember Miss Mindy for many a lonely night to come and foolish or not, convinced himself that she too felt a small twinge deep within her heart (and pants, he hoped) for the freckled twerp now exiting her life. Never to return.

As his eyes refocused and thoughts returned to that of a more innocent variety, he noticed that his dad had also been wistfully stealing one last stare at the waitress who was now seating a new father and son at the booth they had just departed.

*Back off, old man; she's mine!*

# Chapter Eight

A little over two hours of being back on the road, the fuzzy voice on the radio crackled something about a blizzard tearing its way across the land, enveloping small towns with its icy embrace and devouring the smooth, hot tarmac with the cold, white crunch of layered snow.

The announcement came just as the radio blew out. *Crapped out* was how Mike described it, causing Charlie to chuckle under his breath. Mary almost cracked a nail readjusting her glasses after that one.

About an hour before the radio gave up the ghost (just where did all these weird and wonderful phrases come from?), the heater had died a sudden death and so, both Mike and Mary were becoming increasingly angry, with each other it seemed, but neither had the energy for the type of slanging match that had become the norm back home. The white beast swirling outside the car had forced a ceasefire inside, fleeting though it would inevitably be, but Charlie would take what he could get.

He quite liked snow; in circumstances where he got to bunk off school and freeze his fingers making snowballs with Nick and Denny, but he never imagined he would be thanking a snowstorm for its help in making the trip at least bearable, that is if he forgot about the icicles that were sure to form on his pubes, all three of them.

The most his parents could muster now was an old timey shootout, but with scowls in place of pistols. The arguments back home where their bullets were encased with cruel, cutting words had indirectly led to Charlie's love affair with music.

He had spent many nights with his Walkman strapped to his hip and the accompanying headphones nearly glued to the side of his head. With the volume cranked way, way up to drown out the battle royale taking place in the living room, Charlie would drift off to sleep to Queen playing sweetly in his ear, dreaming that one day he too may be a musician. He just knew he had a song in him.

Music was a welcome escape on those stormy nights when the feeling of being trapped rushed him in waves, shrouding him with its darkness and becoming his inside shadow. Music was one thing that his beloved mother had yet to dismantle; at least, not completely anyway.

He could only play in his head, neither parent saw fit to indulge his eagerness, and so, he would never be near the level of his icon, Freddie Mercury, but hey, a boy could hope. Dream even. Charlie hoped for a great deal as his teen years crept up on him, much of which, it was dawning on him, would come to nothing. Each booming argument with its floorboard rattle made him surer of that.

Mike never came out on top during the arguments; Mary was too much of a sharpshooter to let him win. Not even once. Not even on his birthday.

The day his Walkman broke, almost definitely from overuse, and his parents' refusal to buy him a new one was the worst day of his life or rather the worst day of his life so far. Despite the fact that he did learn a few cool swear words, mostly on his father's part of their *conversation*, he was quite shaken whenever one of his mother's lead-lined bullets ricocheted its way up from the living room and penetrated inside his innocent little mind.

Never to leave, no matter how vigorously he shook his head. The realization that many long and sad nights lay ahead of him made his stomach queasy and his skin ripple for a fleeting second as the shrapnel shifted his thinking.

He had been a nervous wreck whenever thoughts of the trip pestered him as the days counted down. Without his music to soothe him, the car ride, and the holiday as a whole for that matter, was guaranteed to be a living nightmare. Now that it was here and he was trapped in the car with Mummy and Daddy, he suspected this was one nightmare that he could not wake himself up from.

Charlie had all but forgotten the dread that awaited him back home as he was consumed with a fear that the beastly blizzard would grow too strong and swallow them whole before they reached Aunt Eve's.

# Chapter Nine

Mary prayed they were still heading in the right direction but with this weather and Mike's pig-headed reluctance to use a map, praying was pretty much all she could do. Why did Eve have to move so far away for this new job? Well, she was only the next state over, but it could have been the other side of the world for how lonely it left Mary. All she had now was her reliance on Father Stringer. He would not let her down.

She much preferred when her sister was a register girl over at Super Savers. It was a nice enough job; sure, the pay was crummy and the customers, on the whole, were themselves a bunch of holes, but it was close. And they got a family discount card thrown in.

Not too shabby and it meant Eve was only a five-minute drive down a nice, respectable suburb, not like those spoiled ones she read about in the national newspapers where apartment buildings were a breeding ground for maniacal drug addicts and every bus stop shelter was routinely graffitied by the hopeless artist.

Heathens, the lot of them, Father Stringer had rallied one time and she found herself agreeing on cue. Going from five minutes to five hours was not her idea of a pleasant drive, hence why she had put it off these past two years. Though with Captain Lost behind the wheel, five hours would have been a miracle.

The car trundled its way along the snowy surface with each gear shift now a struggle when Mike spotted it. Or in actuality, Mike spotted him. But was it a—him? Or even an 'it'? It was certainly something.

Everything had to be something. Admittedly, his eyes were wearing thin and he could feel the occasional nod of the head, a long drive will do that to a person, but he was not so delirious that he was in the habit of imagining people who weren't there.

Mike knew of beaten-down travellers being afflicted by mirages in a scorching sea of endless sand in faraway deserts; he had seen a documentary about such things on the tube. God he missed TV, maybe as much as Charlie did, or maybe more so now that there were dirty channels readily available to the more perverted gentlemen. Or so his friends had rubbed in, presumably not long after rubbing one out. Lucky bastards.

But surely, those hazy, heat-stroke fantasies were caused by fatigue and dehydration. Weren't they? He wished he had paid more attention to the documentary rather than thumbing his way through a hardware catalogue.

This was December 23$^{rd}$ and mirages had simply no business being here. He told himself that snow must have been some sort of winter equivalent, but with every snail inch closer down the road, Mike got surer and surer that what he was seeing was the real deal. A McCoy of the highest order.

Up ahead, at the tail end of what his headlight could show, was a man. Just standing there at the roadside. The mother of all snowstorms beating down upon them, the way a good mother should, and in the midst of it stood the snow-covered shadow of an ordinary man in what was absolutely not an ordinary situation. A silhouette etched against the murky white.

The figure shuffled expectantly in his direction as Mike drew nearer. Definitely real!

"Fuck me, is he actually waving us down?" The words jolted from within, taking him by shock. Breaking their way through a chilled seal that was trying to form over his dry, cut lips. And nearer still.

Mary, who normally found it impossible to sleep in cars, what with the constant churning motion battering her senses and her growing fear of anything remotely car-related, had managed to settle in for a rest. A diet of constant reprimanding and rolled eyes had left her exhausted but her days of feeling wholly rested were far behind her and her husband's outburst had awoken her in a startled daze.

The rest, as brief as it was, did nothing to lift her mood. Perhaps because her dreamless sleep had been so rudely interrupted or perhaps at having the peaceful silence, which had been within touching distance of chiming a full hour, broken. Silence was golden and right now, Mike's voice held nothing but brass notes.

She was about to chastise her beloved, though still in her groggy, sleep-deprived state, the rasp in her voice would not nearly have cut as deep, when she saw what they were slowly advancing upon. She gripped her seatbelt tightly as a feeling of unease washed over her ghosting face.

Nails, unfiled and stained by an unremarkable shade of grey, tore their way through the leather strap as rising fear bore through her shaking muscles and set up camp. It was here for the long haul.

Charlie, snoozing away in the back with his feet curled up beside him, was dreaming about happier times when he watched a taped repeat of Queen performing on something called the 'Top of the Pops'.

# Chapter Ten

"What is a hitchhiker doing way out here? We're miles from the nearest town," Mary forced herself to ask before closing her eyes and praying.

It was true. It had been almost two hours since they had stopped in at the diner, with its sickening medley of aromas now frozen onto them like some repulsive deodorant and they hadn't found a single town since hopping back on the road. Scarcely any cars either for that matter. Not everyone was as brave, or stupid depending who you asked, as Mike was to plough on through a blizzard.

Mary fell into the latter category.

"Maybe he's had car trouble or some shit and got himself stranded" Mike said as he observed the mysterious figure as it twitched and battled the wind from its solid stance. "Relax, will you? Charlie's still dozing away. You know he can sleep through anything," he added quickly as he sensed the rage build and boil within the lovely Mrs Rose.

With a quick glance back at her son, now trying to sprawl but being pinned down by the belt, Mary saw this to be the case (thank the Lord for small mercies, her inner monologue whispered), though she still did not approve of anyone cursing near him, conscious or not.

She was quite aware that she would never be accredited with being the world's best mother but nonetheless, he was her little boy and with every year that passed, she could feel him slipping away from her. Just lately, however, with all the time he spent in that infernal *clubhouse,* it wasn't so much a slip than a pull.

Mary heard the way Mike had said 'anything' and she could feel a rope inside her slowly loop and twist its way into a full-blown knot. She just knew he was talking about their endless bickering. Though she would never outright admit it, she hated the arguing, but the longer Mike persisted in his arrogant, selfish and sinful ways, then the farther away the sound of a ceasefire would get.

But still, she was aware that having battle-scarred parents was not an ideal environment for a child. If her face had not been practically frozen by the chill, she might have felt her eyes tremble and jerk as they released one lone tear.

Maybe she would buy Charlie a new Walkman after all. It was near enough Christmas after all, and what use did a boy his age have of pocket squares. Embroidered no less, but still not high on the wish list of a sweet and simple twelve-year-old.

With a sudden crack of the engine, she sensed her husband more than ease off the gas. Yes, the weather was bad, horrid in fact, but she did not like the ill feeling this braking caused. They were slowing down. Not for the blizzard and not for the good of their health, but for the haunting figure staring them down. She had to end this ludicrous plan before it was too late.

"We are not STOPPING, Michael!" She cried out in a raised tone, so he knew she was serious but hushed enough so as not to wake Charlie. The last thing he needed was to be awoken by a madman hammering away at the car doors. Or hammering away on them if father of the year here got his way and actually let him, whoever he was, inside the car.

*Honestly, why can't he just use some common sense?*

Just as she thought she had broken through the wall of ineptitude that was clearly occupying his brain, the car slowed and when the—hitchhiker—thief—psychopath—whatever, was a mere ten feet from the iced over bumper, the car came to a shuddering halt.

They had stopped.

Mike, with his act of defiance, was visibly pleased with himself. He was, after all, a grown man capable of making his own decisions, despite what his single friends would sneer. His rebellion, however, lasted for less than a jackrabbit's coupling as he found the sideways glare emanating from the passenger seat too damned hard to evade. Like a moth caught in the glow of a bug zapper. Not caught, more like trapped. Impossible to ignore the light or escape the enchantment of its clutches.

Not fancying his chances of being strewn across a graveyard of electrified flies with the stench of their cooked carcasses, he ignited the engine. Mercifully, it kicked into action. Independent thought never did end well for him.

Mary stayed in her battle-ready position; one hand clutching the belt that had become like a makeshift safety blanket for her on this trip (her fingers slotting nicely into the chipped nail trenches) and the other now clinging to her imitation gold necklace that had a small figure of the Almighty, engulfing him in her sweaty palms.

If only she had a third hand, then she could promptly give her beloved a dutiful smack across the head for even contemplating such a notion. In an instant, she knew what the topic of their next argument would be and so did Mike. Happy Christmas indeed.

The car now ushered its way past the strange fellow outside and for one fleeting, harrowing second, his macabre, frost-bitten face aligned perfectly with that of Mary Rose. Despite the lasting chill in the car, beads of sweat raced down her forehead and she tasted the unpleasant salt of them as they curved around her quivering lips, then fell to her shoulder blades and finally puddled out of sight beneath her butterfly-adorned blouse. An effort was made to be bright and wholesome, but it was bland nonetheless. Everything about Mary was bland.

The grip on the seatbelt had never been tighter. A moment longer and her nails, now on the verge of splintering, would have cut clean through the material. Staring straight with her gaze fixed sharply on the snow as it battered down upon the cheap and flimsy wipers, she could feel the knot in the pit of her stomach had grown to be a fully functioning noose that was constricting around her heart as it filled, all too quickly, with sheer terror.

"Please Lord, I'm too—" she began to say but the whispered cry tailed off when the cold air stole her breath.

With the wind picking up, she and Mike saw a heap of snow fall from her frozen nightmare, revealing the mad man's identity. He really was just an *it* after all. Her frost-covered demon was nothing more than a novelty scarecrow. Someone's idea of a practical joke, she assumed, but she did not take kindly to being humiliated. Especially in front of her husband.

With her mind racing between fear and relief, she didn't know whether to laugh or cry. In the end, she fell back into the warm embrace of her reliable friend. Anger.

Charlie, unaware of the panicked hate taking hold of his mother less than three feet in front, with her heartbeat racing and rising, found himself rewinding the tape and smiling to himself.

*Ladies and gentlemen, Queen.*

# Chapter Eleven

Charlie's dream was going swimmingly. Queen had now taken a well-earned break as Miss Mindy came into view, and he whisked her away from the horrid, airless diner and off to the beach where they could share a blanket one size too small and lie in each other's arms.

He knew some people called this *spooning*, but he didn't know why. He would much rather be forking (even in his dreams, he was starting to think like Nick), but Miss Mindy was very obviously a classy girl and so, patience was key.

*Let's not rush the rest of our lives.*

"This is j-j-just swell," he squawked, trying to hide the virginal tremors in his voice. A dopey grin was painted on his blushing face, with his eyes fixed on his darling date, now stripping to a barely-there two-piece.

The sand was as hot as she was and the shapeless clouds floated lazily above in the bluest sky he had ever seen, or ever likely to see. His beauty tossed him a bottle of sun lotion (the expensive stuff, no own brand for her) as she flipped over and nestled her breasts into their new sandy home.

A faded flower tattoo could be seen on her right shoulder; however, his gaze was much more concerned with the pert posterior that he was now inches away from drooling over.

"Don't leave me waiting, Charlie."

Her voice whistled with the faint wind and caused his untouched body to burst out in goosebumps. Everywhere, all at once, and he burned with a rock-hard anticipation.

He was less than a moment away from laying his hands on Miss Mindy and gently caressing her every nook and cranny while he rubbed in the lotion with his trembling fingers when the beach took on a sour note. His dream became infected with a looming, dark presence; the white, soft sand was now made of serrated stone, the fluffy clouds now jagged shadows, and the rhythmic flow of the tide was no longer soothing to the lustful lovers, but took on the form of torrential waves as they crashed over Charlie and his now erased goodtime gal.

There was no time for a mournful groan as the beach scene dissolved as Charlie now had the unmistakable feeling of being trapped in a small space (he didn't know the word for that fear but he felt it all the same) as it filled with water. Slow at first, a mere trickle, like a leaky faucet to wet the ankles but as the water started to steadily rise, so did his fear.

In the time it took for his unspent wood to rot, the trickle had become a gusher. He definitely knew the word for death by water; it was drowning and as the water surged past his hips, he knew it would take him sooner rather than later.

A small, flickering light appeared above his head. Was it the light of freedom or the light at the end of the tunnel? Was there any real difference? His futile thrashing sealed his fate as the more he struggled in his childlike panic toward the blinding light, the quicker the flood quickened its pace.

In just a few minutes, he would be drowned. But it was not the cloaked figure of death that revealed itself as the water reached his chin and the first gulps of water flowed past his absent tonsils. It was the unsettling feel of a hand around his ankle, pulling him downward into the dark depths of that too small a space for a boy to be. The hand gripped him so tight that its cold and clinical feel cut into his water-laden flesh.

All Charlie could think of in that moment was the certainty that it was real. Not just the hand grappling him as he tried to kick it away, but also the water rushing his extremities and drenching his clothes. He knew the difference between dreams and reality, but the panic was as real as anything. He was almost certain that it would not be long before he stopped breathing, not just in that tube, but everywhere.

Charlie, surprising himself, was able to free himself from the hard grip but just as quickly as he was released by that hand, another sprung from beneath the murky surface and clawed at his shoulder.

The hands, possessing an unnerving clamminess, were scrambling around, trying to hold him still long enough for the water to do its job. If it got its way, then he soon would be still, rigid even, for a great deal more than just a few moments.

The tube echoed with the cracking sound of flexing fingers as the unknown hands of death made desperate grabs for the boy struggling to keep his head above the water.

Charlie was being pushed and pulled, prodded like a lab rat, under the water's rising surface by the hands, with skin now tearing with every thrash. Try as he might to break free, the inevitable was, well—inevitable. Charlie, exhausted, gave up as the hands pinned him against the wall. The air in that small space became overrun by his own heavy sweat as his panicked twitches ran wild. Though his lungs were flooded, his body was screaming, desperate to be set free.

Before he could react, his body convulsed and the light of Charlie Rose dimmed just for one second before being extinguished. Sweet, innocent Charlie was swallowed up by the dark waters. His last thought was of the lovely Miss Mindy and without meaning to, he found himself smiling in the face of death. She may not have saved him, but she had stopped him from dying alone.

# Chapter Twelve

It was almost a whole ten minutes after their harrowing encounter before Mary's anger subsided, giving way to the slow hand of fear that now crept delicately around her throat.

The sound of her brittle neck spasming toward the wing mirror whipped her into overdrive and convinced herself that a great, dark mass now rode on the icy wisps of the winter wind, stalking their path and waiting to strike them down. One sharp snap of a breeze was all it would take.

It would just be typical for them to be stopped, for good she feared, when they were this close to Eve's house. She prayed for a safe final leg of the journey, but it was only her fear that could be heard echoing back at her. Michael dared not speak first, too fearful to even risk an apologetic squeak. He had known from the second the car had clanked to a halt, brief as it was, that he had wildly fucked up.

His wife, who was always so put together, held in place with a stick up her tighter than tight ass, had completely fallen apart. Visibly shaking as the mysterious figure had seemingly waded toward them. That sort of shit stayed with a person.

His manly man attitude shrivelled to a husk when he saw the sweat was still raining down on her, flooding her pores. Though she had been an unbearable bitch for the better part of a decade, in that moment, Mike struggled to see that side of her. He pitied her, yes; but in his own shit-for-brains way that made him remember how he had fallen for her in the first place all those years ago.

He had been fresh out of college, flunked out more like because he was a little too fond of the all too available beer less than a skip from the campus's main gate. There would be no more midnight poker games in the adjoining dorm, no more cheap as chips pot as a joint snailed its way around the room during his *study* sessions, and no more languishing in lecture halls with the future stuffed shirts of America either side of him ferociously scribbling every word, huff and wheeze uttered by Professor Windbag Von Dullsack III.

A few days after his dismissal, he ventured out to the library to return some books that he reckoned would be worthless on the open market and that was when he met her, Mary Smythe, in all her prissy, refined glory. She was standing across the room from him with her hair held in place by a bronze butterfly clip and some funky glasses on a beaded chain. He half-chuckled/half-snorted at the sight of her but there was just something about her that drew him in.

Like a moth, he too, was all too helpless to resist her glow.

"She's in the right place," he said to himself, though he wasn't listening. He was far too distracted by the way this enchanting maiden was scolding at her superior.

Their conversation, or more accurately, the lecture the head librarian was unwillingly on the receiving end of, echoed around the grand, old room. The snipes catching a current of dust billowing through the air and weaving in between the aisles of the untouched and unloved (books and patrons alike) before finally coming to a rest in the history section.

Mike was able to catch a couple notes as he approached the desk with his books almost slipping from under his arm, his attention now stolen. He was now quite glad he did not sell the books or indeed just trash them, which had been a very tempting option even as he pushed the pull door at the library's entrance.

From what he could overhear, she was sniping at her boss over the very idea of a children's story-time hour where the staff sat on sinking cushions and read to the young. Mike caught 'ludicrous' and 'sappy' being propelled through her sullen lips.

*This is a woman who knows what she wants or rather what she doesn't.*

The closer he got, the clearer this chestnut-haired dame became and he could make out the name badge pinned on what appeared to be a handmade grey cardigan.

"Mary."

"Happy to help."

This produced another chuckle and snort as this Mary looked decidedly unhappy. Ordinarily, he wouldn't give a passing glance to a girl like this but there was just something about her that he couldn't quite put his finger on. She certainly did not have the prettiest of names, but it seemed to fit her well, so Mike didn't stop his unspent libido from scooping up this turbulent Mary with her slender frame and woven scowl and plotting her down in all manner of pleasing scenarios. Well, pleasing to him certainly, but who knew what women wanted. It seemed far too straight forward to simply ask.

Mike waddled, off-balance due to his awakening bulge, straight up to her and was determined to turn on whatever charm he could muster. He had never charmed a lady before, but there was a first time for everything. At twenty-two years old, he was desperate for his first time, and that nervous frustration made itself known as he sweated profusely with every step forward.

Maybe charm and charisma were just instinct. He had seen it in movies but that was all pretend, he told himself. Maybe it's just something you're born with and lies dormant until the happy, happy day arrives when you meet the girl you're fated to wind up with, and the beast inside awakens.

He wanted to believe so, it would make things a great deal simpler and take all the pressure off him, knowing that he could put in no effort and still come away with a spring in his step. That scenario suited him just fine.

"You better make it quick, Sir. I'm about to quit this sad excuse for an establishment," piped the definitely unhappy Mary to the quivering mess of a man standing before her. The books dropped to the ground the second she spoke to him. Sweaty hands, no doubt. *Typical man,* she thought.

"So, I guess that means dinner is on me tonight then," Mike quipped, shocked that he was able to form actual words and not just a series of stutters and drools.

Forcing himself to ignore not just the pile of unread literature now crowding his feet but also the developing bruise on his shin from where the largest book had thunked down on him (damn you, Dumas), he noticed that he had caught her attention.

The soon-to-be former library assistant was taken aback by the directness of this stranger who had just sauntered into her life. She was a plain woman; her hair, though washed regularly, was dry and thin, an unremarkable smile lay behind her seldom decorated lips and her cardigan concealed a flat bosom. Not that anyone was hunting for it. The only noticeable curve on her entire body lay on the ridge of her nose.

Against all her rationale, a second in his company was all it took for her to know that she liked this man. Up until that moment, she had slipped through life unseen but then in walked Michael Rose, who looked at her in a way no one ever had before. He saw her with his third eye.

# Chapter Thirteen

Charlie awoke with a start as if someone or something had jolted him from his nightmare and thrust him back into the real world. It was those kind of nightmares that made him suspect the line between dreams and reality was as blurred as a winter-battled windscreen. But what did he know about such things. He was just twelve.

His skin prickled with a strange heat that was becoming far too common and the cold remnant sweat of his nightmare was now lashing off slimy skin, clinging to the cheap fabric of his clothes. The icy air surrounding him could not touch him now.

He rubbed his eyes to wake himself fully, blinking away the fluorescent spots that danced their merry way around his eyelids. He arched backward, felt his shoulders crack and held out his hands in a direct line to his eyes as his vision readjusted to the rising moonlight starting to glare down on them, disturbed only by the running shadows of the snowfall.

Studying every indent and groove on his adolescent hands, he came to a chilling conclusion; the hands that just moments ago had held him under the water as the air was pumped out of his lungs until his body became limp and lifeless, had not been childlike.

Those hands had belonged to a grown-up. He felt that feeling way down deep in his gut and he trusted his gut. Only an adult could have produced the force needed to hold someone underwater until their life became forfeit.

*It was just a dream.*
*It was just a dream.*
*It was just a dream.*

He had died in the dream, yes, but woke up in his actual life, unless being trapped in this car with his feuding parents was, in fact, the afterlife. Charlie desperately hoped not. What kind of Almighty would play a sick joke like that on a child?

*It was just a dream.*
*It was just a dream.*

The more he repeated it to himself, the less confident he became of it. Doubt was slowly creeping its way inside. He shook his head furiously to try and free himself of this torment but it had burrowed inside his naïve mind and set up camp next to his love of comics and his bizarre, yet convincing, idea that he didn't quite belong. He was a normal twelve-year-old boy but still, this thought plagued him.

The mood in the car did little to assuage (he had word of the day toilet paper back home and that little nugget had been today's offering) the nagging sense of doom inside his head, feeling the silence in the car as it pulsed through him. It was a stronger, stranger one than the simple uncomfortable one that had existed earlier in the journey.

He had enjoyed that one, even if did only last a short while. This one was deeper, somehow sucking out not only the joy, little as it was, but also the very air itself. It made him sick to his stomach and strengthened his fear that his dream had escaped into the real world. Maybe dreams really did come true.

If you die in a dream, you can just blink and wake up in real life, but what happens when you die in real life? You stay dead. Even if you die with your eyes wide open, they just become cold and grey. Forever open to a world you can never see.

Charlie was trapped in his own fear and restrained by the silence, not daring to break it. He wasn't even sure he knew how to speak anymore. One of his childhood fears was that one day, he would lose his voice and be stuck screaming into a void, his face contorting as it turned purple from frustration, with no sign of anyone coming to help him.

Being under the *care* of his parents, it was easy to coast through life unheard. They visibly resented his normal, everyday voice with its shaking tones. It may have been a nuisance to them and everyone around him, but it was his and not only did he accept it, he liked it.

He convinced himself that if he were to open his mouth now, the dark water that stalked his dream would flood his lungs once more. He could feel the rapids starting to slowly swirl in his foot-well and so, he hoisted his feet up; no way was he going to let those sick, slippery hands get a second chance with him. No sir-e-bob. He had no clue who Bob was but if he helped him to stay alive, then he was probably an okay guy, even if he was a stranger.

Charlie had been warned about strangers once too often, but needs must.

*It was just a dream.*

# Chapter Fourteen

The snow was still coming down in thick, rushed masses and the car, which had braved the beast valiantly up until now, was showing signs of failure. Perhaps the engine, now spurting a chalky black smoke as it pushed on helplessly against the elements, had fought its last battle.

The car, now inches from ghosting and stranding itself and its occupants in the hellish frozen wilderness, gave a flick of the headlights and shone over a sign which was being quickly masked under the white blanket.

*ALMOST*
*A Town…*

At long last. The journey was over. The end of the line. Almost. The remainder of the sign was obscured by the snow, but it was just enough to restore the bare bones of hope. Another couple of minutes and the whole sign would have been neatly buried in its white tomb and Mike would have ushered the car blindly past the turnoff. It would have been as if the sign, and perhaps even the town itself, had never existed in the first place.

Almost had the feeling of a very old town. Eerie and unsettling, as if constructed to be the backdrop in some cult horror film. Like the house in *Psycho*. Lurking in the background and casting long shadows as unspeakable acts were committed centre stage. Charlie had always wanted to visit a movie set and so it seemed Christmas had come early this year.

For hours and hours and what seemed like forever, snow had blitzed its way across the land, maybe even the whole world at this rate, but there was little evidence of any kind of storm as they drove deeper into the pits of the town that Aunt Eve now called home.

There were no buckled branches or street signs slain by the fearsome wind. The town was, quite remarkably, untouched. The small scattering of snow that was present was a mere dusting compared to the rest of the journey though; somehow it seemed fake, decorative even.

"Thank the Lord, we've made it. I thought we would be driving around aimlessly all night," crept the voice of Mary Rose, causing everyone, herself included, to jump and recoil in the way that a person did when they had a half-dream about falling, waking themselves in mid-drop after the safe ledge slipped away from under their feet and they felt their bodies drop through the air as they rushed to a sudden and smashed landing on the cold, unforgiving ground below.

Wile E. Coyote made it look so easy on the television. But this was the real world and that sense of whistling doom never truly left a person. Her comment had been intended to be a casual one, but Mike knew better. He saw the point of his wife's barbed thorn glistening in the moonlight as the hour broke free from single digits. He felt the piercing jab, sharp to begin with as it made first contact and then crooked as it worked its way inside, teasing and twirling as it spiralled.

"Have a little faith in someone other than your precious Lord, dear; we got there in the end. All roads lead somewhere if you give them a chance," Mike rebutted through gritted teeth, his tongue coarsely running over a dented groove in one of his back teeth.

A nerve exposed.

"Michael, it is only by the grace of the Almighty that we have made it here in one piece. I felt for sure the car would have given up long before we reached Eve's, who, by the way, is probably thinking we decided not to come after all and just happened not to tell her.

"We were meant to arrive by 6pm at the latest and it is now just after ten, thanks to your idiotic timekeeping and pig-headed ignorance. I will have to deal with her hysterics. I love my sister dearly, but honestly, do you even know what it's like to deal with a maniacal woman, Michael. Well, do you?"

He twitched and blocked any discomfort that started to rise within him, in parallel to Mary's tone, but that's okay, he told himself. He was married to her, so he knew far too well how to repress even the most painful of feelings. After thirteen years of marriage, he was a seasoned pro.

He knew all her tones and almost all of them spelled trouble for him. This one, he knew, meant she was just getting started. She could never leave a wound alone. A sense of dread rushed him as his tongue continued its mini-marathon.

"By all means, feel free to doom yourself in future; you're an adult, even if you don't act like one, but I, for one, do not relish the thought of repeating this abominable journey with you again and freezing my a—" she continued, cutting herself off as she suddenly remembered there was a kid in the back seat. A kid who was pretending to sleep but was actually staring mournfully out the window.

Their kid.

"I will not allow myself, or our son for that matter, to be stuck in this claptrap of a car with someone as stubborn you. We shall be taking the train home."

A false sense of relief started to wash over Mike's face; his eyes brightened and his tongue paused mid-stride, but even after more than a decade of marriage, his timing was still a bit skewed.

"You do remember our son, don't you?"

She couldn't help but drive that last sting in deep, and Mike, with his face now struggling to hide its contortions as his tongue retook its place on the starting line to carry on its thrashing (eroding enamel as it neared the last dash with blood starting to scurry out from his gums), conceded.

"I'm sorry, Mary," Mike said, after composing himself and felt the mangled ivory in his mouth breathe a sigh of relief.

*There we go, we can all move on now.*

# Chapter Fifteen

Charlie, who for the past several minutes had been looking out the window watching the unyielding town unfold before his eyes, failed to hear what might have been the one genuine apology his father had ever produced. He certainly had never been on the receiving end of one, sincere or otherwise.

With his eyelids low and arms stretched out over his head, it was a cinch to make his parents think he was asleep, albeit in a strange position, if they bothered to look at him. A low risk but stranger things have happened.

He lay slumped against the rear passenger side door, head tilted to the outside world and with a finger in each ear. Driving them in deep to drown out the car crash in the front seats. It seemed you couldn't go on vacation without taking a little bit of home with you.

The louder they got, the deeper he plundered, causing a horribly familiar sensation but he never once fought the urge to release himself. Sadly, it was necessary. It was all he could do just to get by. His body was accustomed to this form of self-abuse. The pain and discomfort was the price he had to pay for having been born into that *family*.

Mary, in shock of the apology falling from her husband's lips, was silent and numb. She didn't think it was exaggerating when she thought that it was the single most unexpected thing that had happened on that journey. Perhaps even in their whole marriage.

Michel Rose simply lived his life wanting the same day on repeat, never having to think beyond the moment he was in. He was desperate for an easy life that was always just out of reach, which left Mary irritable and unsatisfied. He was not a spur-of-the-moment man and so, there had been no surprise orgasms; sometimes one would feel unheard of. Not even flowers at the end of the week.

*He's a gardener. He works with flowers every day. Would it have killed him to bring just one home with him? Just once!*

65

What good was an apology now? She had built up so much tension, too much, during her one-woman show from a moment ago and she needed an escape. A release valve for all the hot air that had overwhelmed her. She needed him to bite back.

Isn't that what a marriage was? An ebb and a flow. Mary had become acclimatized to a warring marriage. What was she to do if peace suddenly broke out? She simply was not conditioned for it, maybe once upon a time but not now. Not anymore. She had moved on, evolved, because she had to. Being married to a lay-about had left her with no alternative. Adapt to survive.

She was battle-worn and incapable of slipping back into her sedentary life of long ago. Who was she without the fight? All her ideals of a happy life with a loving husband had been cleansed years ago. Too long ago to sound a retreat now.

Fractured and miserable, that was her comfort zone, and that is where she saw herself spending the rest of her days. Not really living, just existing in the same space as the man she had pledged herself to in front of the Almighty. The church would not have tolerated such fantasies as divorce and so that desire was quickly neutralized when it reared its ugly, seductive head. A marriage was a life sentence.

Her brain was not wired for a complete turnaround. The idea that Mike, who she had known for almost fifteen years and married for thirteen, could somehow redeem himself simply by saying two words, two measly, meaningless words, just did not compute with her.

Any love she once had for him had been burned out of her as the years of frosty animosity trudged on. Slowly wearing her out until all that remained was the shrill shell of a woman she knew she was. Some days that's all she knew about herself. About anything. So just what in tarnation was he doing saying *I'm sorry*?

*You cannot just press reboot on a whole marriage, Mike.*

Just no, she said to herself repeatedly. Each time with a little less conviction in a voice that was becoming increasingly shaky. A voice she failed to recognize with its desperate, uncertain twang.

*You just can't.*

"It's okay," was all she could muster in retaliation and even that was a struggle as her brain was too busy breaking down at the thought of something new.

# Chapter Sixteen

Mike slowed at an intersection, passing a boarded-up hardware store and what was most likely a haunted children's play park that were positioned either side of his turning. It reminded Charlie of one park back home where he had once fractured his arm by tripping over the sandbox.

Some kids broke their bones by doing daring stunts from atop the big jungle gym but not Charlie. Clumsiness and inconsistent muscles were enough to give him cause to pay a visit to the children's ward at the local hospital. To this day, he can still hear the sound of his little bones crunching under the weight of his eight-year-old torso. He never knew he was so strong, but maybe it was just a bad angle.

The sounds coming from this spooky play park, however, were not ones of shattering bones but rather the sound of a swing set creaking through the howling wind. A haunting rotation that began with a slow rise and finishing with a sudden crash as it swung wildly back.

Up ahead, Charlie thought he saw the curtain in one of the nearby houses twitch, just for a moment. A light then flickered inside and although it was the most normal thing in the world, it took him by surprise. It was the first sign he had seen that there was anyone living in his ghostly town. The hairs on the back of his neck stood firm as his dad stopped outside this particular house. Aunt Eve's house.

"We are here," cried his mum, making no attempt to hide the disbelief in her voice.

Charlie shuddered as he exited the car and took in the joyless home in all its insufferable dread as cold air cut through him as easy as a knife slicing its way through a piece of cake or meat.

"Stop dawdling, Charlie and get a move on. Now. It's straight to bed with you and no arguing."

Charlie lumbered his resisting body up a path littered with weeds sprouting from beneath the cracks. *Huh, his aunt and uncle had the same weed problem as his parents,* he thought. Funny that.

Mike pushed the hefty door and felt it give, and for the first time in what felt like a long time, felt the warmth as it swamped them all with its unnatural cling. The ungodly atmosphere of the town had seeped its way into young Charlie's skin as what he expected to find was cobwebs strung across the strip lights above, stairs that squeaked under the weight of a single rat's tail and shifting floorboards to take him this way and that way through the house of horrors.

What greeted them, however, was an ordinary home, decorated with basic and bland interiors. The front door led directly to an open plan kitchen and living area. A woman, draped in a flowing black robe, clutching a burgundy handbag and with a tight blonde bun sitting on top of a miserable face, rose from a small side table by the window.

The way she breezed across the floor made Charlie think she was floating and the small light shining through behind her made it seem like she was more shadow than anything else. This sight did little to dampen his idea of witches and spectres.

It had been a good couple of years without seeing his Aunt Eve, in every sense of the word, and while he may have been initially shocked by her ghoulish appearance, he found himself nodding. This was, after all, the image he had built up of her in the wonderful absence; his dad had even called her a witch one time when he thought Charlie was out of earshot during one of his many lively debates with his mum.

Although Charlie couldn't be certain it was 'witch' he heard, but looking at her now, it made perfect sense. Of course, she's a witch; why else would she subject her family to this town? Halloween was almost two months ago but it seemed Almost hadn't quite got the memo on that.

"Mary, darling, lovely to see you!" Eve exclaimed with a smile that looked painful as she turned immediately to Mike. "You really ought to be a better timekeeper, Michael. All the kids are asleep and Brian limped away upstairs almost an hour ago. Or did you just did get lost? Again?"

"I've just driven through hell to get here. There is a blizzard raging away, in case you hadn't noticed, Evelyn," he retorted, trying to punch every word.

"Oh, now then really, I can see your fanciful imagination has been running wild as per usual. It's no wonder Charlie gives the pair of you such grief. Look outside, barely a flake in the sky," she tutted in a put-upon French accent. All of Mike's jabs had clearly failed to find their mark as she remained fully capable of pushing words out through her polished jaw. "And how many times must I correct you? It is Eve, not Evelyn. Mary, darling, you really should learn how to keep him in check. It'll stop all that nonsense. Trust me."

It had been less than two minutes in the door and Mike was about ready to turn around and head for home. Safe, dependable, boringly predictable home.

Eve ushered them up a set of stairs at the back of the open room and swiftly dropped the news that Charlie would have to doss down on a rollaway bed in their room, bringing a collective sigh from the three of them. Mike and Mary were too tired to complain and Charlie was too disheartened.

No kid wants to share a room with their parents, especially when that kid was in dire need to explore his body with a helping, guiding hand from Miss Mindy as thoughts of her dashed behind his silvery-blue eyes.

Despite his confused and fearful mind, the nightmare in the car had failed to ruin his craving for the sweet treats Miss Mindy had stowed away beneath her clothes. Showering the first chance he got tomorrow was going to be his special mission. And like a good little soldier, he would see his mission completed. With bells on, whatever that meant.

Eve toured them past pictures of her drab children in their matching uniforms, hung at a perfect angle and showed them into an already cramped room at the end of the hallway where a rollaway bed had been placed on what little floor there was.

Without waiting to hear their views on their yuletide abode, said goodnight ('bonne nuit' in actuality, drawing a snort of derision from Mike) and left them to collapse into their beds. So far, none of them were in the holiday spirit.

# Chapter Seventeen

Eve Prentice, whose real name was Evelyn but took it as personal disrespect whenever someone, mainly Mike, actually called her that name, played the part of an insufferable woman exquisitely. In her eyes, she was a nobody from a nothing town until she moved to Almost.

Now, she was a somebody. The only saving grace about her former life was being able to witness the passion of Father Stringer first-hand, week in and week out but even that was not enough to satisfy her hunger for something more. A grander purpose.

Working at Super Savers was not in her endgame and so, after a long conversation with Father Stringer, he was able to pull some connections in Almost and landed her a job at Apollo Prep, a specialist boarding school, where the next generation of devout Americans were sculpted in the vision of a higher being. She may only be a glorified filing aid but it was better than the tedious job in her previous life.

Some families might have discussed the upheaval, both physical and emotional, that moving would bring, but in their household, one voice reigned supreme and it was not the timid squeaks of her husband, Brian.

While only the students who were over eleven could be housed in the compound adjacent to the school, it offered elementary life-improvement classes starting from five years old. Children of employees had tuition paid in full, courtesy of the investors; so, it was perfect timing for the Prentice's as their first child, William, was almost five years old and due to start proper education.

There would be no risk of corruption from lesser establishments. His mind, untouched by man, would be like a beautiful uninhabited island, just ripe for the ruining.

The move proved fruitful for them all as within a year, Eve gave birth to a girl, Jennifer, and so, all of Brian's mousy protests of stolen youth were self-muted as he had now found his purpose; a stay-at-home dad while his wife's nose was free to grow an extra unseemly inch with every passing term she spent within the joyless walls of her newfound paradise.

Father Stringer had briefly prepped her before she took on the job, so she knew to expect a slow climb to the top, but spending six years without ever leaving the confines of the administration office could take its toll on the body and her arms were beginning to ache.

Eve worked throughout her latest pregnancy, refusing to listen to colleagues when they advised her to rest. The unfortunate few who presumed to know what was best for her, were blasted with harsh truths she had acquired about them. Her eyes may have been a calming, silvery-blue but her tongue was coarse and fiery and one scolding from Eve Prentice was all it took for the matter to be settled. Indefinitely. She secretly hoped that her superiors were pleased with her dedication and that it would encourage them to see her true potential.

She had given birth during the summer break and come September, was back in her little cubicle. Eve (despite all outward appearances) loved her children, intensely, but she was not about to let the trials of motherhood stand in the way of her career. Even love had its breaking point.

A little shit machine named Frederic (not an ounce of French in his veins but a hell of a lot of inherited snobbery) was welcomed into the arms of the family and Eve suspected that Brian and the new baby shared a similar intellect. They were both needy and helpless after all and so, it was the perfect pairing.

With both William and Jennifer now being coached under the same roof, Brian only had little Frederic to care for during the daytime but with the two-week break from their rigorous education fast approaching, Mummy dearest knew the baby, along with her two other delightful bundles of joy, would be too much for her dope of a hubby to manage.

Eve alone was more than poor, defenceless Brian could cope with and so, she did the one thing she had sworn never to do; she reached out to her sister for help.

Eve was aware of the problems taking place in her sister's marriage and was apprehensive at inviting that breed of chaos to her doorstep but needs must, though she did quietly pray that Mary would leave dumb and dumber at home for the festive period.

While Mary's marriage may have been turbulent, Eve viewed her own as one of convenience, looking upon Brian as more of an object than a partner. Safe and reliable. Like an old cardigan. A good fit.

The two star-crossed lovers had agreed that three children was their lot. They had arrived into the world screaming and her eardrums could not handle another note of a shrieking child. Having Eve Prentice for a mother, it was no wonder they squealed like corralled sheep before feeling the sting of a bolt dead centre in the head.

There would be no escape for William and Jennifer as she had freely offered them up to the clutches of Apollo Prep where they would be moulded and shaped into the arrogant, lonely people they would inevitably grow up to become but Brian wanted to hope their latest child would fare better.

That hope, however, was crushed out of him from the second he let (as if he had an actual choice) his wife name the new-born. Powerless to stop her, he resigned himself to the life God had gifted him. Turned out there were times when a bolt through the head was preferable.

*Why God, why?*

# Chapter Eighteen

It was a troubled night's sleep for Charlie, but even though there was no visit from the nightmarish hands, their absence was somehow all the more menacing. He had refused to let himself drift off into the grey unknown but exhaustion quickly took hold of him and he found his eyelids falling and his mind slipping.

A feeling of being trapped in a dark pit and being stalked by the very shadows themselves stole his concern. A strip of sunlight crept in through the window and rested on his face, bringing sweet relief as his caged mind was freed.

He awoke and took more than a fair moment to readjust his mind to the unfamiliar surroundings, noticing that his parents were already up and about. No doubt woken by the intermittent wailing coming from the adjacent room. Most likely the baby but he was sure his uncle had more than enough reasons to let out a scream once in a while.

From the hush of footsteps to the prolonged sighs at 3 am and then again at 4 (and 5), it seemed as if everyone had suffered from a restless night.

Unperturbed by his tiredness, he sprang out of bed, working free the loose knot in his PJ bottoms and darted to the bathroom only to find it locked. A cry of 'beat it', coming from within. Were they ignorant or just cruel? That is precisely what he was intending to do in there. The voice had the needy, cloying airs of his cousin William, who, moments later, strutted out with his hair oiled and combed to within an inch of its life.

Before he could dash inside and make the intimate acquaintance of Miss Mindy, he heard the shrill morning blues of his mother as she called him down for breakfast, causing a stomped strop as he bundled down the stairs two at a time with the smell of crisping bacon and spitting sausages luring him away from his unseemly desires.

The best breakfast he got back home was toasted stale bread smeared in cheap, watery butter. It was no surprise that it was neither of his parents manning the helm at the stove this morning; his father had conveniently buried his head in a newspaper and Mummy dearest was bustling away in some cupboards with his aunt looming over her.

Maybe a couple weeks with the relatives wouldn't be so bad; sure, he would be chastised and degraded but what else was new? At least here he would be well-fed if his uncle's breakfast was anything to go by.

As the adults mulled over the dreary events of their lives, reopening badly sealed wounds as they did so, Charlie wolfed down his plateful and noticed through his shaggy hair that William and Jennifer had barely touched their plates of big breakfast goodies, not daring to let more than a morsel of greased meat slip past their polished teeth.

Charlie felt sad for them, but that quickly passed as he took the chance to chow down on their leftovers. He was happy as Larry, whoever he was. His cousins were not like the kids he knew; they did not slouch when they ate, their elbows rested gracefully by their hips and their upper lips remained stiff as a chilled wind blew in from an open window at the opposite side of the room, with the morning dew riding strong. He supposed that was what happened at their fancy school. A child entered and a shell departed.

After breakfast, they busied themselves around the house for an hour or so; Mike surveyed the garden and deemed it an inhospitable environment for something to be nurtured, bringing a hushed chortle from Brian. William and Jennifer did chores, maintaining the same degree of entitlement they exuded during breakfast, and Mary and Eve planned out the next two weeks, with the occasional glance in the baby's direction.

Just enough activities to keep the kids occupied without being a nuisance. Charlie disappeared back upstairs and promptly entered the bathroom, adamant not to throw away yet another chance to be the good little soldier.

Stepping inside, he immediately locked the door and within a flash, he was as naked as the day a doctor pulled him free from his mother's stomach, displeasing her from day one by all accounts. Standing awkwardly, he found himself surrounded by lime green cabinets as he waited for the water pressure to kick in.

Charlie swayed on the spot and studied a fish-themed rug in front of the shower unit but quickly diverted his train of thought. This was no time for fish, he told himself sternly, even if there was a humpback whale waving its fin at him.

The next ten minutes, or however long these things take (two minutes max if you're lucky, according to Denny), were to be entirely about Miss Mindy. He was sure she would appreciate the devotion.

*A boy enters and a man will depart.*

He closed his eyes as water rushed over him and the cubicle filled with gloriously hot steam. A hand reached out and beckoned him to join her. He was ready, putting his hand in hers and letting her guide him into the unknown.

The steam was thick, yet he could see her perfectly. The outline of a slender beauty etched against the hot wisps. Her naked body was less than three inches from him and he could feel the silky weight of her breasts brush against his absent chest hairs.

His whole body shook and throbbed as a lump in his throat descended. She took one step forward and with one hand now positioned on the back of his head, toying with his hair, she kissed him. Passionately, intensely, lovingly. This was what he had wanted from the moment he saw her in the diner; it may not have been a hillside in summer or a beach under the stars, but it was a start.

Her tongue danced with his tonsils as her free hand softly grazed his torso before migrating south. He had never known a sensation like it, but he tingled and pulsed with excitement and expectation. His whole body was on fire.

He discovered the confidence and the know-how to place one hand on her rear, tenderly feeling the curve as water continued to splash down on his tensing fingers. He stiffened when her hand slowly wrapped itself around his dingle. He had put his hand in hers when she led him into the steam, and now, he would put his trust in her as she led him through this wonderful journey, exploring his body and awakening a dormant beast. Hungry for its new desires, craving every last drop of her offering.

Charlie sensed something bulging within his shaking frame. It felt like a slow build of thunder that gathered in the dark before exploding. The boy of twelve had been left at the door; for now, he felt ten feet tall and an age to match hers for the perfect connection.

*A boy had entered, a man would leave.*

He dared to let his quivering lips find their way to her soaking breasts. Their love was special, intimate and all too brief. Before he could fully enjoy her, his eyes had opened. His thighs ached, his wrist had knotted and any remnant of his love was being swallowed up by the drain.

Charlie stood dripping with a growing smile that beamed the sin of pride in all its naked glory and jerked out a hand to turn the shower off. His insides were streaked with beautiful lightning. His work here was done.

Mission complete.

He exited the shower and immediately, his head started to pound before he had set foot in the now muted room. Red, hot pain seared through his body. Everywhere all at once and he felt his legs give way, almost high-fiving the rug whale as he tumbled and knocked an elbow on the nearby sink.

He tried to call out, but the words refused to come. His mind was once again exposed to his nightmare and he felt the weight of a hand close tight around his throat. From the inside.

Charlie convulsed on the bathroom floor, all the euphoria that had been unleashed in the shower now seemed like a distant dream and the image of Miss Mindy was fading into the graceful wisps of the dissipating steam. Blood spurted from his writhing mouth and splattered the whale, who now swam in a sea of sickly red.

With his hands pressed firmly on the sink's rim, Charlie rose with his legs still shaking. Looking into the mirror, he caught a glimpse of his torso that was now scattered with bruises, probably from all the thrashing, he told himself, though in a voice that shook in parallel to his limbs.

His head throbbed as if something was trying to crack his skull from within and he ran his hands over his body with aching fingers, tenderly caressing the splotches of black and blue.

As quickly as the pain had taken him, it left him as he collapsed. The tension in his throat and skull vanished and he lay naked on the marble-effect tiles with fear and confusion once again rearing their ugly, yet all too familiar, heads. Tears streamed down his trembling face.

In his haze, he couldn't even remember one ounce of the joy Miss Mindy had brought him and in that moment, struggled to even remember her name. The fantastic ecstasy of the memory was now corrupted as it fell beneath the surface. Sinking into the dark recesses of his once sweet, innocent mind.

A voice, small and croaking, told him he was being punished for his indulgence. After a few minutes, the initial shock passed. Charlie repositioned the rug, so the whale's bloody seabed was shrouded under the sink.

He dressed quickly when he heard noises in the hallway outside and scurried into the bedroom to rummage through his bag until he happened upon the perfect item to hide the bruises. Luckily, none of them were visible above the neck, not even the abrasions left behind by the rock-hard hand in his throat. It had been just moments away from turning his skin a foul purple and Charlie was certain it was the same one from his nightmare.

Almost certain.

Charlie hurriedly changed into an assault-on-the-eyes turtleneck his mum had insisted on packing for him before making his way downstairs, determined to put the whole ordeal out of his mind. To leave it undisturbed and just hope it showed him the same courtesy.

He may not have understood the how or the why, but he was not so naive as to expect a miracle and praying would only lead him down a path adorned with the judgmental eyes of his mother and the image of Father Stringer waiting for him at the end with his skeletal arms opened. Just waiting to swallow him up in his crippling embrace.

Did every boy thrash and convulse so violently after their first *playtime*? Something told him not. Why was he so special? A boy had entered the bathroom, but exactly what had departed?

# Chapter Nineteen

With his aunt and uncle's car being too small to accommodate their ever-increasing brood and what with the newfangled car seat taking up two whole seats, William had the honour of being forced to ride with Charlie as they headed out of town to a Christmas market.

Away from his mother's constant scrutiny, William seemed to relax a little, even daring to slouch an inch in the back of the car. Clearly not as uptight as Charlie first suspected; he should really stop judging people as quickly as they judge him.

Maybe they could even be friends. Nick and Denny were great, but it would be a hoot and a half to have a third friend. Maybe William could visit during holidays and then, Charlie could introduce him to all the wonders of the clubhouse.

Maybe William, Will as he would be known forevermore by the geeks, could be their fourth member. Maybe Will could sneak a couple of comics out for him, as a thanks for having shown him this whole new world. Not that he needed a thank you, having a new friend would be thanks enough for Charlie.

As they made their way along the road, he could not help but notice how much the town had transitioned as daylight hit. The horror show he had encountered last night seemed like a distant memory as Almost was now just an average town, filled with the same breed of unremarkable people as his own.

Not so much Halloween town anymore, but Plainsville, USA. The monsters may have been in his head but their ghoulish hold over him as they had crept through the town last night had felt painfully real. The chill in his spine had faded and the hand around his throat had loosened. He could breathe again.

Their car pulled up alongside his uncle's in a field strewn with collapsible stalls that bustled with ornate novelties and tacky must-haves to entice the bickering families in. It seemed the perfect time to pick up last-minute Christmas gifts or, as Charlie suspected of a man with a child strapped to his back who

79

lurched past them in a perspiring daze, the only chance to shop. Tiny Tim in the back was bobbing along to the panicked rhythm.

His uncle disappeared down a makeshift alley, with enough of a quickened step that he was unable to hear his wife's bellows to take Frederic with him. The baby was only a few months old and already a pawn between its parents. Welcome to the real world, kid. That was one hell of an early education.

Charlie ambled about next to a gothic stall selling handcrafted jewellery while his mum grew fascinated with one that specialized in crockery donning the Almighty and his kin. Just what every household needed.

"That's a c-c-cool necklace," Charlie said as he eyed up an item with a pointed star in its centre. "It's a shame I don't have a si-s-s-sister or I might have g-gotten it for her. I do have a girl cousin though, but I think she might be a bit young for jewellery. I have two b-b-boy cousins and one girl c-cousin."

"This isn't the type of necklace that's just for girls, young man. This is for anyone and everyone."

Charlie was taken aback by being called *young man*. Usually it was *boy* or just simply *oi* but this term brought on a smile he chose to hide. More out of habit than anything else.

"Really?"

"Why yes. So long as it fits." The seller chuckled and saw a light in Charlie's eyes grow brighter.

The man, who had looked past the stuttering bag of nervous bones, let Charlie try on the necklace and as it dropped down to rest against his quickening heartbeat, he saw his reflection in a wood-framed mirror next to the stall. He found that he really did look cool and could feel the hidden smile creeping up on him again.

With a quick glance over his shoulder to make sure neither his parents nor relatives were near, he bought the necklace with his allowance. You sure do save up a lot of pocket change when no one will let you near a comic book store.

With a final look at himself in the mirror, he let out his smile, another thing which had been long saved up. He had little reason to smile these days, but the pain and horror of the morning was forgotten for those fleeting moments in which he saw himself. A really cool dude indeed.

He began to walk away with a spring in his step, strutting as if he were on cloud nine itself, when the wailing call of his mother brought him crashing back down to Earth. The hairs on the back of his neck stood firm and he could feel his torso ache once again. As if his mother's voice, riding strong on a brisk current, had pushed his bruises in deeper.

Knowing, and fearing, her reaction to his new ungodly purchase, he discreetly tucked the necklace beneath the turtleneck. Maybe he didn't hate the clothing as much as he first thought when he had gotten it for his tenth birthday. Turns out he could hide a great many things beneath it. Winter warmers had their uses.

The milestone of turning the big 'one oh' and all his parents thought a boy would need was a good, strong, dependable sweater. Jeez, did parents know anything about children? His certainly didn't. Nick got a remote-control helicopter AND a baseball bat for his tenth birthday, for Pete's sake.

First Bob, then Larry and now Pete, who next? Although Peter did also happen to be the name of Nick's dad, so maybe Charlie could let that one slide.

Birthdays and Christmases were so unappreciated in his household that they almost became non-events. Charlie dreaded what was lying beneath the plastic tree this year, if anything. Aunt Eve would not hear of such a thing as bringing a real tree indoors. It would stay where the Almighty intended, thank you very much.

He re-joined his family and saw that they had been busy ransacking the stalls that specialized in higher quality crafts and specialty foodstuffs. Charlie had never been to a market like this before, but he just knew this one seemed posher than what would be considered normal.

No wonder they were here. He saw a bottle of Worcestershire sauce poking its way out of a stuffed wicker-like bag and had absolutely no clue what it was or even how to pronounce such a thing.

His uncle returned, looking a little worse for wear; no doubt from trying the free samples from the home brew stall toward the rear end of the field. Luckily for Brian, his darling wife knew how to drive. Unluckily for Brian, however, he would not be allowed to suffer his oncoming headache in peace.

Eve's neck bulged and a vein in her forehead pulsated as she let a rage build within her. A public shaming would show him, remind him more like, of who was boss but that would not be respectable and so, she let her emotions simmer, just enough, until later when they would be alone.

If Brian were smart, he would cling to Mike, or anyone for that matter, until Eve either forgot she was angry or died of old age. Whichever came first. Image was everything; even here, Charlie noted as they all walked back to the cars in silence.

# Chapter Twenty

They returned home a little before lunchtime and to Charlie's dismay (and his stomach's sorrow), his uncle made a sullen retreat upstairs to the spare room with his head in his hands. Aunt Eve followed with a purpose in her heel and seemingly ice in her tongue from the way her lips curled under themselves. Clearly, it had been a gruelling ride home; something Charlie knew a great deal about.

He also knew it meant someone else would have to conjure up their lunches. Mercifully, a plate of cheese and ham sandwiches greeted him and his cousins. It was quick, simple and required no effort (the holy trinity for the indifferent parent) but by the look and taste of it, it was most definitely the posh stuff. The sort of stuff they would never have back home.

He steeled his mouth, put on his brave boy hat and found that it wasn't entirely horrible. Still not as good as the ordinary stuff but at least there was no mayonnaise. Small mercies. He imagined a posh person's mayo to be a vile attack on the senses and one that left a puddled mess in its wake.

Now, all he had to do was work out what a gentleman's relish was and his tongue could rest easy. William noted that it was similar to the sandwiches off their lunch menu at Apollo Prep, leaving Charlie relieved that his school was comprehensively ordinary.

"What's that sparkle?" Jennifer asked as she walked past him and saw sunlight catch on the twisted chain of his necklace. In the growing fear of dribbling the *good stuff* down himself, he had removed the turtleneck, forgetting what secret treasure was buried beneath.

"Oh, j-just something I got earlier. At the m-m-market."

His answer was hurried, with his shoulders up to drown out the conversation but with a quick peek, he saw that his mum was busying herself with dishes over in the corner. His dad was typically absent. Fear rose and dipped in quick succession.

*Good. We are safe. For now.*

William, with his interest piqued, reached for the chain and before Charlie could stop him, had yanked it out into the open air.

"A necklace? Ooh la-la," he sniggered, carefully dabbing a drop of butter from the corner of his mouth with one of his mother's new napkins that displayed interlocking vines at the corners in a neutral grey. *The French lessons were clearly going very well,* Charlie thought.

"I got it b-b-because it lo-ooks cool. The g-guy selling it said so himself," Charlie fired back in an attempt to be firm but all the while struggling to free himself from William's grasp.

"Charlie got himself a necklace," howled William, who was now almost choking his cousin.

From the sudden stop of running water, Charlie just knew his mother had heard the outburst. Fear rose again like the slow ascent of a rollercoaster.

"Why can't you kids just be quiet?" Mary barked.

"Charlie got himself a necklace," William repeated with all of the taunt but none of the humor, as he finally released his grip.

Mary snatched the necklace before it could rest in the cushion of Charlie's chest and felt her face contort as confusion, mixed with annoyance, washed over her.

"What is this ungodly junk?" Her voice was stern and growing. She pushed her spectacles into their perfect position.

"I g-g-got it today, at one of the s-stalls," Charlie said quietly, avoiding his mother's eye as he spoke. He would not be pulled in.

"If this is what you spend your allowance on, then your father and I might just need to have a conversation about cutting it off completely," she said, still with the centrepiece of the necklace in her hand. "Honestly, Charlie, sometimes I feel like giving up with you. First the comics and now, this heathen thing. It's just rubbish after rubbish with you."

Cool air wafted in through an open window and cleansed his face but he just felt cold. A strange feeling was brewing inside him. It wasn't fear, not exactly, but it held him nonetheless with an unrelenting hook. The rollercoaster was almost at its crest and he could feel the scream rise inside him; but so far, he was holding firm, refusing to give in and hoping the scream would die before it reached his throat that still ached from hours ago.

From the corner of his eye, Charlie could see William sneering at him, obviously elated that he had a front row seat to his scolding. Poor William had just forfeited any chances he had of becoming the next forgotten geek, whether he knew about it or not.

Charlie decided that he was not going to be showing him all the cool stuff about the clubhouse and he would never share their secrets with him. Now, he just wanted to wipe that stupid smirk off his equally stupid face.

"If you're not going to learn how to act respectfully, then perhaps we will have to consider sending you away to a school like the one your aunt works at. Where the word of the Almighty will be drilled into you morning, noon and night. You can see the wonders it has worked on dear William here."

She gestured with her free hand to the now prim and proper William who gave a graceful nod in return for the adulation.

"NO!" The rollercoaster fell, crashing down hard toward the unforgiving Earth and birthed the scream that had been twelve years in the making. For as long as he could remember, it had been there, bubbling just below the surface until the fateful day arrived when he was able to unleash everything that was concealed within.

The strange feeling in Charlie was now blended with anger and refused to let go. He stood to face his mother, who was momentarily stunned by the gall of his outburst and looked up, directly into her eyes. He yanked the necklace from his mother's vice but was unprepared for one of the pointed ends of the star to strike him hard on the jaw when she tried to resist his pull.

Blood trickled out from the side of Charlie's face and before he could dab himself dry, he received another strike; this one cold, yet hot, and flat, yet sharp, as the palm of his mother's hand connected with his cheek. With his eyes watering and his face rippling, he heard not just the dull ringing that he came to expect after such a reprimand, but also the piercing howl of his cousin.

William, fighting the urge to punch the air in a twisted celebration, wept with laughter as Charlie almost lost his footing. It was undignified of the gentlemen figure that was being disciplined into him but in that moment, he didn't care. His aunt would undoubtedly tell his mother how he had revelled in another's suffering and she would discipline him harshly for it, but it was worth it.

Seeing his snively, pathetic, shit-for-brains cousin taken down a peg would satisfy his warped idea of fun throughout the whole Christmas break and another ten more after that, he reckoned.

The peculiar feeling let Charlie's anger take the reins. Its grip cut deeper than the bell tower rope. His skin boiled and cracked before turning a choking purple in places and a scaly, sickly green in others. His muscles tensed expectantly and promptly matched the thundering beat of his young heart.

With his body now inflamed and his mind swinging between what was normal and what was not, he failed to notice the pain in his cheek was dimming, as if about to take a back seat. He staggered forward from the dizzying trauma, caught his arm on a chair in a futile attempt to soften the blow but instead, fell clean through. The chair split in two, wrecking the delicately patterned garden engraved into the back of it and a single rose was skewered by one of its own wooden splinters.

"Really, Charlie? You can stop all this horseplay this instance, young man. Now, get up." There was a hint of regret in her bite, but it was buried deep within her bark that it went unnoticed, even by her.

The ringing in Charlie's head stopped just in time to hear his mother drip her poison over the one phrase that had made him genuinely happy. It had not even been two hours since the market seller had seduced that smile out of his resisting body. Sadly, that was still his personal best and one which he supposed would now go unbeaten, even if he lived to be a hundred years old.

*Why can't he have nice things? Why can't he have a mother like the ones he sees—saw on TV?* God, he missed television. It was a strange moment for him to be thinking about such things, but it was his creature comfort. One of many that had been cruelly snatched away from him, and boy howdy, did he need some comfort right now. Just a drop would do but since he was left to spasm on the dining room floor, he suspected that his thirst would go unquenched. He was naïve, yes, but he wasn't stupid.

Charlie rose to his feet and felt his whole body shake and burn as scores of small, sharp thorns drove their way out from under his goose-bumped skin, tearing through his already fragile body. Some were curved, some jutted through others, doubling the already immeasurable pain, while some made barely an attempt to feel the free air.

Along the centre of his head was a misshapen line of nearly a dozen, almost all of which shattered upon being birthed, leaving tiny fragments of crooked, bloodied bone embedded in his skull with a chilling look that was not all dissimilar to someone standing on a broken mirror and seeing the tiny shards of glass sparkle against the underside of their socks. A circle of small thorns

85

appeared on his now discoloured throat, almost in the shape of a grown man's palm.

"Charlie, what are those?" His mum asked in a voice that was growing with disbelief, but her confusion was quickly swamped by a primal fear and she stepped backward, away from her wounded son.

With blood trailing its way down his face, eventually pooling around his mouth, Charlie went to wipe it away from his eyes but pricked himself on one of the many thorns that now littered his hands. "H-h-help m-m-me."

"You're a freak!" William exclaimed, reaching out to prod his cousin.

Charlie saw the hand extend toward him and without awareness, grabbed it with his own, now swollen. William yelled in pain as Charlie crushed his cousin's hand without meaning to. The taunting had stopped. It was as if someone had flicked a switch, turning William from crying with laughter to just plain crying.

Eve emerged at the bottom of the stairs and with a quick scan of the room, she saw her flawless dining room floor was now tainted with a puddle of blood and fractured wood, before her eyes landed upon her eldest child who was cradling his crumpled hand.

William whimpered with wide, glassy eyes while Jennifer ran and hid behind her mother's legs. Frederic, resting comfortably in his basket in the corner, didn't even rouse at the scene unfolding before them. He was the only one still incapable of judging Charlie.

He had yet to be taught how to fear that which was different, how to hate that which you couldn't understand. Given time, Frederic's moral skin would be forcibly shed under the careful direction of his mother.

"What is the meaning of this? Mary?" Her tone was direct. Empty of emotion but full of design. "How could you let this happen? No doubt your delinquent son is responsible."

Charlie was hunched over with his hands shaking but he saw the terror in her eyes while she was blinded to the shivering fear in his. All she could see were the thorns that had ripped through him, the purple and green skin that lay below his now tattered clothing and the blood skating down his face like some kind of amateur war paint. As far as she was concerned, there was now a beast in the place where her nephew should have been.

"Get away from my son, you freak. You monster," she said firmly despite the shaking anguish slithering its way into her throat.

Charlie sprinted past them all and ran upstairs, making a dash for the bathroom. Immediately locking it. His mind went hazy and some voice inside him, not his, but older and deeper, told him that being locked in meant safety. Whether the stranger meant his safety or theirs was yet to be seen.

In the reflection, he saw something horrifically ridiculous staring back at him through blood-soaked eyes. Looking devoid of all moisture, his laugh lines appeared to be constricting into thin, piercing slashes and his lips were spoiling to a bright red. Halloween had long since passed and this wannabe clown howled anything but laughter.

The cool dude from the Christmas market was long gone and now, all that remained was what? A freak? A monster? He didn't know and he didn't like not knowing. Tears flooded out of him, mimicked the lines of treacle red and stained his formerly pale face.

Once again, Charlie Rose collapsed to the floor and felt the unwelcome embrace of the cold marble tiles.

# Chapter Twenty-One

The fear failed to dilute Eve's anger, her emotions swelled in tandem with her son's now brutalized hand. Both were ready to burst but Eve set aside her favoured emotion and chose instead to nurture her firstborn, burying him in her cushioned chest.

After William found the strength to come up for air, he saw his mother dart out of sight and they all heard the hardened thuds of her knock-off heels on the stairs.

While Mary waited for her sister to return, she stood rooted to the spot, wanting the kitchen lino to turn to quicksand and swallow her whole and looked at anything but her nephew. Charlie had broken the hand as easily as snapping a wishbone at the Thanksgiving table.

She remembered what her wish had been that day; that they all have a straightforward holiday season and hustle along the best they could, but she knew something would come up. Something always did, but this was not in the playbook. Nothing seemed straightforward now; it was all a greying matter of fear and uncertainty.

*Why has he done this to me?*

She had seen the thorns and the scaled skin, but it was the look in Charlie's eyes that burned into the back of her mind now. As confused and scared as they had all been, it was Charlie, sweet little Charlie, who had looked the most terrified. What kind of mother would allow a child to be that afraid? She had smacked him just before he turned into whatever he was now. Was this all her fault?

*No. Don't be silly. Every mother hits their child. They can be little shits, we all know that. And a motherly smack is the only thing a nuisance child understands. This can't be my fault. I need to tell Michael. Where is he? The useless lump.*

*Charlie deserved that smack. He stood up to me. You never disrespect your elders like that, let alone your parents. I had to learn that lesson when I was half his age. Since he is so unwilling to get with the program, then the blame must lie with him.*

*Please Lord, make William stop crying.*

*This is not my fault.*

*Charlie deserved that smack.*

*This is not my fault.*


Eve reemerged in the doorway, bringing with her a dishevelled Brian who looked more than a little worse for wear. The Christmas market had gone strong with their ale stand this year.

"Look, will you? Stand up straight and look at our son," Eve spat with a scowl stretching across her hostile face.

Brian, readjusting himself and leaning on a chair for balance, followed the line of her finger until his addled view fell onto a weeping child.

"Will? What? What have you done? What's happened? Jeez, how long have I been out of it?" His voice may have been coarse and despite being unsure as to whether what he was seeing was real or imagined, he was able to slip in notes of genuine concern.

Not waiting for a response, he dropped to the floor beside his son and took the limp hand in his and stroked the back of his head while William caught his breath in between shudders.

"We need to get you straight to the hospital, buddy. I'll take—" he began to say before the sad truth dawned on him. "Your mother will take us. Then afterward, how about some ice cream? I know there's some Fudge Ripple around here somewhere. Maybe it's in your mom's 'secret' stash. How does that sound, champ?"

William managed to push a small smile through the pain.

"Eve, get your coat; we need to leave immediately."

"I'm not leaving until I've dealt with Charlie. I can't exactly trust you to do it," she replied with a hard stare in Mary's direction. Nature had retaken the reins.

"I don't know what you're talking about, but our son needs to see a doctor. Right now. So, grab your coat and let's go," Brian said with a hint of glee from someone else being on the receiving end of her fangs. "I'm guessing a simple case of rough housing that got out of hand, but you can explain on the way."

Eve was still for a moment. Poor, defenceless Brian had just told her what do to. She was both surprised and impressed and so, she did as instructed but insisted on bringing Jennifer and Frederic with them. Refusing to leave them under the same roof as *that thing*.

She could deal with *it* later. They dashed out the door and Mary heard the hustled burst of an engine and then, the sound of footsteps approaching from the garden. A moment later, Mike sauntered in, with a smug look spreading across his face.

"You should see the state of their garden. Untreated wood on the deck and a rockery that looks so bad, it could have been designed by our own Charlie. Anyways, what were they in a hurry about? I thought that schedule you've put us on was pretty jam-packed. No time to shit from what I saw."

Mike seated himself at the dining table, propped open the newspaper he had pretended to read during breakfast and chuckled to himself, sitting obliviously next to the wrecked chair.

"Michael, something's happened with Charlie. He—he—um—I don't know what exactly but it's bad. William got hurt and had to be taken to hospital."

"Shit, no wonder they looked like crap. I thought that was just Brian's hangover kicking in early. Or is it your sister that will be doing the kicking?"

Another chuckle left him as he thumbed the bottom of a page in the sports section. It breezed past his lips but grated on Mary and her already heightened nerves almost quivered against the hot air. She used to love his laugh, the craving tones of his once silky voice, but not anymore. Whenever he opened his mouth, it now felt like someone was scraping rocks across solid steel inside her head.

"Is Charlie okay?"

"I don't know. He ran upstairs in one of his moods and I heard the bathroom door lock. I haven't been able to bring myself to go and see him. I'm worried, Michael."

"What happened?" The look-at-me swagger in his voice was fast deflating and being replaced with a concern to match his wife's. If she was confiding in him about her fears, then shit really had hit the fan. The fact she was confiding in him at all told him now was not the time to push.

"Charlie was acting out like he always does. I swear, Michael, he has picked up this lazy, stubborn attitude from you and I do not thank you for it. I need your support handling him, but all you do is tie one hand behind my back. It has to stop."

Mike should have known not to trust his wife's tremors by now. Not completely at least. She could be an immovable force at times, and even now with some apparent incident hanging over them, she still spoke with the same cold rasp he was familiar with.

The helpless space that had crept into her nerves had dissolved and it was time for Mike's favourite game, the blame game. He had the all-time high score in his marriage. Nothing was ever Mary's fault.

"He needed a smack to remind him of the way things are meant to be. He is the child after all, but something went wrong. His body reacted funny, I guess and—oh, I don't know how to say it."

A feeling of unease gripped Mike's quickening heartbeat.

*She's finally done it. She's killed him.*

*No, that's ridiculous. She said he was upstairs sulking. He always doing that. Heard some loud noises. Sulk. Being told off. Sulk. Spanked for having a strop in the supermarket. Sulk.*

*But why would Will need a hospital because of Charlie's tedious cycle? Oh God, he must have bitten him or some shit.*

*I'm getting sick of this. All of this.*

"Just say it, Mary and will you please stop pausing? You don't want to know what I'm imagining."

"Okay, but you won't believe it. I saw it happen with my own eyes and I don't believe it. He started having a seizure or something and then he grew thorns. There's no other word for it. Charlie grew thorns. They sprouted up all over his body from what I could see, and his skin turned purple and green, with actual scales on it. And then, he crushed William's hand like it was a can of diet pop."

The voice was clear, but her mind was absent. Unburdening herself had taken her eyes away, driving them up toward the heavens where they received all the answers she needed. A switch inside her head had been turned on, or off, and a calming glaze now washed over her as she came back down to earth, just in time to see her husband adorning the same dumb look when the time came around for his annual taxes. Mouth open, eyes apart and just a hint of a head tilt.

91

"That's ridiculous, Mary. You're making him out to be some kind of animal. Normal people don't just go about turning into something else," Mike said, sitting in full disbelief, the newspaper now carelessly discarded.

"I think it is quite clear that Charlie is not normal. He has always been a little peculiar."

"There is a big difference between the two. He may be odd, naïve and annoying at times, but he is just an innocent little boy," Mike said, with one hand rubbing the side of his head, struggling to take it all in.

"No, you're wrong. He is different now. Something inhuman. Something impure sent from the pit of hell itself has lain siege within him," Mary began with a voice that rose in purpose as she walked toward the stairs, her eyes daring to look up and around before she continued, "The Almighty has judged us, Michael, for our battles and our sins. This affliction in Charlie is here to test our strength and we must overcome it. He needs an exorcism."

It was now the time for a switch inside Mike's head, cluttered in dust and webbing, to be flipped. Seeing how easily his wife was willing to poke and prod their only child made him all the more intent on protecting him. Standing up for his son and being a real father, maybe for the first time in sweet, little Charlie's short life, he was ashamed to admit.

He looked over at Mary and saw the same daggers in her eyes that he knew very well. They were serious, confident and dangerous. She had always wanted to be Father Stringer's second-in-command and it seems now she had just given herself a battlefield promotion.

"No. You're not going near him until you've cooled off." Panic snuck its way into his voice.

"HE has spoken to me, Michael and now, everything is clear. Charlie needs an exorcism to rid him of these demons and cleanse his soul. Only then will he be welcomed into the guiding arms of the Almighty. We all will if we repent and do as HE commands."

"Don't you dare! I'm not going to let you or any of your whack job churchies touch our son."

Mary, with her ears cottoned off to her husband's pleas, started her ascent. It was do or die time for the world's greatest father. Words had failed him and so, he would have to become a hands-on parent. He grabbed one of his wife's arms and pulled with enough force to launch himself in front of her.

He skated past her and stood firm at the top of the stairs, his shadow engulfing not just her, but the whole staircase. The hanging pictures of his niece and nephews now obscured, though the smugness remained as if it was woven into the very fabric of the house.

"You will never understand, Michael. Your lack of faith is my gravest sin. I thought by now you would have submitted but still, you press on with this futile errand. Do you even realize that the longer you resist, the stronger my faith has to grow? Are you so blind that you cannot see that it is exhausting trying to keep up with your disgraceful morals?

"The Almighty entrusted me to be your wife to save you but still, you fight me. You have to know that you will lose, because only I can win. I have to, Michael, because my faith is real, true and pure. It will not falter when the time of judgement comes and HE has come today. It must be done.

"HE also entrusted me to be a mother, so that I can save Charlie, from himself. I see that now. You MUST see it too. Michael, this is the only way. Charlie must be purged."

Her voice came in soft waves that rippled below the surface of the darkened stairwell, but they carried the bitter sharpness of her delusions. From behind him, Mike heard the sound of a door unlocking and felt a shrinking chill wash over his back.

A glimmer of light shone upon the maniacal face of the woman he had devoted himself to all those years ago. It lasted for less than a moment but he saw the sheer, unyielding sense of duty clouding her eyes. Still with his arms outstretched to block any passes, he angled his head to see his son, now trembling in the doorway behind him.

His eyes glanced over the abnormalities and found their focus on the bloodied, little boy who looked a great deal littler than he had just hours ago.

"D-d-dad, w-w-what's going on?" Charlie asked with his innocent, if a little croaked, voice intact.

Mary moved forward, her body pushing with full assurance that absolution was within her reach. Mike grappled with one shoulder as she tried to slip through but released when she dug her fingernails into his neck.

Mary looked at her son's damaged body with her inhibited eyes. "Impure. Impure. Impure."

"Mary, stop it. You're hysterical," he said, struggling. "He's our son. Just STOP!"

His voice punched outward and the air knocked her off-balance just enough for her to lose her footing and slip backward, her legs gliding over the crest of the first few steps before her body went crashing to the bottom. Mike stood motionless, it was tax return time all over again, with the initial beads of sweat beginning to trickle down his temple.

The hard-shell composure finally cracked as Mary Rose was welcomed by a solid wood finish at the bottom of the stairs. Her voice thinned in mid-air before dying completely and her last screech now hung in the air, incomplete. Her splayed legs were battered by the stairs and strands of carpet fibre collected around a shattered kneecap.

Blood was already starting to trickle out from a head wound, smearing a grin that, even in the fall, had refused to die. Once again, a light glimmered, just for a second before being extinguished.

# Chapter Twenty-Two

Eve pulled up to the hospital's emergency room, discarding her car next to an ambulance bay and hurriedly ushered William inside, leaving Brian (still in disbelief at the tall tale she had tried to relay to him) to wrangle their other two kids.

Her story had shocked some sobriety back into his system and so, he was able to correct her parking before wondering how a child could possess such gruesome appendages. Kids scrap all the time, but they don't become monsters with bloody thorns and vicious fangs. There was just no way she was telling the truth. Was there?

They had abandoned the baby seat in their driveway back home so that they could all slot in nicely, but this brought the knock-on effect of Brian being forced to hold the baby for the whole erratic ride. Little Frederic's screams growing louder with every bump and jolt as Eve had driven with a panicked foot on the gas pedal.

Heavy and shaking, like her heart. If William hadn't been in such pain, then he would have enjoyed the racing views from the front passenger seat. When Brian caught up to his wife and injured son, he saw her berating the woman singlehandedly manning the nurse's station.

"Listen, my son is in tremendous pain and needs to see someone immediately," she snapped, gesturing to William's deformed hand.

The nurse in question, elderly and with a passive face, told Eve she would have to take a number from the ticket machine and wait their turn like everyone else. She timidly extended one weak arm and pointed to a box mounted on the wall opposite, never raising her head from above the bulky computer on the desk in front of her. Her eyes transfixed on its blinking lights and purring motions.

Brian, struggling to hold a squirming Frederic in his arms, led William and Jennifer away to the seating area, taking a number like an obedient patient on the way. A tolerable '7'.

Eve fumed at the gall of it all. Her child was in agony, so surely that trumped everyone else's kids, no doubt in lesser pain and therefore less important. William, and by an extension herself, should come first.

Before she retreated, the old woman pushed a form toward her. Reaching out to take it, she could see beside the nurse's computer was an in-tray with a buckling mountain of papers, while the out-tray on the other side grew tired and lonesome. Dust bunnies mingled around its corners and a ready-to-hand stamper yearned for its seal to be broken.

She joined her family in the uncomfortable chairs with her hope now in shreds, sighing as she scanned the form with its mundane questions. If pushed, she would be unapologetic to admit she was tempted to answer the nature of injury question with a response that would fully shame Charlie for the freak that he was but thought better of it, simply writing 'broken hand'. There would be time enough to get her justice. Her revenge.

Against a twelve-year-old boy.

Time ticked by slowly, endlessly. Numbers were called but none of them the right one and fellow patients would disappear into consulting rooms down a painfully white corridor behind them. People of trivial value stealing the attention that should be on her son.

Each passing minute drew an array of silent slurs from Eve. Her eyes never left William's scrunched-up and tear-saddled face, assuring herself that he would no doubt pass out from the pain the second she dared to blink. All of time itself would run out before their number was called.

Before she could berate her husband for his throaty breaths, the stench of beer struggling toward a slow death, a man in a white coat with a flimsy haircut appeared, announced himself as 'Doctor Logan' and escorted them into an examination room, mercifully only two doors down the corridor.

She instructed Brian to remain seated with Frederic, now grappling for a plastic plant just slightly out of reach, and Jennifer, merrily whistling with her focus on an already completed colouring book, while she dealt with the doctor.

*He looks far too young to be an actual doctor. William needs the best, not this wannabe. He probably hasn't even finished medical school yet. He still has acne! Why is the whole world against me today?*

"I can tell someone has been in the wars today, but if you're a good little soldier, I've got just the thing to cure what ails you, little man. A lollipop with all the colours of the rainbow," the doctor said, removing a plastic wrapped treat from a drawer in the cabinet behind his desk, and then immediately returned it to its rightful place. He seated himself on a swivel chair, had a quick scan of the patient form and then gestured for William to hold out his hand.

"Are you a real doctor? Or did I mistakenly walk into the middle of a fancy dress party?" Her question was cold and the dopey grin on Doctor Logan's face was swiftly retracted.

"I assure you that I am fully qualified, Mrs Prentice. The sterile environment of a hospital can be daunting for small children, like your son, and so, I suppose I am guilty of having a whimsical nature with my younger patients. It helps put them at ease. It's important for them to be calm."

"Do not underestimate my child," she replied harshly, in the full knowledge that her family thrived in sterile places. "His freak of a cousin broke his hand. Crushed it in less than a second. Now, if you will kindly do your job, then we will gladly leave and let you grin moronically at your next poor patient."

Doctor Logan swallowed a retort and began the examination. He saw the fragile hand awash with bruises, the black and blue growing out from the wrist and galloping toward the knuckles. William's digits were limp and twitched softly when the doctor prodded them with his gloved hands.

"When did this incident occur, Mrs Prentice?"

"Today, almost an hour ago now. It would have been sooner if not for the infernal wait time you inflicted upon us."

"Hmmm."

"Hmmm? Is that your medical opinion?" Eve sneered, rolling her eyes and sharpening her vocal chords for the main course.

"It is unlikely that this level of bruising would show so rapidly on the skin. Was your son in good health prior to this? Any bumps or scrapes that you were aware of?" The question was clinical, all remnants of his jovial manner swiftly exited the longer he observed William.

"My son has excellent health. All my children do. He does not get into *scrapes,* as you call it. He goes to Apollo Prep where they make fine young gentlemen and ladies. He is not the sort to roll around in the mud all day getting black and blue. So, you will abandon those thoughts and actually focus on the issue at hand."

Doctor Logan examined William's hand again, swallowing a half-snort as he did so, not daring to be caught in Eve's coiling anger.

"While the nature of the bruising is suspicious, I believe I have good news for you, Mrs Prentice, and you too, scamp," he started, removing the surgical gloves and running a hand through William's hair, ruffling the plain, oily strands. "The hand does not appear to be broken."

"I told you his cousin was a freak, did I not? Who knows what horrors he is capable of? Of course it's broken, you incompetent fool. Just look at it."

"No, Mrs Prentice. While it does appear to be in quite a nasty state, and no doubt your son is in considerable pain, it is only bruised. The nerves and tendons in your son's hand and fingers responded just as they were meant to. I can, of course, prescribe him something for the pain."

His manner had relaxed but his fill of Eve Prentice was drawing dangerously close to overflowing and so, he glanced over the cruel way in which she talked about her poor nephew.

"Can't you X-ray the damn thing or are you just too inexperienced to deal with the matter? I want a second opinion. I heard the bones crunch myself," she said with nostrils flaring. Doctor Do-Nothing was dressing himself up as her next victim and with the mood she was in, she would gladly snap.

"But Mum, you weren't even in the room when Charlie grabbed me," piped William, now angling his head behind the doctor toward the drawer where he had replaced the lollipop.

Eve's focus was lost; her eyes shifted, her nostrils calmed and her mouth went dry. The grin on Doctor Know-It-All's face was beginning to reform.

"Don't interrupt, William. I—well—"

"Mrs Prentice," Doctor Logan began, leaping upon the gap with a placid voice. "I can see that you are clearly in great distress about your son's condition, understandably so, and I know how easy it is to let our imagination run wild and exaggerate a few truths in stressful circumstances, but I need you to hear me and to trust me.

"The bruises, though irregular, will heal. If they do not, then by all means, bring him back for further examinations but the bones are not broken. Any doctor will tell you the same. There is no good reason to X-ray the hand. To do so would be a waste of hospital resources, everyone's time including yours. Was that your family out in the waiting area?"

"Yes, my husband and two younger children."

"Then spend your time with them, not me. It is Christmas Eve after all."

"But Will—"

"Your son will be just dandy in a week or two, but in the meantime, stay off the battlefield, little man," Doctor Logan said, debating whether or not another ruffle was on the cards but opted to simply write the prescription for some pain meds, struggling to contain the grin as it returned to his lips. He had battled Mrs Prentice and her slithering temperament and came away victorious.

He noticed her mouth was still fighting against the idea of conceding and a scowl ran along the line of her eyebrows when she realized it was too late to retaliate. First, Brian telling her what to do back home and now, this jumped-up little know-it-all refusing to do as she commanded. Her snap was slowing, becoming less of a threat. Maybe she was the one in need of a doctor.

The doctor grabbed a lollipop for William and did one full swivel in celebration, and then another for luck as Eve and William left the examination room in silence. William's silence was one of childlike glee at the sight of the rainbow-swirled sweet, while his mother's was one of a deafening defeat.

Once the door was closed, Eve snatched the lollipop from William's good hand and promptly tossed it into a nearby waste bin, proclaiming the dangers of sugar to a young boy's dentistry in a new, unusual tone that was riddled with sulk. William's glee swiftly turned to sorrow, but he maintained his silence. He knew his mother too well to try and raise even a syllable right now.

They re-joined the others and Eve batted away all of Brian's nagging questions, telling him coldly to get all the kids into the car while she made a stop at the pharmacy.

When she had entered the hospital, full of panic and despair, she had sprinted past the pharmacy with its gaggle of drug-wielding patrons and had failed to notice that to the right of its counter lay a vestibule with pay phones inside. Now, she was filled, or refilled, with anger and a lust for vengeance.

She may have lost her fight with Doctor Logan but the day was far from over. Refusing to let her nature wither and die, she hurriedly picked up William's prescription before dashing to the nearest phone. There was still time to come out on top. She may have lost the battle, but she would win the war. By any means necessary.

# Chapter Twenty-Three

Mike stood frozen, his feet dancing precariously over the ledge of the top step, willing himself to descend the stairs, whether to help his wife or to join her was unclear but either way, his mind reverted to a basic setting, preventing any action.

He saw Mary's broken body, sighed and felt only fear. There had been moments, and dreams, where he had imagined this situation and the emotion that had dominated his subconscious had been relief not fear. Joy not shame. Euphoria not dread.

But now that his dream had come true, the reality of the situation hit him as hard as the stairs had hit his dearly departed wife. His freedom had come at a price and it would be the scared little boy who had sprinted to their makeshift bedroom the second his mother had slipped from view who would ultimately have to pay for his sins.

Mike bowed his head and wanted to cry. Nothing would be the same again. Nothing would be normal again. He wanted to separate the woman he had married from the woman whose silvery-blue eyes had turned to glass before the fall but he knew it was hopeless.

They were one and the same, maybe they always had been and maybe he had just been blind to it all these years. Indulging her fantasies little by little just to keep the peace. Charlie twisted his fingers in his ears when the warring became too intense, doing whatever he could to make his life bearable and his father was no different.

Mike may have willingly walked down this path but he had done it with his eyes firmly shut. Strolling out into no-man's land, oblivious to the carnage he was advancing upon. The carnage he had encouraged by his do-nothing attitude. Perhaps if he had fought back more often, pushed back, then he would not have been forced to push her down those stairs.

Mike may have won their final showdown but the last thing he felt was victorious. He turned away from the woman he had once been devoted to and headed for the bedroom to be with his son.

Entering the room, he saw a small, scared boy sitting on a rollaway bed, head pressed painfully into knees that were now crammed into his chest. Mike had refused to believe Mary's story of thorns, just adding it to a growing list of her delusions, but something awful and traumatic must have happened to their son.

It wasn't all venom she had been spewing. He could see that now. Sitting in front of him, he saw the thorns, every single one of them. They glistened in the dying afternoon light that was pushing in through the window. His clothes were in tatters and Charlie's white skin was now bathed in a red shroud.

"Son, I need you to tell me what has happened to you. How did all of this happen?" His question was riddled with confusion but that was quickly swamped by distress when his mind fixated on just how much blood there was. "Are you in pain?"

Charlie failed to lift his head, only answering in mumbled heaves.

"It's okay. You don't need to talk if you can't right now. We will figure this out together." His thoughts were panicked but he managed to keep his voice steady. At least on the surface. He had to be strong for his son, even if that meant faking it.

"Wh-h-at's wrong with me, D-d-dad-d-dy?"

"I don't know, Charlie, but whatever has happened to you, we will find a way to undo it."

"Mum cal-lled me—"

"Never you mind about any of that. Your mother was just a little confused, scared. She didn't mean any of the things she was saying. There was too much of Father Stringer in her head to think clearly."

"Is M-m-mum d-dead? I s-saw her fall."

Mike was prepared for the question but was thankful that his son had said fall and not *I saw you push her*. There would no doubt be a great multitude of people who he would have to convince of that fact.

*What is Eve going to say when she comes home? What will the police think happened? Will they believe it was an accident? What will happen to Charlie if they don't? What will happen to Charlie full stop? What were people back home going to say?*

101

None of them could resist a bit of gossip. To hell with the ones who were hurting, grieving.

*Well, they seemed like the perfect couple on the outside but who knows what goes on behind closed doors.*

*Oh, let me tell you, it has been a nightmare living next door to them. The arguments were endless. Screaming day and night. They think I can't hear them because I'm old, but I can.*

*He was probably knocking her about for years. He never wanted her to have anything to do with the church. Confession and all that jazz. Was probably scared witless that she would sing like a canary to Stringer.*

*It's always the quiet ones.*

*The eyes unsettled me.*

*He was like a ticking time bomb. It was just that poor woman's misfortune to be around when he went off.*

*Of course he went mad, have you seen the kid? That little freak is enough to drive anyone insane.*

He had the world and its mother to convince that what had happened to Mary was an accident, but how could he make everyone else believe he was innocent when he didn't believe it himself.

"Yes, Charlie. Mom's dead. I'm so sorry. For this. For everything," he spoke through panting breaths, trying to cradle his crying child with one arm while ignoring the piercing pain as a mass of thorns met his flesh. "I have been a crappy dad since day one and all I have are shitty excuses for it.

"I guess it was just easier to be lazy than to actually get involved in anything that was going on with you. I'm so fucking sorry that you have suffered so much because of my selfishness."

"Did you h-hate her?" Charlie asked with his head now raised and his hands flexing over his legs as he straightened them. He asked the question in a bland matter-of-fact tone, already assured of the answer.

Sensing the gates were about to burst wide open, Mike raised his free arm up to his eyes. A futile attempt to repress the flow. "No, Charlie, I didn't. I know that might be hard to believe because we argued a lot, maybe more than a mummy and a daddy should do, but it was never hate."

"I heard a l-lot of n-nasty stuff. A-after my headphones broke," Charlie pressed on, hammering away at his father's dam with his relentless unburdening.

Mike looked at his son who was trying to scrape off some of the dried blood from his hands and felt more shame wash over him. He knew he was never going to be father of the year but never in his wildest dreams had he imagined this level of negligence. Had his lack of care, love even, caused Charlie's incident today? He hoped not. He didn't know whether he could live with the guilt.

"Sometimes, Mummy and I used cruel, unforgiveable language toward each other, but that's because we made little things into big things. We fuelled each other's fire but in a bad way. Does that make sense, Charlie?"

"You set ea-ch other off, like f-f-fireworks."

"Exactly. And there's only one thing a firework can do once it's been lit."

"Boom."

With his lips now quivering, his mouth wanted to laugh but he resisted its urge. If he laughed now, he would surely cry.

"Yup. There's no telling it no once it feels that first spark. It needs to explode. But not only were we stoking each other's bad moods like that, we were also idiots because neither one of us could see that we had the perfect little family right in front of us. We were annoyed at our own stubbornness, our own blindness. I never hated your mum, Charlie. I loved her. I promise you that."

Charlie, who for the past several minutes had been looking at everything in the room apart from his dad as he asked the cold truths he would never dare to ask on a normal day, felt the pain that was ripping through his body like fire lessen as a new sensation started to rear its head; concern.

He angled his head, fought off the familiar and comforting twitches and looked his father directly in his eyes. Their eyes met for the first time and Mike saw the tiny fleck of silvery-blue he had only ever seen in photographs. Seeing it up close gave him that calming sense of relief he had been craving for as long he could remember.

The flood came. It had been years in the making but it drowned his face in less than a minute. Mike's arm returned to its position under his eyes and became quickly soaked under the weight of his own tears. The dam had burst and a torrent had been set free.

He stood to try and relax himself and as he stretched his arms out to crack his joints back into position, he felt the strange cling of an embrace around his chest. Looking down, he saw Charlie wrapping his arms around him and his head was now buried into his chest. Thorns struck him all over but he didn't care. He deserved this pain.

His normal, fatherly instinct was to push Charlie away and he had to kill the urge before it developed into action. A hand on Charlie's shoulder flexed an inch but he hoped it went unnoticed. He had been pushing Charlie away all his life. Maybe all he needed, what they all had ever needed, was just one long hug. Not the fleeting drive-byes they were familiar with. The pitiful shoulder taps as they breezed along this road they had forged for themselves.

Everything used to seem so simple but now he had wandered into unknown territory and no matter how tempting it was to return to normal, or what passed as normal, he vowed never to push his son away again.

He told Charlie to stay put, to busy himself with whatever he could find in the bedroom, while he did the adult thing. He couldn't put it off any longer. He had to face up to what he had done.

Mike paced his way down the stairs and saw Mary slumped on the hard floor. He had half-hoped to be able to slide past one side of her but she had landed badly, though it wasn't really her he was blaming, and so, he had no choice but to step over her. With one leg either side of her splayed torso, he struggled not to catch her eye. He saw the shattered glass of his wife's dead eyes.

They had always been cold but now, those frosted daggers would forever hold the ice that she had masterfully, painfully, slowly driven into his heart during their many happy and unhappy years together. One bleeding into the other, obscuring his memories of the only woman he had ever loved.

Looking at her unflinching face was ruining the image he was trying to build of her, the image he would cling to in the days to come. How was he supposed to remember that her eyes had been the first thing he had loved about her now? Image was everything but that particular one, taken before he had even spoken to her and before anything had ever gone wrong, was now distorted. Her eyes, now drenched in blackening rings, would forever hold a look of righteous horror.

Even in death, she wouldn't let him have this one thing. But still, he continued to hold onto the promise he had made his son not five minutes ago. He may have failed as a husband but he was determined to be a good father. Mike made a grab for the wall telephone, punched in the numbers for emergency services and gave only the basic of responses to the probes coming down the line with his voice on autopilot.

# Chapter Twenty-Four

Charlie appeared at the top of the stairs just as an array of flashing lights pushed in through the polished window of the front door below. His mother looked as if she was twitching where she lay, where she fell, but he reassured himself that it was just the lights strobing over her body. Her corpse.

Charlie shuddered at the ugliness of the word. There was to be no pot of gold at the end of this chilling rainbow. His dad was fidgeting on the spot, his feet nervously clicking together and his palms sweating. The rap on the door was not subtle, but rapid like a machine gunfire. Even now, with the battle won, the war raged on.

"You better come in. I called about my wife. She's there by the foot of the stairs," said Mike with his voice suppressing all emotion. It was mechanical, almost clinical. He had scraped the bottom of the barrel but his mouth was dry.

He stepped aside and allowed two paramedics over the threshold. Now, it was real; now, it was happening. From the doorway, he could see one police cruiser by the sidewalk, the driver door ajar and a semi-muscular policeman straddling the gap as he spoke into his radio.

Probably just routine for one cop to show up to a call of this nature but every glance in Mike's direction sent shivers down his spine and he retreated back inside the house. He had never had trouble with the police before, not even a parking fine. He got enough trouble at home with Mary without inviting more. Now, she was gone and the police were here.

The paramedics had brought everything needed to aid them to breathe life back into a person, to pull them away from the tempting light that lay beyond and back into the comfortable darkness, but there was no helping Mary. They pronounced she was dead on arrival and then turned their attention to the pale, jittery man standing over their shoulders.

"We are very sorry, Sir; there was nothing to be done."

"I know," Mike said with his head down, his eyes resting on Mary's shoe that lay almost two feet from her body. He walked over to her and replaced it. "She was always such a neat and together woman. She wouldn't be caught de—"

His mind caught up to his words and let them trail off before he said anything that would bring back the emotions. He had a feeling they wouldn't return slow, it would be an explosion but right now, he felt numb, and that was just fine by him.

Mike felt Charlie's shadow hovering and saw his tiny stature at the top of the stairs. He could not see his son's eyes but from the heaving shoulders to the writhing hands, he knew his son was crying.

*Maybe Charlie can cry enough for both of us. I must be empty by now. Oh God, what are we going to do?*

He hurriedly gestured for Charlie to go back into the bedroom when he saw him inch forward for the first step down. The two paramedics left the house, but their absence was quickly filled by a policeman who, with a toothpick gyrating its way around his mouth, gave the room a quick scan.

His eyes moved from the dead woman by the foot of the stairs to the broken furniture (which, from the angle he was standing, neatly hid the small scattering of blood) before resting on Michael Rose.

"My name is Sergeant Woodley. So, would you like to tell me what happened here, Sir?" It felt like a rhetorical question as his demeanour was quite clearly, 'you can either tell me calmly or I'll shove your ass against the wall and still get what I want. I'll see this through to the bitter end, just you see if I don't'.

"We were arguing over something. She wanted to go upstairs but I got ahead of her and stopped her. Then, she fell," Mike spoke slowly but never paused, his eyes still on Mary. He now noticed that her glasses had broken in the fall. The frame was in two halves and the glass itself had shattered into a more than two pieces. Considerably more.

He would never again feel the sting of her reprimands. Of course, he already knew that but seeing them lying there in that state, somehow helpless, made him sadder than he was expecting.

She could be unbearable, but he needed someone like that in his life. Now, he was alone. Left to fend for himself with no one to show him the way. Now, she was the free one and he was the trapped one. Even in death, they perfectly balanced each other. Who would do his thinking for him now that she had left him?

This time, the chuckle escaped his lips and took a smile with it as it pirouetted through the air. It squeaked out of him and the high pitch was caught by Sergeant Woodley.

"You stopped her and she fell?"

"Yes."

"Are you quite sure of that, Mr Rose?"

"It all happened in a second but yes. She just fell."

"I see. What was the argument about? Must have been quite a heated one." His tone now shifted from questioning to probing as his nose found the small patch of blood by the broken chair and his eyes surveyed the distance between there and the stairs.

Like a dog with a bone, he would not relent until he had worn it down to a frayed strip. Only then would he have his answers. He was just a simple man with a simple need. Closure.

"It was about our son, Charlie." Desperation tried to worm its way into his voice, but he kept it at bay. Bland colours painted his unmoved face and bruised his features as he fought to contain everything that wanted to escape.

"Kids can be a handful. I don't have any myself, but if I did, I very much doubt that I would feel the need to argue about them with their mother on the stairs of all places. Dangerous place to be hollering. Accidents can happen, Mr Rose. Was your son here at the time of the *accident*?"

"He was in the bathroom."

"Uh huh, uh huh. I suppose that explains why your wife was so intent on going upstairs. But it does nothing to explain your motives in trying to stop her. Did he see the altercation itself?"

Mike felt himself pause. Up until now, he had been answering coldly but not untruthfully. He could live with that. It kept his emotions in check, frozen beneath the surface. He could not let them thaw. Not in front of the police.

"No, he didn't see a thing."

"I see. Is your son still here? You didn't send him off to the neighbours or anything. I need to speak to him."

"No, well, yes, he is still here. But no, you can't see him."

"Excuse m—"

"And this isn't our house. It belongs to my wife's sister and her family. They're out at the moment."

"Mr Rose, I will be speaking to your son about this business because he is a potential witness. Kids see and hear a great deal more than we imagine." Mike was bitterly reminded of his conversation with Charlie about the headphones.

Mike felt his palms flood with sweat and fought hard to stop his legs from giving way. Charlie was fragile right now and did not need to be intimidated by the police. The longer he could delay that, the better. He assured himself that was the right thing to do.

Mary had always been the idea person in their marriage, all he knew how to do was stall and he wasn't very good at that. And garden, but that was not going to help him right now.

Sergeant Woodley excused himself, returning to his cruiser and Mike choked on a sigh of relief as one of the paramedics, looking disgruntled, reappeared and just lingered in the doorway. He was being watched, their eyes never leaving him as sweat now clung to his clothing like foul glue. Winter was no time for a wet t-shirt contest, but Mike would have come away the big winner regardless.

# Chapter Twenty-Five

"It's alright, ma'am; we are aware of a situation at your address. Emergency services are at the scene now."

The news took Eve by surprise. With the wind knocked out of her, the hot air she had brewed now floated uncomfortably in the air around her before evaporating.

"I see. Well, good then. The sooner that little creep is locked up for what he did to my son, the better. I don't know how William will ever recover from this ordeal," she spoke in a curt tone, displeased at having her moment of glory snatched away from her.

She never imagined Mary would have the nerve to do what was right. She was too soft on that boy, she and Mike both were and now, it was her son that had paid the price.

It was now the time for the 911 operator to play the part of the stunned caller. "Uh ma'am, may I ask what incident you are referring to?"

"My son was viciously attacked by his cousin. I'm calling from the hospital right now. The doctor said he was lucky I brought him in when I did. If it had been any later, he could have lost the hand completely. Why? Wha—?"

A low buzzing came from within the earpiece and then, an unpleasant, clattering sound in the wall behind the row of phones. Around her were fellow callers who had also been rudely cut off mid-sentence though she doubted their call was as important as hers. Or indeed the callers themselves.

Confusion gave way to a rising irritation and Eve quickly high-tailed (and high-heeled) it out the vestibule and headed for the main reception, momentarily forgetting her family was waiting for her in the car. To her relief, a shift changeover had taken place and the incompetent nurse was nowhere to be seen, no doubt causing havoc in some other part of her life. A man skirting the edges of his forties with fidgety fingers was now manning the helm, ruffling through the weeds of the abandoned in-tray.

"Excuse me," she began. It wasn't polite, it was cutting. "Your phones over there aren't working. Is this how you run an entire hospital? How are people supposed to believe you can work those unseemly scanner machine things and all the other nonsense if you cannot even keep a working telephone?"

"Oh, sorry missus, we're undergoing some routine repairs to our wiring this week. I told 'em the place would go to 'ell in a 'and basket, but no one listens to Ed here. My grand mammy was always saying that, come rain or shine. The 'and basket part, not the Ed part, if you catch what I'm flingin'."

"Imagine doing them sorts of repairs on Christmas week. I told 'em Christmas is when we get the busiest. Mostly winos and the like but still a healthy inflow of the general pop, you know. Ha-ha, a healthy helping of the unhealthy. How do you like that, missus? Ha-ha."

Eve, again, was silenced by the ineptitude and senseless drivel that seemed to be contagious in this infernal place. All she wanted was simplicity but the Almighty continued to throw her curveballs the size of basketballs. Testing her patience more than her strength. She had no doubt how strong at heart she was, but her patience was another matter entirely.

It faltered on a regular basis but that was only because she was surrounded by mindless idiots. If it wasn't Brian, then it was her colleagues at the school who failed to live by her standards or the man in charge of her local parish (not a drop of Father Stringer in his veins) and now to top it off, she had had to deal with a doctor who probably still wore diapers in medical school and the unhelpful, wittering man behind the desk.

"I don't care about any of that. Just fix the phones." Her mind may have been tired, all thanks to the idiots in her life who were themselves, tiresome, but her voice was as heated as ever.

"I can't do that, missus. I wouldn't know where to begin with fixin' stuff like 'em phones. I'm surprised they even let me answer 'em, let alone tamp'ring with 'em. I would let you use this one here, but I got in trouble for that b'fore. 'Office use only', they say."

Eve raised her hands and constricted them around a throat that wasn't there in the air. A look of exasperation was growing across her stern face. Giving up before hearing more endless gibberish, she turned and headed for the exit, blindly passing a sign that read:

*Attention!*

*Repairs Ongoing. Possible Disruption to Electronic Devices.*

*Apologies.*

She entered the car and Brian was busy entertaining Jennifer and Frederic with one of the silly voices that he did. A French pirate that she could hear from three cars away. William was sitting in the front, stroking his hand.

"We were beginning to think you had abandoned ship," Brian said with his voice wearing thin. The kids loved the bit but even pretending to be French took its toll.

"I had to make a call."

"Everything okay?" He sensed the flatness of his wife's tone and knew that it wasn't but still he asked.

*If you're struggling for a pirate name, my love, you should go with Captain Tedious. Or mundane. Just a thought, and one that you'll learn about later when I've sorted things back at the house and the kids are in bed. Once Charlie is dealt with, then you will have my full attention.*

"Do I have to take a pill now?"

*Why are police on the way to my house? The operator was confused about Will's assault, so Mary probably neglected to tell them when she called them. Typical, protecting the wrong child. But what else could it be? What else had happened? What else has that monster done?*

"Mum?"

"Yes, dear? Sorry, it's been a long day." Her concentration refocused, temporarily steering away from an emerging vendetta and centring on the here and now.

"The painkillers," William said, gesturing for the bottle poking out of her jacket pocket. "Do I take one now?"

"Oh, yes dear. Here you go. There is a bottle of water to swallow them down with in the glovebox." She turned out of the hospital parking lot and sped off toward home, unaware of what was lying in wait upon her return.

111

# Chapter Twenty-Six

"Hey Becca, you there, hon? Rebecca? Get off the damn can and pick up, woman. Earth to Becca."

"Jeez Bill, what goat climbed in your bed this morning?" A voice that wheezed the coarse tones of a woman who was clearly in the latter stages of lung cancer.

She had taken the news in her stride. It had hardly been a surprise to her cohorts; her toxic lifestyle had to have some repercussions. Smoking a couple ten packs a day since her early teens was now as natural as breathing, even if those breaths were long and throaty.

What did she have to lose now? She routinely asked the people who strode through her life with fishhooks in their eyebrows. A running joke at the station was getting second-hand smoke through the radio but she always failed to laugh at that one; instead just calmly stated that she would haunt the shits out of them once she had gone to meet her maker. Literally.

"That's no way to talk about your mother. But enough of your lip, woman, unless you're finally going to take me up on my offer." The wink was already implied but he still made a crude attempt to sound it out down the radio.

Normally, when he was on the job, he was as serious as anything but there was just something about Rebecca that let him relax. He had his shot with her over a decade ago but he was too much of a flake for her to contend with at the time.

They had muddled through the uncomfortableness together and came out the other side separately. Colleagues, friends and not a damn thing more. He had matured since then but it was too late now to try again. Surely.

"You know, maybe dying ain't gonna be so bad after all, if it means finally escaping your, oh let's call it *wit*. So, what can I do for you, I say through gritted teeth."

"Ha-ha. Now, down to business; I'm over at 23 Bridlington Lane and there is no way this is just an accidental death. It's looking like the big one."

"You're not saying murder, are you? We haven't had a murder in Almost since two summers ago. Remember that backpacker in the sewer?"

"Remember him? I was the one that found him. Never did find the backpack though."

"Oh yeah, I thought you just took credit for that because it was juicy. You know, sewer juicy. Ha-ha."

"Stop your yammering, woman. Now, something is not quite right here. There are clear signs of a struggle and the husband is shifty as fuck. He's hiding something. I'm going to need you to get in touch with district and have them send the lab boys down for this one. Becca, you still there?"

"Sorry, Bill. That address you're at, 23 Bridlington Lane. We've just had something flag up from the central dispatch office."

"Oh, do tell, my dear."

"Apparently, the woman who lives there, a Mrs Eve Prentice, just called in about an incident that happened at her house earlier today. Her son had to be taken to hospital because of an attack and the cousin is involved somehow. CD says she was confused when they told her you and the medi-boys were already there."

"The husband in there, Michael Rose, said his in-laws were out for the afternoon, so that probably makes this Eve Prentice the dead woman's sister. If she wasn't expecting us to show up, then she probably isn't aware of what's happened here."

Even through the radio, Rebecca knew Bill was radiating a glow of puzzlement. It was the same look he always gave whenever his cogs jammed. His face always gave away when he was disheartened by any new hairdos she trifled with.

He secretly thanked the cancer for saving him from having any more of those awkward moments. Not a lot of women could pull of the Homer Simpson look but she was one of the lucky, or unlucky, as it happened.

"Oh jeez, does that mean she doesn't know her own sister is dead? And you think murdered? Oh, how awful. Just awful."

"Strong heart, Becca. Now focus. What was she calling to report?"

"You know, we should really poach whoever is on shift over at CD because this information is glowing. You know what most of them are like at this time of year; only a small, nondescript line in the call log unless there's a limb hanging off or a priest on fire. Anyone else would have swept this report away, filed it under *who gives a crap* and that would have been the end of it."

"Yes, I know it's shitty. God help any cats in trees for the next two weeks because we all know no one else will. Now, if you please, Rebecca. What does the report say?"

"The information that came through was that her son was badly hurt. She was calling from the hospital, but the line was cut short before she could go into detail. She did say, however, that it was all to do with her nephew. That would be the dead woman's son then? Awful, awful."

"Hmm, Mr Rose was closed right up until his son was mentioned. Then, something in him switched. Refused to even let me see the kid though, not that he has an actual choice. This is an inquiry into a suspicious death and the son could be a key witness. Or—"

"Or what, Bill?"

"Or his son could be responsible for the mother's death. If he attacked his cousin, maybe the mother tried to discipline him, and so, he lashed out at her too. The dad is probably trying to protect his son."

"Oh god, that is a horrid idea. I know how much you like your intuitions, Bill but please, please be wrong this time. It's Christmas day tomorrow."

"I know. Maybe you should call Ben in to cover the rest of your shift, so you can take one of your *herbal* remedies and have a rest. Stress isn't good for you."

"I might just do that. I'll add it to the list of unending calls I have to make today."

"Good but honestly, Rebecca, what on earth made you decide this job was the one for you?"

"Oh, I don't know, there was this young, toned police officer. He didn't just swing his truncheon wildly like the rest of them, he actually had good aim with it. Well, nearly good aim."

"Sounds like quite the catch."

"He was, but would you believe it? I ended up catching cancer instead."

"Life's a bitch, dear, and the—"

"And then you die. Heard it all before, from you as it happens, Billy boy."

"Indeed. Right, I'm heading back inside. I have a few more questions for Mr Rose and this elusive son of his. If you send the men in white coats to my location with their dusters and micro-wotsits, that would be great. Better get Burrows

114

here as well, they are technically her lab boys and you know how she gets when she is kept out of the loop. Oh and one of our guys as well. Better to be safe than sorry."

"Will do, Bill; take care."

Rebecca killed the radio but in the dead air, two or three unsaid words hung between them. Stretching and repelling in the distance.

# Chapter Twenty-Seven

Mike saw the bulky sergeant making his way back up the garden path and felt his limbs tremble again. A panic rose in his legs, shaking with the cold wind sweeping through the open doorway and settled in his chest.

*I can't let him speak to Charlie.*
*Can't let him see Charlie.*
*Shit. Shit. Shit.*
*They'll do God knows what to him.*
*Shit.*

The paramedic was relieved of his guard duty and looked doubly relieved to be able to return to his ambulance buddy. Spending his snack break (without any snacks) babysitting this potential criminal. Personally, he thought Mr Rose was suffering from grief, not guilt.

*All his years dealing with people at their most distraught had obviously taught him nothing,* he thought to himself, shooting a cold glare in the sergeant's direction as they crossed on the threshold. Sergeant Woodley returned and Mike's figure shrank down to the size of a mouse. Now, he knew how Brian must feel in this house every day.

"Well, Mr Rose, it seems you have not been entirely honest with me. Can you explain why your nephew was taken to hospital earlier today?" He spoke with clear intent.

The question stunned Mike into a dumb silence, his lip quivered until it felt a sharp bite to hold it steady. His teeth ripped through flesh and he swallowed the bitterness of first blood.

"And what all of this has to do with your son?" Woodley said, refusing to break eye contact despite Mike's best efforts.

"With Charlie? N-n-nothing," he replied unconvincingly, blood now oozing from the wound and slipping down his throat as he gulped.

"I strongly advise that you stop wasting both of our time. Specialists are on their way here to examine every inch of this house. If there is a secret here, we will find it." Mike's face flushed, all the nerves into the open, his anxious grey now a ghostly white. "And I reckon that your son has the answers I'm looking for. How old is he?"

"Twelve."

"Okay, so, either you let me speak with him, here casually, or I can place you under arrest for obstruction and take you both down to the station. Believe me, it will be better for everyone if we can get to the bottom of this without putting him through an interrogation."

Mike thought for a few moments, his mind racing between what was best for his son (he didn't have a clue, he wasn't a thinker) and what was right. Again, no clue.

"Charlie, you can come down now," he called up the stairs, positioning himself awkwardly around Mary's body to shield Charlie's view the best he could.

A minute later, they both heard the soft sound of footsteps creeping down the stairs, as only a child could make. That's all he was. Not a monster, but a child. Mike waited for the unholy gasp from Sergeant Woodley when he saw Charlie's affliction, curse, abnormality but none came, only a rudimental hello; though Mike suspected it had been laced with a forced gentleness.

He looked at his son and almost stumbled back over his wife's body. There was not a single blemish, scar or graze on Charlie's head or body. The purple and green scaled skin had receded back to its original milky white and in the time he had been confined to the upstairs, he had changed out of the torn clothing and washed the blood off him. His hands were now immaculate. Mike wished the same could be said for himself.

Charlie stood at the bottom of stairs, visibly thankful for the human shield and appeared to be the spitting image of a perfectly normal boy.

"You must be Charlie, my name is Bill Woodley. I'm a police officer and I need to ask you some questions," Bill said as he approached the boy and gestured for them to come away from the stairway. He may employ rough tactics from time to time (the job called for it) but he was not so insensitive to try and hound a grieving boy. He knew he would need to play this carefully. "Is that okay?"

"Y-y-eah, I g-g-uess so," Charlie answered with his head twitching up to the ceiling and back again, avoiding everything in between, and continually jittered one hand under his sleeve.

Bill, leaning against the work-top in the kitchen, felt his nerves tense up, just an inch. There was something about this boy, but he couldn't quite guess what. He didn't like not knowing but nevertheless, he viewed Charlie with the same stereotypical filter that almost everyone who met sweet, little Charlie used.

Mike took his son's hand and walked Charlie over to the far end of the kitchen, his own nerves dancing the soles off his shoes. They rested in front of the fridge and felt none of its freshness. The cool air locked inside, leaving them to stand sweating in the wooden kitchen.

"So, Charli—"

"Are you go-going to l-lock me up?" Charlie interrupted, tears now forming around the corners of his eyes. He reached out for his dad's hand, surprising them both and squeezed it.

"What makes you think something like that then?"

"Bec-cause I'm evil. I h-heard M-mum say so." His voice was without imagination or exaggeration. It was simply matter-of-fact.

Mike felt Charlie's hand begin to slip away but he held on tight, not wanting to let go. He never wanted to let go, not now. He didn't know why the thorns had vanished, but he was grateful that they had, though he wasn't sure if even they would have stopped him from holding his son right now.

There was a first time for everything and with his heart racing and his mind plaguing him with intrusive thoughts, it could also be the last time for all he knew.

*He's not taking him. He's not taking him. He's not taking him.*

*He can't take him, Charlie did nothing wrong. Didn't even touch his mother. Not his fault. I was on the stairs. Not Charlie. Not his fault.*

*Oh, Mary, what have we done to our little boy?*

*It's my fault.*

*It's all my fault.*

"Wha—? Stop Charlie, you could never be evil or any of the things Mom said today, okay?" Mike interjected through his breaking heart, desperately trying to sound reassuring. To convince himself as much as Charlie that he could actually make a good parent now that he was flying solo. He was learning on the spot that parenting did not come with a parachute.

"Can you tell me about what happened here today, Charlie? Did you have a fight with your cousin?"

"No."

"No? I heard he was taken to hospital. I'm sure he will be just fine, but I do need to know what happened to him."

Mike was about to butt in again and tell him to go and ask William himself if he was so intent on finding out the truth, but stopped himself when he realized William would only relay whatever *truth* had been drilled into him by his mother. She had never liked Charlie, not since that one Thanksgiving.

*Bitch. Get a sense of humor.*

"He w-was laughing at me. He made fun of my new n-n-ne-ecklace, then Mum s-sl-l-apped me for h-h-having the necklace, and then he po-pointed and la-laughed at me again. I gr-gr-rabbed his hand and it just sorta cracked."

Mike stood shocked, with anger drowning the panic. Anger toward Mary, himself, the world and finally, Mary again.

*All of this was over a necklace? A fucking necklace, Mary. That's what kicked all this off? Are you fucking kidding me?*

"I see, that is why your mother said you were evil? Because you hurt your cousin's hand? Sounds like it was unintentional to me. I didn't know my own strength when I was your age either." Sergeant Woodley lowered himself to Charlie's level and saw the boy drop his head in tandem.

His voice was calm but still running with the same nagging prod that he had perfected over the course of his career. He backed off an inch, hoping to draw the boy out of his shell and into his net. Soon, he would have the full picture. A smile formed behind his wet lips. He was beginning to taste it.

"N-nno, I'm a m-m-m-onster," he began and allowed another squeeze of the hand before turning his attention to his dad's flexing shoes, the time for eye contact seemingly over. "I heard everything she s-said. S-he w-wa-wanted to p-p-purge me."

Bill swallowed his smile and let a startled look sweep its way across his face. Whatever he had been expecting, it was far from this. He may not have had book smarts, but he liked to credit himself with a certain degree of intelligence. He knew when people were lying to him. The kid was clearly traumatized but not a fantasist. Charlie was telling him the truth.

"Okay, thank you for telling me that, Charlie. It can't have been easy to do. But I need a little more help here. Maybe you can answer this one, Mr Rose. To accuse her own son of being a monster is not exactly normal behaviour. Was your wife suffering from any psychotic breaks?"

"She was religious, if that counts. Dangerously so."

"Religion in itself is not a delusion, Sir."

"Maybe so, but I think she crossed the line between fantasy and reality when she planned on sacrificing her only child."

Bill paused for a moment, taken aback with the forced, gritted tone of Mike's rebuttal before hearing a sound he knew well; a van spluttering chalky smoke had just pulled up. "Ah, I think that is the forensic team here now. Charlie, can you go wait outside for a moment? I need a few more words with your dad. We'll be with you in a couple minutes."

"Okay."

Charlie headed for the door, shrinking at the sight of the four new people already suited and booted in their spaceman clothes. Strange people with strange clothes gave him the kind of uncomfortable itch that you just couldn't scratch.

"Ah Stan, great, you're he—uh, sorry I was expecting DI Burrows' team. Who are you exactly?"

"They were called off. District wanted us on this job."

"Why would they do that? Stan and his men are quite capable—"

"Look pal, we were called in at the last minute. If you have any problems, take it up with district."

"Don't worry, I will. DI Burrows should be arriving anytime now but she will no doubt want a full work-up of the scene carried out. I assume she is still on her way."

"Not my place to know."

Bill gritted his teeth and turned his attention back to Mike while the specialists began surrounding Mary's body. "Mr Rose, I didn't want to ask you this in front of your son. Did you push your wife down the stairs?"

120

It was a question he had been expecting since the moment Mary fell but his reply still stumbled in the air of Sergeant Woodley's blunt tone.

"No," he said without confidence, his mind too concerned on Charlie. "I told you, we argued and she fell."

"Yes, you did say that but after speaking with your son, it is clear that your wife was acting erratically, shall we say?" He walked over to the window and watched as Charlie paced nervously on the porch. "If your wife had gotten hold of Charlie, then it may very well have been his body being photographed as we speak."

"What's your point?" Mike asked coldly and glanced at the men busying themselves around the spectacle that was his wife.

"That you were protecting your son from a possible violent attack. The people further up the chain may be inclined to be lenient if you own up here and now. It will be classed as self-defence or even accidental death. The last thing they want is a murder on the records. All they care about is numbers and something like this will screw up their averages."

Before Mike could consider this forbidden fruit dangling seductively in front of him, Sergeant Woodley placed one hand on his shoulder and gestured toward the boy now sitting cross-legged out on the lawn and twiddling a single piece of grass between his fingers.

"You were protecting your son then and I can see that you are still protecting him now. It's admirable, you must be a good parent to risk perjuring yourself but take my advice, Sir—Mike, prolonging this process will only do more damage. You have both suffered enough today."

Mike sighed and felt himself reaching out toward the branch, the smell of the gorgeously red apple now wafting through his nostrils.

"Let it end, Mr Rose."

"I pushed her. I killed my wife," he said as he plucked the apple from the low-hanging branch. One bite was all it took to unburden himself, freeing himself of the tension that had been simmering just below the surface. His eyes remained dry, but his face creaked in the strain of his confession.

Sergeant Woodley, disguising a grin as he mentally added another tick to his tally, produced a set of handcuffs from his back pocket. "Just a formality, you understand."

Mike nodded in silence as he was read his rights and led out the door. The cuffs were rough and applied with a heavy hand, but he failed to notice the weight of them. His only concern now was Charlie who angled his head as the two men stopped beside him.

"D-d-dad? Wh-a-at's going on?" Charlie asked as he stood up, the seat of his pants now muddy. His voice failed to hide the rising fear when he spotted the cold, steel cuffs.

"It's going to be alright, Charlie; just stay calm."

"Your dad is coming down the station to help me understand a few more things. It will all be okay. One of my officers is on their way to look after you until we get this all straightened out." He wanted his speech to be soft for the boy's sake but a glimmer of pride was beginning to shine through.

Charlie heard all of this and none of this, his brain failing to separate the concrete words of the police officer and the twisting air now consuming his adolescent mind.

"No. He d-d-didn't do anything w-w-wrong. You can't do th-this," he said, shaking his head vigorously and latching onto his father's arm.

"Charlie, listen to me. It will all be okay, I'll be back soon," Mike said as he tried to angle himself in a way for Charlie to feel like he could be hugged. "And then, we can just go home."

Before Bill could drag Mike away, they all heard a car pull up on the roadside. A slimmer, younger officer emerged and began walking toward them. Charlie, with his eyes now watering his trembling face, felt a shiver run down his spine.

"Charlie, this is Officer Mendez. He is here to look after you while your dad and I sort things out."

Woodley welcomed the new officer and instructed him to remain here and look after the boy until DI Burrows arrived on the scene. When the officer grew disgruntled at the prospect of babysitting, he was sharply cut off. Bill's speech had now lost all of its approachable charm. It was as cold as Charlie's spine and the handcuffs grazing against Mike's wrists.

"C'mon, kid. Inside. I'm not paid enough to just stand about in winter," said Mendez, placing one hand on Charlie's shoulder to lead him away. When the small boy resisted and refused to let go of his father's arm, he resorted to a grip that Charlie knew very well. It had a motherly firmness to it.

"Charlie, you have to let me go. The sooner I go, the sooner I'll be back."

"No," he said with a gulped squeak and grabbed a hold of the handcuffs.

"Charlie, this isn't up for discussion. Your father is coming with me."

"If the little shit stain won't let go, then take him with you. No skin off my nose."

"I have already given you your orders, Mendez, so you will see them complete, without question; unless you want to face a disciplinary before the New Year. Now, take the boy back inside."

Mendez let out a silent scoff and yanked Charlie the best he could. As a young man who exercised regularly, primarily within the confines of his bedroom with whatever unlucky maiden took his fancy that week, he became quickly annoyed at how easy it was for the snotty brat to endure him.

"I s-said NO!" Charlie's voice exploded out of him. His skin rippled and tore under the thunderous cry. The thorns were back, this time sharper and with a swelling pain, his body failing to adjust to the torment the second time around. The handcuffs buckled under the weight of his grip and his dad's hands swung awkwardly in the free air with each ring of the cuff now an unseemly bracelet.

"What the f—" said Mendez but his sentence went incomplete and he fell to the ground in a shocked agony. The arm he had gripped Charlie with was now in the hands of the little boy who had just torn it clean off.

Eve's lawn had been trimmed to within an inch of its life and even managed to stave off the approaching frost, but three seconds was all it took to be smothered in the blood now pouring from the severed wound. Mendez screamed and the pain now surging through him felt like a poisoned ecstasy. His nerves were on fire and he squirmed uneasily in the growing red pool.

*Oh Charlie, what have you don—?*

"Noooooo," screamed Mike, his emotions now flooding back into him as he saw Charlie convulse wildly on the spot before dropping to the ground and spasming uncontrollably.

Mike felt a sweaty hand tightly clasp one of his own and when he looked up, he saw Sergeant Woodley, with a look of horror mixed with confusion developing behind his eyes, holding the Taser in his other shaking hand. Officer Mendez's right arm dropped sluggishly from Charlie's grasp and fell a mere two feet from its former owner. Mike looked down and felt helpless at the sight of his trembling son.

Charlie's body jerked painfully on the grass, all thoughts now drowned out by the piercing screams inside his head. His thorns retracted and bulged in equal measure and the soft scales that had stretched in parts over his body, transmuted to a dark fury that now lacerated its way from head to toe. His wails were like a gathering thunder and his skin flared with lightning. A storm was brewing inside his unstable body and despite the agonizing torture, this was indeed the calm.

# Chapter Twenty-Eight

Sergeant Woodley lumbered into the holding cell that now housed the frantic Mr Rose. His feet shuffled with a new, disillusioned purpose. A look of confused terror was still etched onto his face, frozen against his once admirable features. A headache began its descent behind his weary eyes. It had already been a long day and he was too switched on to fool himself into thinking it would soon be over.

As far as the storm gathering overhead was concerned, the day was just beginning.

"How is Charlie? You've refused to tell me anything since what happened. Please, he's my son." Mike was sat upright, his spine firm and bolted to the seat but the rest of him resembled one of Mary's Thanksgiving concoctions; jellied and dripping in a bland transparency. If he were to stand, he would crumble. His mind was already in pieces.

Woodley maintained a vacant, heavy stare as he paced the room, his hands clenching around an invisible string, pulling and stretching. Desperately trying to twist it into something recognizable. "He was still unconscious when he arrived at the station." The reply was cold. "But do not forget that while your son has some irregular features, Mr Rose, he is responsible for the death of one of my officers."

"Well, yes, bu—"

"And you should look around you. This cell is not for show. It is not a waiting area. Your wife is dead, because of you."

"I realize that but I thought we had that pretty much sorted. Accidental death, you called it," Mike rebutted.

"That was before a fine, young officer lost his life. Except it wasn't lost, was it? It was stolen from him. A deeper probe into the events surrounding your wife's death may well be required."

"I don't understand."

"It is unlikely that anyone higher-up will want to look leniently on you now, given the loss our station has suffered at the hands of your family."

Words became stifled in Mike's mouth and died in his throat. Only hollowed air escaped him.

"It may well be the case that your son was responsible for his mother's death. It would certainly explain why you were so insistent that I not see or speak to him back at the house. Was it because you knew how dangerous he was, Mr Rose?"

"That's insane."

"Or was it so that you could confess to the crime yourself and spare Charlie a further ordeal? Either way, he screwed up your plans by attacking and killing one of my men."

"Charlie didn't do anything to Mary. It was me, it was me, it was me," Mike now pleaded with frustration and desperation marrying unhappily in his throat.

"Perhaps but like I said, further examination will be needed. You need to understand the seriousness of the situation. Either you pushed your wife to her death or you made a false confession to protect a dangerous individual. Both scenarios end in trouble for you."

"And you need to understand that I don't give a flying fuck about what happens to me in here. All I am concerned with is that Charlie is okay."

"Okay?" It was almost a laugh, but his face was too constricted to notice. "You want him to live in a world where everyone believes his father killed his mother?"

"The world can go to hell."

"Let's not forget his new beastly appearance. He's never going to be okay again."

Mike, failing to avoid the grating sting, felt his spine finally relent and he shrank down into the chair. His own shadow folding in on itself in a futile attempt to escape. To run and hide. Before today, it was all he ever wanted but as he so often credited himself to his boat buddies, he had stayed. And this was his reward.

Nothing would have been better than this shit show. Literally nothing. A big, steaming pile of sweet nothing was preferable to a dead wife and whatever Charlie was now.

*A monster? No, that's just ludicrous. Monsters belong in horror films and under the bed.*

"Charlie is just a kid, he would never have hurt that officer if he hadn't been stressed. You taking me away from him made him panicked and that is when those things, abnormalities appeared. It's not his fault."

"Are you trying to say it was mine?"

"No, no. I don't know who is to blame for it all. Maybe me. Maybe Mary. Maybe no one."

"These abnormalities as you call them obviously give him strength well beyond reason. Is that how he hurt his cousin earlier today?" The opposite end of the see-saw now came back into view as his voice changed. Not softened, more flattened. He was running on adrenaline but even that seemed to be in short supply. His whole body was wearing thin.

"I don't know. I didn't see that."

"What did you see today then that might add some shred of value to these proceedings?"

"I saw Mary. She changed," he replied bluntly. "Not like Charlie, it wasn't anything physical. This was just in her eyes but it was deeper, darker. It was like something had taken hold of her. She was delusional, talking about sins and sacrifices. She was going to hurt our son. I just wanted her to stop but she wouldn't."

"So, you stopped her." Sergeant Woodley was playing the parts of good cop and bad cop all by himself. Two sides of the same coin in his eyes, though which side would come out on top was anyone's guess.

"It's all a blur. I don't even remember putting my hands on her. Please, you have to believe it was an accident. I did this and I would do it again a hundred times over to protect Charlie. He might be covered in thorns from head to toe but his eyes are still his.

"He is still the same little kid he was before all of this shit happened. Only now, he is frightened and you saw what happened the last time he panicked, so please, just let me see him. I don't what anything like that to happen again. Do you?"

Bill considered this for a moment, a flash of conscience washing over the simmering rage, but he continued to twirl the coin between his fingers regardless. "I cannot do that but prior to our interview, I informed my superiors about the incident. I relayed every horrifying detail about your son and they are sending a doctor to examine him. He should be arriving anytime now."

"Thank you."

"Save the gratitude. There is something seriously, dangerously wrong with your son and while you might want to bury your head about it, I would not put another one of my team in your son's path until whatever is wrong with him is put right." Penny in the air.

"There is nothing wrong with him. He is my son."

"No? Are you quite sure it was your wife who was the delusional one, Mr Rose?" The coin landed with a strong, affirming thud and with that final quip, Bill ended the interrogation and strode out of the room, now with a quickening heel.

# Chapter Twenty-Nine

"We're just turning into the street now, William. Once we're inside, you can go straight to your room to have a lie-down. You have had an awful day and that useless doctor has just made everything worse for all of us."

Their journey from the hospital had been delayed by insufferably slow drivers in front of them and Eve, desperate to get home where everything was prim and proper, spoke with a rushed air in her voice. Today had been far too much displacement for her and what she needed was to lie back in a steaming bath with unscented bubbles and feel her hair float effortlessly at her side.

A glass of white wine in one hand while the other went scavenging for treasures untold beneath the water. A well-earned reward for keeping it so together up till now. The family would surely have floundered without her lead.

First, however, she had a certain monstrous nephew to take care of, knowing full well that her weakling of an older sister would have failed in her duty. She loved Mary, dearly, but she was faltering. She had failed as a wife and it was now crystal clear that she had failed as mother. Perhaps she did not have what it takes to be a part of Father Stringer's trusted circle.

*I would do what is right by the Almighty. I need to give Mary a good talki—*

Eve's inner monologue dropped out of conscious thought when they approached their driveway and saw a whole squadron of emergency vehicles encroached on her property. She had expected one, maybe two (at a push) based on the tone of the dispatch receiver she had spoken to but not this.

A whole fleet operating out of her comfort zone. In her head, the glass of wine slipped from view and a calm, undisturbed waterline came frustratingly into view. The depths of her treasure would need to go unexplored yet again.

Official police tape barred them from parking in their driveway and so Eve, with eyebrows descending over her narrowing eyes, abandoned the car in a jutting angle in the middle of the road. She exited the car and her face turned to shock with a hint of fear when she read the endlessly sprawled lettering of *crime scene*. Composing herself for her own sake more than her young children who now stood beside her, she forced her expression back to its dependable stone.

Flashing lights streaked over her house in an amateur light show, similar to the one impure families disgraced their homes with at this time of year. Abusing the rightful need of the holiday for their own self-serving wants. Only this light show showed no red or green; it was all blue. Each strobe had an unspoken urgency as the last of the afternoon glow began to fade, bringing a slow darkness in its place.

There was also no inflated Saint Nick (heathen Nick more like) on the lawn, playfully taking the carrot nose from a hideous, snowy representation of man. Instead, her lawn was flooded with a sickly patch of deep red. Her soil had been stained and she just knew who was to blame.

"Is that a body bag?" Brian asked as he glanced over at a black mass lying adjacent to the ruined patch of red grass.

"Take the kids back inside the car. I'll find out what is going on."

"Okay, just take a breath first, you look on edge."

"I will not allow them to keep me from my own home!" Eve proclaimed, disregarding Brian's concern and abandoning him at the curb side. She marched up to a police officer on the other side of the tape. "This is my house. I demand to know what is going on here. Where is my sister?"

"Ah, you must be Mrs Prentice," the police officer squeaked without knowing why, flipping through his hastily scribbled notes. "I will go and find a superior officer. She will be your point of contact for the time being."

Brian's suggestion of breathing failed to stop Eve from becoming incensed the moment the police officer turned his back on her. The young man walked away, never knowing how lucky he was to avoid her sting, the wind carrying a punched extremity far from its intended target.

In the short moments that passed when Eve was left standing alone in the cold, she saw the body bag loaded up into the back of a private ambulance. Whoever it was in there, it wasn't Mary; the build of the bag's occupant was all wrong to be her weak sister.

Good, that meant she could still educate her on all the things she was lacking. She supposed it could perhaps be Michael, but he didn't seem like the dying type. His sort stayed around forever, long past any respectable expiration date. She had her own version of Michael, currently failing to distract their children with his dancing knuckles.

*Maybe Michael overplayed his hand and said one wrong thing too many. That was certainly possible. Almost inevitable with how irritating he was.*

Despite her feverish resentment toward Charlie, the thought that it could perhaps be him in the bag never crossed her mind.

"Mrs Prentice, I am DI Burrows. Please step this way," said a giant woman too far over the ledge of middle-aged to pull it back a couple years. "We can talk in the house. Forensics are just finishing up their initial finds."

Eve, wanting answers, chose not to scold the woman for having the nerve of inviting her into her own home, did as instructed and followed the policewoman inside. The house was cluttered with people in white coats busying themselves with her everyday trinkets. A man came down the stairs and made a point of avoiding a couple of odd markers on her floor at the foot of the stairs.

*What have you let your little freak to do my house, Mary?*

"Mrs Prentice, or can I call you Eve?"

"No. You can call me Mrs Prentice, then you can tell me exactly what has happened here, who the person in the body bag outside was. And then you, and all of your little crew, can leave my home. My son has just been in hospital, I'll have you know. This is the last thing he needs. So, speak quickly."

"Okay, firstly, the deceased in your garden was that of a police officer. A scene unfolded here in which an officer sadly lost his life," she began in an unchanged tone. With where this conversation was going, she needed to remain calm, even if Mrs Prentice was charging herself up for a fight. "Secondly, I have been informed about your son. Your nephew admitted to being involved in an incident earlier today and—"

"William was not involved in anything. He was the victim of a vicious attack. I hope that little, psychotic monster Charlie has been locked up by now." Her chest rose and fell as she let the barbed wire curl around her tongue.

"Charlie Rose has been taken into custody. That I can confirm," DI Burrows said slowly with a delicate balance. Not too direct, not too placid.

"Good, my son has been traumatized by that little heathen."

"I'm afraid the incident with your son has yet to come into play. He was apprehended for a different matter entirely."

"What! The assault on my son is trounced by what exactly? What could be so bad to warrant such an insult?" The words, dripping in her own brand of motherly love, tore through her mouth but all that she got in return was an uncomfortable silence.

DI Burrows only gestured to the horror show in the garden, electing to let Eve fill in the blanks herself on this one. The slow realization began to dawn on Eve's face. An evil thing had taken place but she struggled to hide the conflict on her face.

On the one hand, it was horrible that a man had been killed, in her garden, but on the other hand, maybe now people would take her seriously about Charlie. There was only one thing to do when a weed infected your garden.

*You cut it out, root and stem. For none shall grow in a garden left to rot.*

"Your brother-in-law has also been arrested," DI Burrows said, breaking the prolonged, painful silence.

Eve disregarded the struggle and allowed a glimpse of delight to leave her face at the news. With no Michael to drip poison in her ear about rationality and no Charlie to kick up a fuss, Mary would have no choice but to listen to her. Finally, things were starting to go her way. Perhaps one man's sacrifice was not such a bad thing after all.

"Fantastic. I imagine my sister is sulking somewhere at how disassembled her life has become and no doubt in desperate need for me to put it back together for her. Where is she?"

It was here that DI Burrows paused for a second but that was all it took for Eve to sense something was deadly wrong in the chilling air.

*Charlie killed the cop, but why had they also arrested Michael? If all this took place outside, then why was a horde of heavy-footed men in white suits desecrating my inner sanctum by leaving their marks by the stairs? Why were the police here in the first place?*

*Why? Why? Why?*

"Where's Mary?"

"I'm afraid that is why Michael Rose has been arrested. I'm sorry to inform you that he confessed to pushing your sister down the stairs. Mary Rose was pronounced dead at the scene."

The news drained all the glee from her face, her mind pounded with a nagging twitch and her insides turned on themselves. Her eyes jerked toward the stairs and she felt the contents of her stomach hit the eject button.

DI Burrows had been doing the job too long not to anticipate the flurry of vomit that sprang undignified from Eve's shaking mouth and stepped away in time to avoid being coated in its sickly slime. Instead, the green bile coiled itself over her pristine floors.

A fellow officer approached, carefully dancing over the now green and grey tiles and motioned for a private word. The two of them huddled away from Mrs Prentice.

Eve looked around the room, all of her keepsake comforts now distorted. The air of control she had relied on, now muddied with the bitter unknown. "Mary's dead?"

"Yes, let's go outside," DI Burrows said as she returned, the balance beam now abandoned. It was pure direct. When Mrs Prentice failed to move, still scanning her crumbling sanctuary, she had one of her men escort her out the door. The officer maintained a firm grip on her arm even once they were outside in the less than fresh air. The smell of cloying blood still strong.

"What is going to happen now?" Eve asked with hints of juvenile uncertainty trying to creep their way into her sickened throat.

"You will need to come with us. I've just had word from the officer-in-charge of the case; they want you over at the police station. You and your family."

"But that is where that thing is! That thing attacked my son, my William and now you want to put him within touching distance of him. If you cannot even protect your own officers from it, then why should I trust you with my children?" Her call was fired off in rapid succession and DI Burrows was left with a chill filling the wide, stuck hole in her mouth. She swallowed a bitter breeze that still lingered with an air of decay.

Eve's need for anger and to hear herself speak slowly began to rebuild itself to a normal level but after the events of the day, she thought she might burst if prodded too hard. Yesterday, her life had been as she had designed, but now the image of a perfect family was crumbling around her. Being washed away under the weight of the storm that her relatives had inflicted upon her.

"Mrs Prentice, I understand you have suffered a trauma but think practically. This is a crime scene. Do you really want your children to be here right now?" She gestured to the carnage surrounding them. "So, please go. They will just need you to iron a few things out."

"You understand nothing."

"I can assure you, your nephew will be kept far out of reach of your children. Sergeant Woodley just needs you to answer some questions."

"That thing is not my nephew. He is the spawn of Satan himself. I need to see my family. Now!"

"I'm sorry, Mrs Prentice, but there is nothing I can do. Your husband complied on the spot, he and your children are already on their way."

"Oh," she replied and the balloon at the back of her throat deflated a little. A thought fleeted past her mind where she contemplated scouring the idea of Brian with hate then and there but instead, found herself praying that he had remembered to pick up William's painkillers out the car before they departed. Her loyal lapdog had just humiliated her and he wasn't even aware of it. Yet.

DI Burrows seized upon the moment's silence, showed Eve into a car and bid her farewell, clearly having had her fill of what Mrs Prentice was serving. In the back of the car was an expressionless man reading a clipboard stuffed with papers and the driver, probably another one of Burrows' subordinates, Eve reckoned, carried the same empty look.

They muttered a few condolences about her loss but the words were stale and their faces made no attempt to hide their distaste. Clearly, she deserved to be in distress after what her family member had done to one of their own boys in blue. These men were clearly indifferent to the fact that Eve's exhausting, mountainous revulsion of Charlie Rose made theirs seem little more than a molehill. After a minute of silence, the driver opted to make conversation out of a forced politeness but Eve was too swamped in her head to notice.

The police station was only a short drive away but to Eve, it felt like an eternity would pass before she was able to hold her children in her arms again. She would have been quicker on foot; roads had no logic when compared to a frantic mother.

A nervous itch grew over her the further away she became from her home. She looked back and felt nauseated at the sight of her tainted temple. The realization that she would never see her sister again now hit her in waves that rippled her face, eroding her stony features but she did not cry. She would not crack.

# Chapter Thirty

Bill entered the main reception area and saw how disturbingly quiet, calm even, the place appeared. During the Christmas week, they usually picked up a domestic situation here and there and the routine drunk and disorderly (nothing ever serious and never requiring more than two on shift), but bad news travels fast and a memo had whipped its way around the county shortly after the drama at the Prentice's house and any and all incoming *guests* were to be diverted to the nearest available station.

No one wanted to risk being near the *thing* and so, the only people under his care were the Rose's. He had a feeling that this was not going to be the quiet festive period he had hoped for.

The front door creaked open in the roaring wind and in bundled Rebecca, smothered in her withered woollen overcoat. The soft white had faded to a coarse grey.

"Is it true, Bill? George is dead?"

"I'm afraid so, Becca. Arm was ripped clean off and he bled out. Right in front of me."

"Oh, how awful. They said that the kid did it. The one we were speaking about just before. But how, Bill? How can a child do a thing like that?" A lump was in her throat.

"This is no regular kid, Becca. There is something unnatural about him. He looked like he had walked straight out of a Hammer flick. You don't need to be here."

"I couldn't stay home. Not with all this happening."

"So, you decide to high-tail it down here with a literal monster three doors from your desk. Smart move but if you get gobbled up, don't come crying to me."

"That's not funny, Bill. I had to come back. I had no choice," she replied with a hesitant squeak.

"It's okay, but if you're staying, then I'll send Ben home. At least one of us can have a merry Christmas. The rest of us are in for a long night."

Rebecca let out a sigh that was quickly entwined with one of Bill's. Only in the cold ether could they allow an embrace.

"So, what is going to happen, Bill? There isn't exactly any standard procedure on this. I mean, we've never had a death on duty before, let alone something like this."

"The dad confessed to killing his wife, so we can hold him, no problem, even if it does turn out to be an accident but after what his bastard kid did to Mendez, I see no harm in letting him sweat it out in the cell a little longer. I wonder how long it'll take for him to realize the clock in there doesn't work. Let him stew."

"Bill."

"A doctor is on the way to take a look at the kid because, let's be honest, do any of us have a fucking clue? I mean, the kid has thorns. Fucking thorns."

"I'm guessing not your standard paediatrician."

"I'll be fucked if I know. The big wigs from district are sending some fancy specialist."

"Looks like you're out of luck then, mister, because you never know anything."

"So that's why I never get lucky," he replied with a familiar bounce returning to his voice. He was glad to see Rebecca return his knowing smile. "I'm heading into my office for now. Give me a shout when the doc gets here. Oh, and if the unearthly child should awaken before he arrives, feel free to give him another dose from our very own Doctor Taser. Trust me, it helps."

Bill gave her a final pat on the shoulder and departed into his office. Once inside, his breathing started to sprint as if in training for a marathon and he felt the rage bubble again. Only this time, it was mixed with the crushing air of grief. He had never particularly liked Mendez but not even he deserved to die like that. Did anyone?

Mendez's panicked, confused shrieks were horrible in the moment, but Bill felt sure that he would be able to tune it out soon enough. He had heard plenty of pained howls over the years and they all died down eventually, but every time Bill blinked now, he saw Mendez lying there. For that split second, he was back there on the lawn, standing ankle deep as a red river flooded out of the hole where an arm should have been.

He had given the order for Mendez to be on the scene, had told him to deal with the distressed kid and he had watched helplessly as his colleague writhed in agonizing pain. As he settled in his chair, his mind was crushed under the weight of his guilt as he drank in more than a few poisoned thoughts.

*Maybe the mother was right and the station now played host to some sort of demon child. No, don't be ridiculous, Billy boy. There had to be some logical explanation. Monsters aren't real. They belonged in the nightmares of children. Not actually in the children themselves.*

Only, this monster had broken free. Unshackled. The nightmare set loose and now, two people would spend their night lying on some cold slab. How many more nightmares would there be before they all just woke up and things were as they once were, or better yet, as they should be?

*Monsters aren't real. Are they?*

# Chapter Thirty-One

Around the time that Eve Prentice was learning she was now an only child, Doctor Herman White glided into the Almost police station, with a face that said it all; here is a man who is ten feet tall.

"I believe I am expected," he said with an effortlessly direct tone as he approached the reception desk, carrying himself with an inflated ego that only came from a lifetime of commanding respect.

"Ah yes, Doctor White, your...um...patient is just down the corridor," replied Rebecca, feverishly adoring the man before her with skin the colour of polished marble. Her stare was briefly stolen by the two diminutive people standing either side of the great doctor. From the way they paled under Doctor White's long shadow, she knew they were his juniors. In every sense of the word.

Bill, hearing the whisper of voices drift through the hushed and solemn station, exited his office and saw the toned outline pushing its way through the frosted windowpane in the door connecting the main corridor with reception. He appeared a moment later and looked less than pleased on seeing Rebecca's intense gaze. He made quick work of the rudimentary introductions and showed Doctor White and his entourage to Charlie's door.

"He's in here. For your sake, I hope he is still unconscious," he said bluntly. "A quick examination and then out. Don't poke the beast, as they say. I can't have any more upset today." He went to open the door when he felt a forceful hand on his shoulder as if he were being reprimanded.

"My team and I will proceed alone," Doctor White insisted, with extra insistence on the me, myself and I.

"Listen, Doc; technically, he may be a child but he sure as hell doesn't look like a little boy anymore. He is dangerous. There is no telling what state he will be in."

"And that is why I am here. To assess him. How can I perform my work authentically if the very person who assaulted him is lurking in the corner of the room?"

"Hey, don't try and start any of that shit. He took down one of my officers and for all I knew, he would attack again. I'll say that in front of a tribunal if it comes to that. I can't let you in there without appropriate supervision."

"No, I shall not let you interfere with my methods. I will not have my hard-earned practices corrupted," he spoke calmly but there was a subtle coarseness to his voice, irked by the insolent officer but he had long since mastered how to weave control so it was always within his hands.

"If you take issue with my work, then by all means, contact your superiors but I am quite sure they will listen to reason. And when I say reason, I mean they will listen to me. Obviously, someone feels you are out of your depth."

Bill, taken aback by the subtle scolding, stood dumbfounded with the doorknob still in hand. The doctor brushed him aside and he was left on the wrong side of the door, feeling like a kid waiting for a good old spanking by the principal. His cheeks turned a disturbingly bright shade of red.

Inside the room, Doctor White observed a shivering mass huddled in the far corner. The boy was awake.

"You must be Charlie. I'm Doctor White."

The boy, with his knuckles curved up over his head, was unresponsive to the doctor's now floating, feathery tone.

"Charlie? I gather you have had a quite a difficult day." Still, the boy remained silent, never raising his head.

Doctor White instructed his juniors to remain by the door and he treaded lightly toward the boy. His shadow, streaked in the barred light of the small window to the left of the room, lay behind him so not to impose upon the boy. Like with any wild beast, the approach was key. Slow and cautious. A delicate, intimate shuffle forward, just an inch at a time. It was only a matter of time, but he always got his prize. The hunter and his trophy.

"Can you turn around, Charlie? I would like to look at you."

"Wh-hy would y-you want to look at m-m-me? I'm a m-mon-s-ster," Charlie spoke plainly but his words were muffled, drowned out by his own tears.

"Like I said, I'm a doctor. I can help you."

"You can't."

"Well, you see, the thing is, Charlie, I'm a special kind of doctor and I only deal with a very *special* type of patient."

Charlie, with a growing curiosity, slowly raised his head before half-turning to face the doctor. From the corner of his eye, he could see that this Doctor White was now crouched beside him, arms down calmly by his side and his two juniors were still rooted to the spot by the door.

Their faces were poised and engaging. One was hurriedly scribbling (no doubt in the scrawl universally adopted by doctors) while the other stood rigid but he sensed no threat from them.

The light in Doctor White's auburn eyes slowly gathered around a pool of clear intrigue as Charlie began to trust him. In an instant, he saw the lightning that had almost scorched Charlie's skin, the countless thorns, some of which were bloodied by a futile attempt to rip them off and the quivering lips of the boy who was now soaked to the skin with a mixture of blood, sweat and tears.

"There we go, m'boy; that wasn't so difficult. Now, come sit with me. I think we should have a little talk."

Charlie rose from his huddled position on unsteady feet and sat opposite Doctor White at the nearby table. He knew he was in a cell, he had seen a few cop shows in the past, but this doctor was giving off a calm and soothing vibe that seemed to quell his nerves. Not like the intense, almost brutal procedures he had once cheered along with at home. They always got their guy in the end. By any means necessary.

The streaks of lightning began to dull, fading back beneath the skin and the white-hot pain dulled as Charlie sat in full view of Doctor White's kindly presence. A hidden smile left his lips and in that moment, all of the fear and anger that had inhibited him over the past twenty-four hours settled. A blind reaction to the doctor's alluring manner.

His mind skated past the horror show as the thorns slowly, and painfully, made their retreat back below the surface of his now-clear skin. The pain, though still noticeable in his creaking muscles, quickly receded to a manageable, almost acceptable level. He had felt worse one time when he stubbed his toe.

"Charlie, how do you feel? Your afflictions, so to speak, seem to have vanished."

"I'm okay, they did that e-e-earli-i-er too."

Doctor White's face twitched with a tremoring glee as his mind abandoned what little logic he had been building at that point. This was something new. Deliciously, seductively new.

Charlie's demeanour during the *phasing* or whatever it was had stayed as dry and hard as the Christmas dinner that would now most likely not be cooked this year. From the outside, Charlie now looked like any other boy his age, but from the inside, Doctor White was sure he remained the wonderfully dark being that had caused this whole sorry affair. This was to be an interesting case indeed. His whole body haemorrhaged in goosebumps, every nerve tingling with a primal thrill.

"Can you tell me everything that happened today, Charlie? It's important that I know. Only then can I begin to help you."

"So, you can h-h-help me? You can stop me h-h-hurt-t-ting people." He was scared. He was desperate. He was a child and here was a man who was here to rescue him. From the station? From himself? Charlie didn't know but he wanted to please this doctor all the same.

The doctor stood and went around to the boy, placing one hand on his shoulder and shot him a look loaded with a welcoming comfort. "Of course I can. That's what I do. I will take your pain away."

His tightly packed shadow was now given the space to breathe. Growing and stretching toward its prey. It was not yet time to go in for the kill but the whiff of the still weeping child, helpless and alone, was just too tempting to resist. Doctor White set his trap and simply waited, willing him to submit. He would have his prize.

It was all too easy. The squeeze on the shoulder was all it took for Charlie to blindly follow this hunter back to his hideout. Old sins cast long shadows and sweet, innocent Charlie was now trapped under this one.

He told the kind-eyed doctor everything he wanted to know and a fair few things he had no interest in, but Doctor White listened patiently with a plan forming in his mind and a morbid smile being birthed behind his false lips.

Charlie surrendered completely.

Foolishly.

# Chapter Thirty-Two

"Ah, Woodley, I shall be taking command of the young boy's case from herein," Doctor White began as he strode into Bill's private office, without knocking. "After talking at length about his affliction and such things, I am confident that only a hands-on approach will suffice.

"He requires specialist treatment and sadly, you are far too ill-equipped to deal with such a situation. If I may have use of your telephone, then I shall be able to take him within the hour." His two juniors, still clinging to his shadow, hung on every valued, chosen word.

Bill stood to meet the doctor's gaze but lasted only a moment before forcing his stare to veer off, wildly and obviously. It came to rest on a harmless hanging picture at the far end of the room, but the damage was done. He had exposed his inferiority to the holier-than-thou doctor. An uncomfortable feeling was swelling in his stomach and making the bitter journey north, but his face displayed only the frail signs of a stunned silence.

Doctor White was not only a skilled physician, he had learned the art of hunting early in his career and was now, in his own proud voice, a brilliant artist. Luring his prey into his trap, embracing them with false kindness before masterfully, expertly, going in for the kill.

"My facility is more than capable of handling a case like the Rose boy's. Under my care, he will flourish."

With colour returning to his face, Bill swallowed a hearty, sickly gulp and quelled the shifting rhythm in his stomach before it put in for another rise to the top.

"Flourish? He killed a man today. Right in front of my eyes. That cannot be overlooked just because he has differences. I will not allow it. That boy is dangerous."

"At times of great stress, we are all dangerous," replied Doctor White with the orange glow from an overhead light darkening above his eyes. "He possesses a great gift. Volatile yes, but great nonetheless. In the wrong hands, his ability could cause more scenes like today but in the right hands, who knows. I believe there to be a chance that he can be cured. After that has happened, then you can do with him as you please. But only after. Until then, he is mine."

Bill, sensing the matter was already out of his hands, retreated back into his silence, with his shoulders heaving and mind swaying. His hard-man stature, carried with ease throughout the years and worn like a badge of honour, crumbled under the looming shadow of this mysterious doctor. He submitted without ever realizing that had been the plan all along.

"I would like to speak with his father before we depart."

"Okay but you're not taking him with you though. He isn't a freak like the boy," he said, sullen.

"You should be careful, Woodley. Words can cut just as deep as a knife. Swiftly too."

*One man's freak is another man's treasure trove.*

Bill squashed down into himself, regretting his words and wanting to turn invisible. If Charlie could have his *ability,* then why couldn't he have his? He escorted the doctor further down the corridor and into the interrogation room to meet the jittery Michael Rose. Again, Bill was left outside in the cold corridor with words unsaid and a face now cherry red.

"Mr Rose, my name is Doctor Herman White. I have just spoken with your son and I am afraid to say that his condition is quite severe," he said, studying every dip and flex in Mike's face as he rattled off his speech.

"How was he? Was he okay? What will happen to him? Yesterday, he was a normal twelve-year-old boy, a little odd perhaps but nothing serious. And now this. How can he go from a sweet, innocent child into a thing?" Mike pushed the words out between a series of nervous, panicked breaths, almost choking on the last.

"After observing him, I believe that he is suffering from a rare disorder which affects his genes."

"Shit. How bad is it?"

"You already know how bad it is. You saw what he did. What he was capable of doing. Mr Rose, how aware are you of epigenetics?"

Mike turned away, unsure if he was being accused of being idiotic or just blind. The only sound whistling through the room now was the metallic clang of his cuffs as he readjusted himself.

"Epigenetics is the study of heritable traits. Or changes in the function of our cells," Doctor White began and concealed a glorious smile when all his words fell on deaf ears. "In terms you will understand, all living matter is made up of genes and these genes determine who and what we are.

"Some of our genes lie dormant and we are able to go about our lives with these potential changes staying undisturbed. While this is the standard for the majority of the population, it only takes a small mutation of the cell and our growth and development can be drastically altered."

"But if it's in his genes," Mike started without knowing how it would finish. He wasn't even aware that he was speaking, just thinking. A million thoughts hurtling through his mind, crashing toward each other and dying on impact. This one slipped through, unscathed. "Genetic? So, this is my fault?"

"Biologically speaking, no; I don't believe so. My previous work has allowed me to conclude that the ones who present with the more extreme mutations, like Charlie for example, had their genes altered by a defect in the mitochondrial DNA. His *variant* was passed down from his mother's side of the family."

Mike, with thoughts of Mary flashing before his weary eyes, went to speak but Doctor White was far from finished.

"He may have inherited this abnormality from his mother, but there was a chance it would have remained inactive throughout his life. He would have lived quite happily with it never rearing its ugly head. Sadly, however, that has not been the case.

"Our environment can bring about changes to our bodies. Stress is a key factor and given the trauma your son has undergone today, it is little wonder that his mutation has made such a violent appearance. He is also at the right age for puberty to start causing instabilities with his genetic make-up and so, the strain his young body was under was simply too much for him to handle.

"After speaking with Charlie and given my extensive knowledge in the field, it is clear that this mutation of his genes has always been there. Hidden within him all these years, lying in wait until earlier today when it exploded out of him. There may have been signs over the years that he was different, shall we say, but unless you were skilled enough to know exactly what to look for, then it would have gone unnoticed."

"But why him?" Mike asked, shifting his concern away from the habitual *why me?* "Does everyone have this thing hidden inside themselves?"

"Everyone possesses a baseline genetic make-up, what we would consider normal but everyone also has the chance of having their genes mutate. It is just Charlie's bad fortune that his is an extreme example of that situation."

"So, we aren't all thorn people then? Deep down?"

Doctor White bit his tongue to stop a howl escaping. "Not at all, Mr Rose. Every person is created differently. Even those who share an epigenetic defect may develop mutations of their own but it is highly unlikely that they would present in the same way as Charlie's. This is simply the life the Almighty has dealt your son."

"So, what do we do? There has to be something," Mike said, with echoes of blame returning back into his voice.

"I run a facility that specializes in the obscure and the unusual conditions that play havoc with the genes of children and I would like to take him with me so that we can observe and study him, and then treat him. Perhaps even cure him."

Hook.

"Cure him?"

"We excel at what we do, Mr Rose. I have an extensive medical career and there has yet to be a case where my team and I have come up short."

"You explained all this to him?"

"Indeed."

"Was he okay?"

"No, but I wouldn't expect him to be. The trauma of losing a parent coupled with his rapidly altering state is enough to drive anyone mad. He is a child with the capability of causing a great deal of harm to anyone who comes into contact with him. Your son has endured more than a child of his age should but with your assistance, we can help him."

Mike sat with a confused hunger. For hours, he had been wanting answers, desperate for them but up until now, he had been left starving. His hunger was brewing a rage but then in came this doctor, with soothing eyes piercing out beneath eyebrows that were almost crooked in the dim light, and Mike felt the rage simmer away. As if to nothing. All that hot air evaporated but through the steam, he could see the redolent face of Doctor White.

"I need to see him."

"Of course, Mr Rose. I will, however, advise caution. The news that his body was betraying him was a heavy pill to swallow. I could see the distress building within him and the more unsettled he becomes, the more his body will react. I fear that if Charlie remains here much longer, then his condition will deteriorate."

Line.

"He can get worse, sicker if he stays here?"

"Indeed, he may. A prolonged phase of heightened emotions lit the spark that caused his genes to reveal themselves and more stress will only add fuel to the fire. I understand your doubts and your fears, Michael, you are obviously a good father but this is what is best for your son. My facility is his only chance. Trust me."

Sinker.

"Then, he needs to get out of here. Do what you have to do."

And just like that, the deal was done. In that moment, Mike surrendered and wasn't even aware of it.

"Excellent. I shall have my team arrange the transfer. You are doing the right thing. Believe me; soon, your son will flourish. That is a facility guarantee." Doctor White departed the room with a sickening smile resting behind a condensed grin, lying in wait until the moment came where it could pounce. Be unleashed.

*Soon.*

There was never a question of Charlie not being transferred. A trophy was no good if you couldn't see its shine.

Mike gambled with the life of his son but when you played against the dealer, the cards were never stacked in your favour. You always came away playing the fool, and in the case of Michael Rose, who sat in his holding cell with his wrists still chained to the table and a look of false relief blossoming over his face, the blind fool.

146

# Chapter Thirty-Three

Eve was escorted into the police station and saw her family huddled in the waiting area. She brushed a kindly woman trying to entertain Frederic out of the way and gripped them with the kind of strength only a mother knew. There was enough force in her grip that she could give a diving sparrow hawk a run for its money.

Her nails dug into their backs but their wails for mercy went unheard. Despite the clawing pain, relief tried to wash their faces of the fear and confusion but like a stubborn stain, the panic stayed.

"Ah, you must be Mrs Prentice. My name is Re—"

"Save it, I don't care who you are. Now, I would like a moment with my family. Alone."

"Yes, of course, I understand," Rebecca said, retreating back toward the safety of her reception desk. Hiding behind its barricade.

Eve's ears fizzed at that cursed word again. No one could ever understand. Not now. With her grip showing no sign of relenting, she nestled William and Jennifer's heads firmly into her chest, burrowing deep. Trying to shield them from the horror but it was already too late.

"How could you let them bring our children here of all places? Don't you realize that *he* is here too? What were you thinking? Let me guess, nothing."

"They said we were needed here. I can't argue with the police, dear. They're the police but it's okay, we haven't seen Charlie. We only got here two minutes before you did." His body was stunned and every word had to be lured out of his submissive mouth.

"It seems you can't do much of anything these days. At least, tell me that you remembered William's painkillers." She finally released her children out of her bosom and back into the stilted air of the Almost police station. As she let go of William's shoulder, she could see his hand was swelling far worse now. Red and blown up, like a balloon about to burst.

"I didn't need to. He remembered all by himself. My brave boy."

"So, you need a child to do your thinking for you. Just look at his hand."

"I can see it perfectly well, Eve, but with things like that, it will get worse before it gets better. But it will get better. Everything always does. In the end."

His calm quality grated on her twitching nerves, inflating her own balloon and she took one step toward him. Her breath was now inches from his but there would be no loving embrace. Her breath, white and hot, slashed its way across the air toward Brian's timid blue.

"Oh, so you're a doctor now as well as a good father?"

"No, but I would have listened to the doctor if it had been me in that consultation room with William."

"Excuse me?"

"William told me everything the doctor said while we were being driven over here. I'm actually kind of glad you were brought separately. It gave me some time alone with our children. They are not the puppets you long for them to be."

Now, it was Eve's turn to play the silent partner as Brian danced circles around her. Neither of them aware he had those moves at his disposal. She lowered her head, looking at nothing but trying to think of everything. He was no competition for her but trying to find the right word to put her beloved back in his place was proving harder than she expected. A mouse did not square up to a snake and live to tell the tale.

"His hand is fine. It's just bruised. Kids scuffle all the time, Eve. It was hardly the first time he and Charlie got into some sort of pow-wow and it won't be the last."

Eve raised her head and Brian saw a twisted smile stretch out over her face. "You know nothing. Why do you think we are here, Brian?"

"I don't know yet. Something must have happened back at the house but all the officer that drove us here said was that he couldn't comment. I suspect we will find out soon enough."

"We are here because I called the police on Charlie an—"

"You called the police on your own nephew? How could you be so cruel, so spiteful?"

"Because I, unlike you, dearest husband, will put the safety of my children above everything else. And that includes that little freak. I, their mother, called the police to remove Charlie from my home, and what do you go and do as their father? Bring them all straight to him."

"I don't believe you sometimes, Eve. You can be strict at times; hell, a lot of the time, but this?"

Eve, realizing the futility of trying to bring him round to her reasoning, decided it was time to win and stop playing with her food. "Mary's dead."

Brian halted on the spot, his train of thought derailed. "What? How?"

"Michael killed her. He pushed her down the stairs."

"Oh Jesus, that's horrible. I'm so sorry, dear," he replied, the courage he had been building now lay at her feet, a pile of rubble, and his voice returned to its normal, passive self.

"Thank you."

"Okay, so now I understand why you are so worked up but please don't take it out on an innocent boy."

"You still don't see it? They had to have been arguing about what Charlie did to William. About what he is. He is the cause of all of this."

"Eve, you're grieving. Charlie is odd, I grant you that, but he is just a twelve-year-old boy," Brian said, pleading with his wife to see sense. The air of doubt sticking to his throat told him he didn't believe she would listen. She would forever be blinded by that which she chose not to see.

"He is a twelve-year-old boy who killed a police officer."

"Oh, come now, this is getting a bit out of hand. Charlie did not kill anyone. He couldn't. He's just a child."

"I'm only telling you what a certain DI Burrows told me. The police came to arrest Michael and Charlie lashed out as they tried to take his dad away. I don't know the details but he did it."

"This really happened?" A coldness was growing over his shadow.

"I'm afraid so, Sir," said a man intruding on their conversation. "I am the officer-in-charge of this case. Bill Woodley."

"But how?" Brian asked, turning around to face the police officer who was backing up his wife's delusions.

"I will assume that you had not been present when your nephew transformed."

"What do you mean transform?"

"Charlie Rose is not the sweet, innocent boy that he appears to be. There is something inside him. Something wicked."

"Oh come now, that's ridiculous."

"I apologize, Sir but the facts cannot be denied. Your nephew sprouted some kind of thorns all across his body. I, like you, would have scoffed at the idea if I hadn't seen the transformation first-hand. There is little in this world that I trust, Mr Prentice but I trust my eyes. Your nephew is no longer a little kid. For all I know, he may not even be human anymore."

"He really killed someone?"

"Yes. One of my officers. He tore the arm clean off and let him bleed to death. If I hadn't stopped him, then who knows how many others would have suffered the same fate, or worse."

"Now, do you believe me, Brian?" Eve interjected, the smug creature living at the back of her throat now given the chance to breathe again. "If that isn't demonic behaviour, then I don't know what is."

"This is too much to take in. And Mary?"

"It appears she was arguing with her husband about their son's *condition* and sadly, she ended up losing her life. A sad affair all round."

"I told you so."

"Oh Eve, I'm so sorry."

"Yes, I imagine you are," she responded without looking at Brian, instead focusing all her attention on Sergeant Woodley. "What will happen now?"

"Michael Rose will remain here under caution until formal charges are brought while Charlie is being transferred to a facility that apparently knows how to deal with this sort of abnormality."

"I would think a bullet to the head would be a better way of dealing with him."

"Eve!" Brian responded, scared of the calmness in his wife's voice.

"What? If a dog turns bad and rips open a babe in the street, you put it down without a second thought. You didn't see him, Brian. I did. Charlie is far worse than just a rabid dog. He is a beast."

"I agree, Mrs Prentice, but it's out of my hands."

"So, he attacks my son, causes the argument that results in my sister's death, and kills one of your men and you give him a get out of jail free card. Seems like quite a nice reward for such atrocities."

Hearing Woodley's passive attitude toward her, and her children's safety, fuelled her rage and she was desperate to let loose on someone other than Brian. Brian was too beaten now for a win to feel anything but expected. This Sergeant Woodley was new. Fresh.

"Believe me, if I had my way, he would rot in a cell for what he has done but I have my orders."

"Tell me, are your orders more important than protecting my family? Why is he being shielded from harm, blame even, while my family is exposed to it? Left to stew in the mess he has created."

"Mrs Prentice, what is important is that he will be contained and our town can rest easy," Bill added with a hint of jealousy toward all the blissfully ignorant people who would have the luxury of sleep that night.

"Can you tell us why our family was summoned here?" Brian asked, desperate for the conversation to change gear.

"There are some loose ends with Michael Rose's story about the events of today. You were all present with him up until a few hours ago and so are all key witnesses to his state of mind today."

"This couldn't have waited? We had just arrived home from the hospital when your people bundled me into a car," cried Eve.

"Ordinarily, a brief statement at the scene and a detailed follow-up in a day or two would have sufficed but giving that your home is a crime scene, inside and out, it was judged best to gather all the facts as soon as possible." Bill was now responding only to the words and not the sharp meaning that lay behind them. It had been too long a day.

Eve tensed her throat. Her home was finally noteworthy but not because of her. Because of him. It. She stood on the spot, shaking, imagining the horror as scores of tourists ambled up to her sanctuary; all for the cheap thrill of seeing the remnants of the red grass.

*No, I can't allow my beautiful home to be reduced to such filth. I will not stoke the fire that keeps the cheap rags fuelled. But what to do? I could have the lawn paved over. Hide the sordid past under a layer of concrete. That despicable thing has ruined everything. Desecrating my perfect lawn.*

*Oh Mary, I need you here. How can I berate you now? How could you leave me? How could you let yourself be tainted by bearing that thing?*

Bill was now desperate to move things along, knowing peace would be foreign territory so long as he stayed in the company of Eve Prentice. After assuring her that her children would be safe in their absence (taking a few hits as her chastising protests bounced around the room), he escorted her and Brian into a private room where they would be forced to scour over the smallest detail in Michael's actions.

From the way he sipped his coffee to the way he folded his newspaper. Wanting to know if there was a slow build before the explosion, knowing full well that sometimes, people just snapped. It only took one spark to light a match.

Despite Eve's insistence that Michael had always been 'rotten' and an 'unfit husband' (drawing exasperated sighs from Brian), Bill was beginning to sympathize with Michael Rose and concluded that he must have just snapped on the spot. If Mary had been an ounce like her sister, then it would have been almost impossible to have a sensible discussion with her.

*Maybe it was an accident after all.*

# Chapter Thirty-Four

Charlie sat alone in his cell, the walls seemingly shrinking around him. Closing in on him. Closer and closer until all the air in the room was as flat as Susie Costello's behind. A couple days ago, he may have chuckled at that thought as it skirted across his mind but now, he didn't know if he would ever laugh again. His head was swirling with a thick greying mass that clouded everything. Holding him with a suffocating grip.

Doctor White had explained everything and Charlie understood only the bare bones of it. How his insides were turning against him and that in a way, this was his destiny. That he was simply too young to begin to control the raw power now flowing through his adolescent veins but it was all going to be okay. Doctor White wanted to take the power away from him.

At what moment does flat air become dead air?

*But we have to act fast, he said, because I'm too vol-a-tile right now. Too dangerous for my own good.*

Yesterday, Charlie Rose was a regular, little boy, but now, everything was distorted. Everything was irregular. His innocence had been muddied and it scared him. Way down deep in his summersaulting stomach, he could feel it. Fear. It grew with every second that rushed past him now. His mind slipping further and further into the grips of the dark unknown that now ensnared him.

His head lolled forward and he snapped back to a semi-conscious thought in time to catch himself before he connected with the table. A feeling of regret swelled within his throbbing body. If only he had restrained a moment longer and allowed the hit, then maybe he would be granted some peace. Slam it hard enough against the table and all of the dread that was blistering throughout his body could have been at an end.

A sweet, longing, merciful end.

The twelve-year-old boy with dry blood on his hands and thoughts of pounding pain plaguing his fragile mind swayed in his seat as tears streamed down his face. A new normal.

He certainly had a tale and a half to share with Nick and Denny the next time he was in the clubhouse. If he ever made it back to the clubhouse. To home. To safety. The only dangers there were the taunts and sniggers. After the past twenty-four hours, that was almost desirable. Right now, he would welcome the jibes if it meant escaping. Not just the room, but the whole damned situation.

*Will I even be allowed to go home after everything? Would Nick and Denny still want me around after they find out what happened?*

*What will people say?*

*What will they think?*

*What will make them not hate me?*

*A cop was killed; that always riles people up into a frenzy. It'll be on the news. My picture will be on the news. I'll be on the news. I'll be the news.*

*Oh God. Oh God. Oh God.*

*It'll probably interrupt some heartstring puller they always stick on around this time of year. Just typical. There's always a psycho that craves the spotlight when the holiday season kicks into high gear. Only this year, I'm the psycho, but worse. A monster.*

*I don't want any of this. I'm not craving anything. I just want to go home.*

His days playing the fool, the patsy, the loser would be at an end. Now, he would be the creature, the monster, the thing. Only difference was these games would not stop at the clubhouse entrance. What happened in the club stayed in the club but this? No, this would be something far beyond his reckoning. Like a beast in a cage, trapped and put on display for the thoughtless drones to gawk at.

"Step right up, ladies and gentlemen, boys and girls. Come and look at the incredible boy who tore an arm clean off and let the poor sap bleed out. Marvel at his scales for skin and thorns for freckles. Come one, come all. Pay at the door. Have a picture of your kid with the Almost beast. Under 5's half off."

Shifting from the point of humiliation to one of a horrified spectacle would come as easy as flipping a coin. Each with the same level of exhausted shame.

Cell. Cage. They were just words that meant the same thing; Charlie Rose was trapped. They could confine him however they saw fit but he would forever be the outsider.

The outcast.

*Happy holidays indeed.*

# Chapter Thirty-Five

Bill paced nervously and without purpose in his office. It had been the worst day of his professional life to date, and all that was waiting for him when the day came to its close was an empty refrigerator. Cold and forgotten. How apt.

After wrapping up his interview with the Prentices, he was grateful to have a moment's peace back in his office. By the end of their discussion, he had grown older and weaker as Mrs Prentice continually bit back at the harmless questions. With every barb cutting deep into his tired body, he wondered if anyone ever came away unscathed after an encounter.

Eve was formidable, far outshining her husband, who had slunk down into the shadows almost like clockwork. The louder she hissed, the quieter and more invisible he became. He only had a moment's grace before Rebecca strolled in. A blossoming smile was killed as he saw a woman in her fifties, with the appearance of someone twice her age, shuffle in behind her. Mrs Mendez.

Rebecca left them to it, but all Bill could offer Gloria Mendez were the meaningless platitudes that would do little to touch the surface layer of her grief. He had watched her son bleed to death and as he looked into her wanting, welling eyes, found himself lacking.

The words, the motions, everything that would have made the situation an ounce more bearable. If it was his worst day, then god only knew how she felt when he told her the one responsible for her only child's death was a twelve-year-old boy.

Last Christmas had taken away her husband when his car skidded the wrong way around a sharp bend not too far out of town and now, this one had taken away her son. Her handyman. Her reason for living. Snow may feel soft and playful in its falling flurries but Bill reckoned the only thing Mrs Mendez would now feel when the air turned cold and the clouds swarmed above was a sharp sting. Striking deep and making way for an ashen shadow to consume all from her fracturing mentality to her broken heart.

During their brief conversation, Bill saw her face, and body, transform from living (struggling but continuing nonetheless) to simply existing. He wondered how long it would be before she too fell victim to the bitter, white storm. He was ashamed to admit the relief that rose in him as she exited the police station.

Bill seated himself behind his desk but felt his authority drain out of him until he was sapped dry. Just a husk of his former self remained, all of the dregs streamed around the man now standing out in reception, talking with Rebecca, a smug infestation setting up camp.

Doctor White was the type of man who took centre stage with him wherever he went. Bill rubbed his eyes raw, desperately trying to kick start his gears into motion when the phone rang. Ordinarily, one ring was enough to bring him back down to earth from whatever dark space he was orbiting but on this occasion, his hand refused to move toward the receiver. He had simply had enough.

With the ringing ingraining itself into his head and pushing against his skull, he regretfully picked up. With a quiver in his lip, he sighed deeply as he answered.

In all the years Rebecca had known and worked with Bill, she had never heard him beaten before. Annoyed, yes. Angry, for sure. But not this. This was uncomfortably new. Even down the line, the strange, unwelcomeness of it hit her squarely in the face. He had been down before but never out. "It's me, Bill. You okay?"

"Fine, fine. Just a long day is all. What is it now?"

"Just a quick word to say that Doctor White has arranged the transfer of the umm, the boy. He says his people should be here in around ten minutes. After that, it should be a smooth transition. I have the transfer forms ready for you. Mr Rose has already signed his part, seeing as how he is still technically the legal guardian."

"Okay, thank you." There was no warmth behind his words. They were just bland and empty.

He put the phone back down and felt the veins in his knuckles pulse out, almost in protest at his defeatist attitude. Once upon a time, he would have fought until his throat dried up and then fought some more with some elaborately indelicate hand gestures, but today's mess was almost at an end.

With the boy transferred, he could at least begin restoring some of the normality back into his station. His officers could grieve in peace without the looming presence of the *thing* that cast this long shadow over them. The fact that Charlie was a child would do little to quell their hate for him. He shared it.

He didn't know how the more resolute officers among them would take the news of his transfer but he was struggling to find the energy to care. They would not see it as out of sight out of mind, but more like sweet, innocent Charlie had been given a free ride straight out of the shit show he had smeared across this town.

That would have to be tomorrow's problem. The day was nearly over. So long as he simply did nothing. The act of doing nothing was foreign to him but was quickly becoming a very attractive idea. The voice in his head dimming as this new, strange notion grew more beautiful with each passing second. Wrapping him in its unfamiliar touch.

If only he could fight past his career-crafted instincts and silence his own inner monologue, maybe then he could feel the warmth of this foreign beauty. There was a light at the end of the tunnel and right now, he felt like falling headfirst into it.

# Chapter Thirty-Six

"You are the doctor that will be dealing with Charlie." It wasn't a question. Eve marched across reception, tearing herself away from her family and breaking apart Doctor White's huddle with his two juniors. Their hushed voices died on impact as her words cut through the air.

"I am indeed. And you are? You don't look like police."

"Of course I'm not police. I am Eve Prentice, my sister was Mary Rose, and I want to know what you intend on doing with her beast of a son."

"Ah yes, Mrs Prentice, I saw you and your children over there but forgive me for not approaching you. I did not wish to intrude on your grief, I could never begin to understand what you are going through."

Eve let her tongue simmer for a moment as she studied the man in front of her. There was something new about him. "Thank you, but I—"

"You have questions? Naturally. I would expect nothing less from a woman of your eminence," Doctor White said with his words on a reel. "Charlie Rose will be taken to my facility so that he will pose no threat to the greater community. You have my assurance on that, Mrs Prentice. He will be contained."

"But why take him at all? He is a dangerous animal. Why not just put him down?" This time, there was no Brian to hold her back as she laid her cards on the table. Here was a man who she could afford to go all in with.

"It is a fair question and one that I myself asked when I heard about his actions today. He is a ruthless, mindless beast without question, but to rid the world of him so simply as a bullet to the head would be doing a disservice to the memory of your poor sister. And the slain officer.

"He is a fascinating case, from a purely medical point of view, of course, and my facility is equipped to deal with beings such as Charlie. There, we can study how his body reacts to certain situations and use those findings to strengthen our world against others like him. The heathens that would put our beautiful, hard-earned humanity to ruin without strict intervention."

"Others?" She squeaked, disregarding every other word. She felt safe expressing her views, opinions and beliefs with him but any sense of solidarity was now dwarfed by a growing panic.

"Oh yes. He is in no way unique or special. I have deduced that his affliction is an abnormality in his genes but there is still so much to discover about his *kind*. Under the right conditions, all their secrets will be unearthed."

"It's in his genes?" She asked this with a lump swelling in her throat. It choked her as her eyes darted toward her children impatiently stretching in the cheap seats of the waiting area.

"Absolutely. My initial findings are that whatever is inside of him was buried deep within his body until the unfortunate incident at your home. As of today, the beast within has been awakened," he said, giving Eve a wide stare before allowing himself to copy her fleeting glance. "I would like to—"

"Excuse me, Doctor White, but your transport has arrived," Rebecca announced with a mousy sigh. "If you could just sign these forms here."

"Excellent. Please excuse me, Mrs Prentice, but duty calls," he uttered, leaving her dejected and with a shade of tainted blue developing over her face.

She hovered in his air for a moment before returning to her family. From their short conversation, she knew not to impose as he turned his attention back toward himself. He took the forms and pawned them off to one of his juniors. "Fill these out, will you Howie? I don't have time for such a tedious formality."

"Yes, Sir," the junior replied and hastily scribbled his way through the forms before handing them back to Rebecca.

Bill may have been right in his feeling that Doctor White carried the glow of centre stage with him wherever he went but he had slummed it here for long enough. These were his hunting grounds but even he, a god among men, could have too much of the forest air. Too much kindling spoils the fire but nevertheless, he would come away victorious with a new string to his bow.

"Soon, soon," he said to himself, salivating. He ordered his men down the corridor to collect his prize for him.

Bill appeared in the room and looked conflicted from the way he was holding himself together. In the doctor's presence, it was easy for someone to feel inferior. Bloated and in the way of his grandeur, yet all the while shrunk down to half their size. No matter what Bill did, he would lose. The game was rigged and he wasn't even aware he was playing. Or indeed, that he had been played.

He walked toward Rebecca before halting on the spot. From his position, he saw only half of her beautiful face, the other being swamped in darkness from her standing so close to the doctor's shadow.

Bill shuffled in place with a strange sadness swelling inside him, his head dropping heavy into his heart before a poking prompt from Becca settled his mind. He took the transfer forms and did his part. His duty fulfilled. Or at least that is what he would tell himself as he failed to sleep later that night.

During every aspect of the day's events, he had carried out his duties faithfully. Maybe that was the problem. In doing his duty, he had failed everyone; himself, Mendez, even Charlie on some level. A level he chose not to see.

But what could he do about it now? In a matter of moments, the boy would be taken away and if he dared to reach into himself and pull out the part of him that actually gave a shit about other people (could Charlie even be classed as people now?), he would find himself struggling to care. Surely?

No, it was too late. The forms were signed. The deed was done. Sweet little Charlie was on his own.

*Sayonara, kid.*

It was at that moment that he came face to face with the monster that had taken down one of his officers. The beast that had set his whole sorry life to ruin. The twelve-year-old boy who trembled as he was led through reception, burying his face into his chest as he avoided locking eyes with his aunt.

"You absolute monster! You fiend. You beast. Your mother should have dealt with you when she had the chance, and now she's dead," Eve screeched, shattering the frozen air. "And it's all your fault."

As Charlie was led past his family, he saw William visibly shaking and cradling his hand out of sight. Jennifer ducked behind her mother's legs for safety and Frederic wailed incessantly in his father's arms. His aunt, with limbs flailing and mouth foaming, tried to break past her husband's human barricade but Brian was doing everything he could to corral them into the corner, away from his nephew.

Doctor White, standing in the corner with a determined yet soft hand on Charlie's shoulder, adopted his comfortable role as the observer and failed to stop a grin from escaping. Let the people squabble. Nothing could interfere with his plan. He was too close to having his prize to allow such an absurdity. He emerged from the shadows and every delicate step forward brought him closer and closer to the prey.

*YES! He's mine.*

Bill watched as the Prentices wrestled with each other, their children suffering under Mrs Prentice's frenzied figure. He saw the struggle and pain that had been caused. He saw the whole circus and felt his insides shift. He had to act before there was a bloodbath in his station.

He very much doubted if Mr Prentice could prevent his wife from ripping Charlie apart if given the opportunity. She was a woman possessed. A deep, merciless revulsion had inhibited her. Much like how Michael had described his wife, he unwillingly noted.

It was as if a switch had been ignited in his brain and all senses of morality had been restored. The alluring fragments of hatred toward the boy vanished and he finally saw him for what he was; just a scared, little boy who was now being led toward the front door by the man who had made his insides curl up in shame and, if he was truly honest, fear. He saw Doctor White display a cruel grin. It was just for a second, but he saw it. His instincts were right. How could he ever have doubted them?

Before he knew what he was doing, his feet were carrying him to the crowd bustling by the door. "Doctor White, you cannot take him. He is staying here, under my care."

The action caused Doctor White to choke on the nothingness that filled his throat. The marksman in his tongue was taking a well-earned rest after a job well done. He felt Bill's palm land on his chest and recoiled at the touch of the run-down townie.

"Excuse me?" He may not have been lost for words but plans and eventualities, strategies and attacks came in short supply as he stood so close to the doorway. Too close to let this mere mortal stop his mission.

"I don't know what goes on at your hospital, but I have a bad feeling about this whole situation. I don't trust you, so Charlie is staying where he is. Any medical attention he requires shall be conducted here. Under my watch."

"How dare you speak to me with such insolence! I can perform miracles with these two hands. No doubt the only thing yours can do is scratch your head when anything bigger than a missing mailbox comes calling."

Bill, running off the adrenaline surging through his veins, felt the crooked, shaming smile he had been wanting to bury, fix itself into one of a conscious triumph. The doctor had revealed himself and that was all Bill needed to match him.

An argument was simply a race. Whoever reached the finish line first and felt the checkered flag breeze through their hair was the victor. The doctor may have edged him out on a few tight bends, but now, he could match him length for length and mile for mile.

Doctor White was no different than the slobs in the drunk tank every Friday night who resorted to their childish defences when you took away their bottle. He knew how to handle their blows and the doctor, now, was no different.

"Listen to me, Herman; this is not your town. You do not make the rules here. You have a few government friends? So what? None of that means shit when you stepped through that front door. I am the officer-in-charge of this case and Charlie is under my care. And I am telling you no. If you want to stay, then you will play by my rules."

Silence enveloped the station as all eyes became fixed on the two contenders. It was set to be a photo finish. Rebecca felt a wave of panicked relief swell within her chest (her Bill was back) and Charlie simply stood where he was told to stand, still with a cowering gait, feeling nothing like a prize to be won.

"Sergeant Woodley, if I may be s—"

"No, you may not. You do not get to talk your way out of this one. If words are your only weapon, then I think we are done here."

"Okay, I can respect a man defending his homestead. If the transfer is truly off, then might I be permitted to use your telephone? I can stand my team down back at the hospital."

"Very well, but I suggest you make it quick. It has been a long day and I am about ready to drop," Bill answered in triumph, almost in shock at how quickly the race had finished. And the winner is—

Doctor White, with eyes never leaving Bill, walked over to the reception desk accompanied by his two devout followers while Charlie stood awkwardly between the challengers, not knowing who to turn to. Who to trust.

"Brian, we have to get the kids out of here." Eve's voice, once shrill but now smothering her in an alien panic, stabbed through the air and punctured the cold stillness that had been holding her family in place.

"What do you mean? We can't just go without being given the all-clear back at the house. We don't even have the car with us."

"Then we'll walk. Just do it," she hissed and gave him a look he knew well and, having doubted her so much already today, he fell back on his only defence; he listened to his wife.

Eve, never taking her eyes off the beast in case of a surprise attack, coiled her shaking arms around her children's panicked shoulders and ushered them outside into the free air. Brian carried Frederick, who mercifully had stopped screaming and followed his family. Charlie was the only one to see their escape; everyone else too engrossed in their own little world to notice.

Doctor White, with his back to the room and unaware that the family of five had just slipped through his fingers, dangled the telephone cord between his flexing fingers as he gave his new orders in short, hushed breaths down the line. The instructions he gave to his juniors (who had their eyes fixed on their boss, mentor and leader) were silent but they understood him perfectly and one dashed out to the transport vehicle. New orders called for a new plan. He would have his prize. A minute earlier and there would have been a pile-up of people departing.

"Where did the Prentice family go?" Howie asked, the remaining junior.

"They're gone?" Doctor White spat as he turned and saw the empty corner where they had huddled mere moments ago. "How could you let them leave, you useless man?"

"Why does it matter to you?" Bill replied, assuming he was the intended target.

Doctor White failed to answer, merely letting his eyes narrow before turning away with his shoulders heaving. He took his remaining junior aside and scolded him in hushed tones.

Bill went over to Charlie and removed his restraints but was still unable to look at the boy who he had cursed and wished unthinkable things about. He would have to live with that. His conscience may have been wrestling with itself but as he finally angled his head, with a gentler push than he expected, and looked at the child, he knew Charlie would have to live with something far worse.

"I'm sorry, Charlie. I made the whole situation worse for you. Back at your aunt's house. I was wrong. I guess I got scared."

"It's o-o-okay, I get sc—car—red too sometimes."

"Like now?"

"No, not anymore. Thank y-you. I thought he was n-nice when we chat-t-ted but he se-s-seemed happy. But like a b-b-bad kind of happy."

"I know. I felt it too. Everything is going to be alright now. Once this lot leave, I'll let you see your dad. Would you like that?" Bill said, trying to sound reassuring. Trying to be the good cop.

"Oh, yes p-please," he said and for the first time in what might have been a long time, a happy tear was added into the pool. "What will happen to me n-n-now?"

"We can figure that out later. Rebecca, you should get yourself off home now."

The missing junior returned from the transport vehicle, now wearing a slick, leather shoulder bag and nodded. Doctor White's eyes lit up, the anger at losing the Prentices now relegated as a new influence took over.

"Oh, I'm afraid no one is going anywhere. Not just yet anyway," Doctor White said with no effort to conceal himself now. A malevolent smile curled around the corners of his mouth. Ready to pounce. He welcomed in half a dozen men from outside, all with the same glossed look of adoration for their leader. They had been dutifully waiting within the transport vehicle but now, they were able to be deployed and complete their mission.

"What do you mea—?" Bill began before everything went dark and he found himself crashing to the ground.

Charlie stood in horror, burying his face into his hands as the men in white coats whisked through the reception room, never missing their mark before departing just as quickly as they had entered. Bill and Rebecca never stood a chance, and Charlie now stood alone.

Isolated.

The trap had been sprung; all that was left now was to close it.

# Chapter Thirty-Seven

Outside the police station, the daylight had bled its last drop and the town was now in the grips of a sweeping darkness. A dark canvas was squeezing out the stars, cleansing Almost of all glimmers of light.

"Wh-what are you d-d-doing? You can't do this. I don't unders-s-stand," Charlie pleaded with a frightened jerk of the head.

Sergeant Woodley had slumped by his feet like a discarded wad of paper. The man, who earlier had tried to split up his family, now lay in the foetal position. Charlie would have pitied the man but he had none to spare for anyone but himself. The kind reception lady was sprawled in front of her desk, wearing a look of confused panic like a mask.

Doctor White smirked at the scene before focusing his attention on the horrified child.

"It's going to be just fine, Charlie. I could not allow anyone to interfere with my work. My plan for you may have been changed, but I would never permit it to be so recklessly abandoned. You will be coming with me."

Charlie stepped backward as Doctor White moved toward him with his arms outstretched expectantly. The hunt was over. It was time to have his prize. Charlie tried to raise his own arms in protest but every vein in them twisted, resisting his pull.

He had been bowling once before, for Nick's tenth birthday, and that day, he could only manage the smallest ball on offer but it was as if he was now carrying around two extra larges. The more he tried to fight back against his own body, the heavier they became, dragging him down.

In his childlike haze, he looked to Doctor White for help but found only his sickening, stalwart glare burn into him. The doctor laughed at his struggle but to Charlie's adolescent ears, all he heard was the cackle of a madman.

The pain coupled with his fear and Charlie, playing the unwanted role of host to this most distressing union, strained for as long as he could, trying to keep the inevitable at bay but his body was against him. He was far too weak to fight back and he surrendered to himself. Once again, his body exploded.

Doctor White looked on with ecstasy running through his eyes as the twelve-year-old boy collapsed and convulsed in front of him. Charlie screamed out, a hapless desperation perforating his call, but Doctor White stood firm. Right now, he was only the observer.

Time would come for his intervention but for the moment, he enjoyed the show that this terrified child was performing for him. Doctor White could utter only one word as Charlie was left to writhe in his uncomfortable panic: "Fascinating."

Howie, the younger of the two juniors (still in their resolute position either side of the great man), jerked his head away from the boy. A feeling of uncertainty was stealing its way up him, rising from his feet and settling in his stomach. It churned against his unmoving stance, as if in a declaration that they should be helping the boy. He was their patient now, after all.

"I can feel your conflict, Howie, but you must put a stop to it. If you let it control you, then sooner or later, *that* will control you too," Doctor White remarked with a nod in Charlie's direction. "Our work is sacred and we are soldiers. Now, hand me a syringe."

Howie reached into the shoulder bag and produced a syringe like the ones that had taken down Bill and Rebecca, concealed within the hands of the spectral men, and handed it to his leader. He closed the bag up and let it rest against his body, the zip softly grazing against his fingertips.

Doctor White began walking toward Charlie's now motionless frame. The tremors were over but he was still whimpering like a wild animal caught in a snare. Every step forward set off their own individual aftershock and he could see Charlie's shoulders twitch as he caught every one of them. Charlie Rose, the epicentre.

"I think it better if I remain in my observation mode until he is confined back at the facility," he said with a clear voice but clouded head, pawning the syringe off to the junior beside Howie.

The junior, delighted with the opportunity to prove his commitment, did as instructed and moved within three feet of their newest prey.

"Do this and the white coat is all but guaranteed," he heard Doctor White whisper, bringing him out of the zone for a moment.

Charlie angled his head toward the man as he felt the paused step and looked at this determined unknown enemy. The eyes turned wild as the junior went in for the kill. Charlie saw the syringe come down toward him, liquid malice oozing from its mouth.

He rolled to his left and felt the needle stick into his shoulder blade. Its venom was released but from its jutted and clumsy angle, he was able to shake it out with ease and rose to face this new adversary.

The junior was dumbfounded. He had observed Doctor White do this a dozen times since being recruited. Hand-selected by the great man himself. He had studied his master's hunting techniques. Everyone at the facility had. The supervisors, the shareholders, even the auxiliaries. Never once did Doctor White put a foot wrong whenever he stepped into the forest of the damned, so how had this happened? How had he failed?

Before he could turn and offer a face of penance to his mentor and commander, his feet left the ground and his whole body was thrown through the front window of the police station. The prey had attacked him!

*Impossi—*

The confusion drowned out the pain as glass shards tore through his clothes, gashing his skin in mid-air before he came to a rest with a broken spine and his head cracked open on the curb side.

Charlie, with eyes turning a sour red, foamed at the mouth and saw a man, who earlier that day had tried to separate him from his family, still lying near his feet. Helpless and vulnerable. His thoughts were not his own, corrupted by the hunter's blundered attack but before he could lash out, the world inside his head grew dark and his body went limp.

All the rage coursing through his seething body had stopped him from feeling the punctured stab of a second syringe to the back of the neck, courtesy of an unnerved Howie.

With the prey now subdued, Howie (without waiting to hear a congratulations from his superior) dashed outside, foregoing the door and leaping through the shattered window. He crumbled next to his friend and knew at once that he was gone.

He may only be a junior but he knew death when he stared it in the face. His friend had died with thick confusion still spread over his face and his body had been overwhelmed by a glassy dust that held no shine. Returning inside, he saw Doctor White standing over the prey's body. His smile dazzled in the grim darkness.

"He's dead, boss. Dead."

"I figured as much, given the ferocity of this beast. But this is no time for mourning, Howie. We have work to do. Load the boy into the van."

"What about—?"

"I should not have entrusted such a momentous task to a junior. Clearly, he was not worthy of such a command but yes, we will take his body back with us as well. We can extract the prey's DNA from his corpse. We need as much of it as possible."

Howie stood motionless, unable to process the cruel emptiness in his mentor's words. Doctor White sensed the hesitant weakness and squashed it out of him.

"If we do not act quickly, then all of this could be for nothing. We both saw how feral he was just now. Imagine that power once we harness it. Imagine what will become of our precious world if we do not. He must be back at the facility by the time that dose wears off. Load him up. Now!"

Howie moved and did as instructed but his mind was disconnected, still focused on the sight of his fallen friend's mangled body. It flashed in front of him every time he blinked. The blood. The exposed backbone. His friend.

Blink. Blink. Blink.

# Chapter Thirty-Eight

"I don't understand," Brian said, trying to catch his breath. They were walking against a bitter wind with only sporadic street lamps to light their way home.

"Of course you don't. We should just have that stamped across your forehead. Let people know what they are getting into in advance," Eve sniped back, wishing she had been given a similar warning. "If it were left to you, our children would have fallen to the same fate as that monster."

"You're not making sense," Brian replied, trailing a little behind his wife and trying to keep Frederick's face out of the winter cold. Cradled in his father's loving arms, he slept happily on their evening stroll, unaware of everything.

"I'm making perfect sense, it's your own fault if you cannot keep up. It's bad enough they are related to that creature but that doctor was actually planning to treat them all the same. If Mary wasn't dead already, I would have killed her myself for spawning such a hateful thing." No shade of guilt touched her vocal chords as she rallied off her disgust.

Brian, stunned by his wife's new form of callousness, said nothing in return but looked to his two eldest children (each holding one of Eve's hands), but they mercifully seemed unaware of their mother's ravings. But he could only see the back of their resolute heads and wondered if their faces relayed a different story.

William, being the eldest, had suspected something bad was happening for a while now but his face had concealed it well. His mother's teachings of reserving emotions (storing them for a later day) still sitting strong in his adolescent mind. Jennifer, however, at only five years old, failed in this lesson and her face was plastered with cold terror.

Though they both had different approaches to their current trauma, they were both smart enough not to complain about how tired they were from walking. Their legs ached and William was sure he could feel blisters forming on his feet, pushing back against every step forward.

"This is all his fault."

"Who?" Brian responded blindly.

"Urgh, who do you think? Charlie's. I have tried telling you repeatedly today but you refuse to hear me. If you had listened back at the house, then all of this could have been avoided but no, you had to put on some fake macho show whereas I was just being a hysterical woman, wasn't I?

"We see one drop of blood and collapse gracefully onto a pre-placed pillow. Well, I have news for you, you simpleton, what I was being was a mother." She gave William and Jennifer each a soft squeeze.

Brian stopped walking, not knowing if it was the pushing chill in the air that had winded him or the cutting swipe of his wife. They were almost home but he suspected that not even in the confines of the normal and familiar would he be safe from her snaps. "I'm sorry, dear."

Eve ignored his words, knowing that was all they were. Brian was about as much use in a crisis as an umbrella stand on board the Titanic and all he could offer her was meaningless, worthless words.

They turned into their street and saw the spectacle that graced them earlier (and disgraced her home, Eve pointed out) had departed. The only thing that remained was the official tape, swaying in the breeze but its haunting yellow message holding firm, signalling to everyone in the neighbourhood that this house now played host to a gossip mill of horror.

Eve's image was destroyed. Her plain, unadorned lawn was finally clear but the grass would never be the same again, never be beautiful again. The sick dread had seeped into the roots. Someone had moved their car to a properly parked position. Both Eve and Brian guessed it would have been the police but that still did not sit right in Eve's head.

*Is there nothing they won't touch? Is nothing wholly mine anymore?*

"Why did I ever invite Mary here? This was my sanctuary and now, it's in ruins."

"Because she was your family."

"This is all the family I need," Eve responded, nodding toward her three children. If Brian hadn't been holding Frederick at the time, then he suspected he would no longer have been included in the intimate gesture. "Take the kids inside, I need a moment alone."

"Do you think we're allowed?"

171

"This is our home. We shall do as we please."

"Okay, if you're sure but don't stay out here too long. You'll catch your death," Brian said, still trying to sound like someone she might love.

Eve watched her children disappear behind the closed door and immediately sobbed as she turned her attention to her crumbling image.

*Lord, tell me. What do I do now?*

She was buried so deep inside her own head that she blocked out everything from the outside world. She called out for answers, for guidance, for orders but all she received in return was cold silence. A void where the only sounds she could make out were her own desperate cries echoing back at her. This had never happened before. HE had always answered when she called but now, she was left in the nothingness.

*No. No. No.*

Slowly, she was brought out of herself and the sounds of life that surrounded her faded as if to nothing. The wind whistled a silent tune and a scattering of birds flapped soundlessly through the bitter evening sky. While the outside world may have been hushed and still, inside her head, she was still screaming against the empty mass.

Collapsing to her knees with tears now washing her face, she could feel self-pity lurk behind her features as she clawed at the grass, frantically trying to save herself but it was no use. The red patch would always be there. On her lawn, under her fingernails and in her mind. The fear of the day was being rinsed away, but the anger was holding steady against the cresting wave.

She had invited Charlie Rose into her home and now, her garden was the one to pay the consequence.

*He is no true rose, flaunting his immorality in the face of all that is right.*

*He is only a weed, come to turn my garden to rot, but I shall prove I am still loyal, Lord. This is just a test and you made me cleverer than this contaminant. You can see I stand strong in the face of his sin. I shall be the one to put a stop to him, cut him out before he can taint us any further. I shall cut him out.*

*Root and stem.*

Eve Prentice stood and rushed over to her car, unaware her shoes were now caked in red mud. When she found the keys still in the ignition, she took that as a sign that this was the only option. The only path she could take to prove herself. She sped off toward the police station; however, this time, she failed to give a final look toward her home or her children.

Devotion to the Almighty was now in full control of her mind (and hands), blinding her to the fact she had just relegated her children to the sidelines alongside their father, her grief for Mary and her trepidation toward Doctor White. She departed without a second thought for anyone other than her saviour.

*This is just a test.*

Eve tore through the streets, skipping corners and jumping stop signs, in her relentless pursuit. Her tires came to a grinding halt when she spotted Doctor White and his men loading Charlie into the back of a van. Trying to steal him away from her.

She was so consumed with righteous hatred that she failed to spot the shattered window of the police station and was unaware that the van already housed a dead body. Another victim of her nephew. All she saw was her chances of redemption being cruelly snatched away from her. Something she would not easily allow.

With a guided hand, she shifted the car into gear and began squealing down the single lane road, her rage-red eyes untouched by the dark night's shine. Doctor White stood proudly at the back of the van while his prize was loaded in alongside the dead junior.

The thought of Charlie waking during the journey (unlikely with the high level of sedative but still, anything was possible with the inhuman) and finding himself within a hair's length of his latest victim caused too much joy; he could not stop a grin from emerging.

That grin, however, promptly retreated back behind his callous face as the sound of an engine revving quickly became the only sound in the world. He turned and saw what should have been certain death thundering toward him. He felt Howie flinch and cower but he had a reputation to uphold. The great man stood firm, his fear so expertly concealed that even he couldn't feel it.

Eve was less than twelve feet from smashing into the man who was trying to deny her salvation. With no weed to remove, she would have failed HIS test and be forever lost. This was HIS plan and her purpose. All she had to do was drive straight for a few more seconds and all her worries would be over. Her doubts unfounded.

But whatever force was guiding her hand must have sensed the reluctance within her and she was discarded. A sense of morality snapped back into her when she could see the white coldness in the doctor's eyes and the terror in his junior's.

Eve crossed her arms over and the car swerved off the road, crashing into a dilapidated bench which she had always thought was unsightly. Her neck jolted forward as the airbag was released, two of her ribs were shattered and both collarbones displaced themselves. She happily closed her eyes as she was welcomed into the land of unconsciousness.

Howie was the first to approach the battered car while Doctor White remained in his stoic position.

"It's that woman. Mrs Prentice," he announced, still with fear and sweat raining down his face.

"I don't tend to like surprises but this just might be a happy one. Howie, put her in the van with the others. She can still be of some use to us."

"Sir? I don't think we should move her. She seems pretty beat up."

"You are not here to think. Follow orders. That is the entire sum of your existence. So, do I need to repeat myself?"

Howie gave a silent agreement and began the uncomfortable task of removing Eve's body from the wreckage. Though she was still alive, she still felt colder than when he had to lift his dead friend's body not five minutes previously. The white-hot rage that had inhabited her, had abandoned her.

# Chapter Thirty-Nine

Bill stirred in his fallen spot; something was knocking against his skull and the impulse to bat away whatever it was quickly died as he realized the hammering was coming from within his own head. It was as if his skull was swelling, pushing out under his skin, trying to break free in an effort to feel the cool air whip generously against the bone.

A ringing in his ears dulled as a new sound took over. A desperate, pained noise. Someone needed help. He rolled over and had to force his eyelids to open. All of his muscles now seemed stubborn, refusing to do the bare minimum. He didn't know how long he had been out cold but the room was coated in thick darkness. The only light in the room came from a flashing monitor on Rebecca's telephone at reception.

*Becca! Where's Becca?*

He knew he had been drugged, he just didn't know what with and all his history of first-aid seminars and active situations told him not to ignore something that serious but those nagging thoughts were quickly suppressed.

Rising to his feet, he was happily surprised to find he could stand unaided. Crawling around the floor, looking for Becca would have been too undignified, though it would probably bring a smile to her face and right now that was all he wanted to do. It's all he had ever wanted to do. He was done with missing his chance. He just had to find her and tell her.

His eyes readjusted to the dark and over by her desk, there she lay. Her body glowed a troublesome red as it was modestly lit by the flashing light on the desk above and from the haunting flashes, he could see she was shaking. He darted over and collapsed by her side, taking her head in his lap and failing to remember everything that he had learned in first-aid.

Christmastime shifts were a hollow, joyless affair and so, there were far fewer staff on duty than during a normal week. By the time he had his showdown with Doctor White, he had sent everyone else away and he gave thanks for small mercies but why did it have to be her on shift? Why did she have to come back?

He tried to hold Rebecca's arm flat to stop her hurting herself but his effort was in vain; the arms flailed, striking both herself and Bill, and her eyes rolled back in her head, giving Bill a clear view of her reddening whites. A dark mass was coming over the horizon and the sea blue of her eyes was beginning to dim. Vomit began seeping out of her mouth and was closely followed by the slow trickle of blood.

The seconds ticked by agonizingly slow and Bill cradled her long after the seizure had stopped. He held her head against his chest, willing her to hear his heartbeat and mimic him like she always did, but she was gone. Slipped away without having the last word, never knowing whose arms she had died in.

Her boss, her friend, her almost someone. He had always been her almost someone, and now that almost had become a never. It hurt like a burden that was far heavier than her vacant body still nestled in his embrace. Bill begged, cursed and even prayed for her to come back to him but soon, his words dried out, leaving him with nothing to do except gasp in the cold air. Alone.

He sat with his crushed body for almost twenty minutes without moving an inch, not wanting to disturb her peace but elsewhere in the station, a noise was growing, starting low and staggered but the pauses were waning and one mighty, anxious cry was enough to swat away the fuzziness in his head and bring him back to himself.

"HELLO! HEY, ANYONE?"

Bill eased Rebecca off him and placed her arms across herself. He took one final look at her and saw the light, his light, had been switched off. The sea had calmed but all Bill could see now was a dark mass stretching out. Forever.

Following the noise, he came to a stop outside one of the holding cells. This one in particular, he remembered, belonged to a very distressed and very disgruntled Michael Rose.

"Sergeant Woodley. I have just been left here for god knows how long. That clock over there is missing two of its hands, you know. You can't just let people stew like that."

Bill stayed silent, his mouth still full of half-swallowed tears.

"Can I please see my son? Or at least tell me what you are doing with him. I heard a lot of commotion before. Is Charlie okay?"

It was in that moment that Bill's thoughts were not solely of Rebecca; he remembered his confrontation with Doctor White and then nothing. Blackness. In his drug and grief-addled mind, he had completely forgotten that Charlie Rose even existed, let alone that he was in his care.

Charlie was just a kid but someone else now lay dead because he came to town. That fact refused to quieten down no matter how hard Bill yelled. Screaming into the void. He could feel the anger start to take hold of him again but this time, it was different.

Rather than simply crashing over him and consuming his every thought, it just rippled. Something inside him, a shining beacon, was trying to hold him steady, trying to keep him afloat. It held him with soft hands that refused to let him sink beneath the surface, into the murky unknown where he knew there would be no coming back.

"Charlie? No, I don't believe he is okay." It was a forced reply and absent of all emotion. "A lot has happened since you and I spoke last."

"Where is he?"

"Come with me. I think I know where we can find out," Bill said as he removed Michael's handcuffs.

The two men exited the cell and headed back toward reception and felt the winter wind attack all of their senses as it stormed in through the shattered window. It carried a hollow cry that echoed through the building, exposing the emptiness.

"What the f—! Please tell me this wasn't Charlie," Mike said as he saw the body in the centre of the room.

"No, Charlie didn't do this."

"Then, what happened?"

"Doctor White happened. He drugged me and Rebecca and must have kidnapped your son while we were out cold. I came away lucky; she, on the other hand, did not." The words fell out of his mouth. Lucky was about as far from the truth as could possibly be.

"Oh my god, why would he do all this?"

"So he could have your son."

177

"But I told him to take Charlie away," Mike replied, every word dripping in disbelief. A horrified confusion was quietly killed as more primal emotions took command. The fiercest among them being guilt.

"That doesn't matter now." Bill grabbed the transfer form off the reception desk. Rebecca lay by his feet but he couldn't look at her. Not anymore. He furiously shut his mind's eye to avoid sinking into the deep and actually read the form this time rather than just skirting over the details like before. He found the line where the junior, Howie, had scrawled the transfer destination. "He is at the Artemis House facility."

"Where in the hell is that?"

"I know the name. I think it's only about forty minutes from here. That settles it then, I am going to this facility and will see justice done against this lunatic. You want your son back, yes?"

"Is that a serious question? Of course I fucking do."

"Good. Then I could use your help in bringing White down."

"Okay but your version of justice might differ from mine. If he has harmed my son, then I'll kill him."

Bill, surveying the damage done to his station (feeling not just the tiny shards of glass tear through his beaten shoes from the broken window but also the massive hole left by Rebecca), smiled. "Looks like we agree on something, Mr Rose."

"Call me Mike," he insisted and they headed out the door, so preoccupied with fear and anger that they disregarded the beaten-up car and the now crumpled bench. The two men jumped into Bill's car and headed off to find their own definition of justice.

*Rebecca didn't slip away. She was stolen.*

# Chapter Forty

"Attention all, I am foregoing the three-day adjustment and observation and moving straight to extraction with our newest arrival. Everything must be in place within the hour. There can be no mistakes." Though his eyes were weary after his travels, his voice remained as formidable as ever. It cut through the silence and drew every eye in the room toward his resolute position.

The surgical team, nodding in unison, erupted into a fine-tuned applause that echoed throughout the theatre at sight of their rigid director emerging from the observation booth opposite the main stage. With every cheer, he was lifted to new heights and the founder of Artemis House had his head in the heavens for too long now to turn back.

For almost thirty years, Artemis House had secretly carried out its mission to rid the world of those who would bring it into disrepute. These impure few would be hunted down, studied and have their contaminate extracted; for only the Chosen were capable of harnessing such power. In the possession of the beasts, it would be a curse upon the land, but in the hands of those who were truly faithful, it would be a blessed gift.

The facility's founder, director and father of all who inhabited her hallowed halls understood what needed to be done and so, sought out those of similar principles, people who would devote their mind, body and soul to the cause, and little by little, he began the arduous task of righting the wrongs of the world as he saw it.

It was six years into the mission when he realized the problem with merely removing the unwanted souls. The Chosen could cut down all the weeds that the good earth may sprout but the people left behind had shown no signs of gratitude for how pure their garden was becoming.

Their work may have been shrouded but every impurity they removed had made the world a more beautiful place to exist. The problem was no one was asking where this new shine was from; they were just content to wallow in its afterglow.

He called a meeting with his benefactors (a consortium of ordinary men whose only power stemmed from the size of their wallets) and proposed scouring the lazy morals of the modern world and replacing them with ideals of what the world should be.

Artemis House was trying to build a new world by removing the stains of human life and to do this, she would need a twin. An institution that specialized in a firm education, rigorously coaching its followers about what to accept from life. And which facets of society were destined for disposal.

The people of Almost were blind to the miracles being performed around them. They were within touching distance of a greatness that they would never know and so, positioned at equal distance outside the town that was judged to be full of the most disinterested people that the country had to offer, the founder gave birth to the Apollo Preparatory School.

While the students of Apollo Prep were being schooled in the ways of the new world, it was only those who were housed in its compound that were honoured with the discipline necessary to carry out the mission when the time came and they were called upon.

The founder knew a war of faith would likely be fought and it was a sad and simple fact that in the modern world, the heathens outnumbered them. Conversion, as a concept, didn't go far enough and if they were to succeed and survive, then they would need to tip the odds in their favour.

While Apollo prepped his soldiers for the coming war, it was Artemis, with her ingenious staff hunting down all the mutant children they could find, that would ensure they were triumphant. Every new prey brought the founder one step closer to a victory he could only envision.

"Excellent. It has been far too long since we have enjoyed a find this rare. Succeed tonight and we shall be remembered by history. No longer will we be confined to the shadows while the world bathes in the shine of our work. Are you ready to step into the light?"

The crowd chanted their agreement.

"We shall be first site in a dynasty that spans the entire globe. Sister sites will be born because of this day and they will look to us, as Head Chapter, for guidance in the new world. All we have to do is build it. Ready the stage and I shall shortly call for the Rose boy to be brought down. Under our watchful care, he will flourish."

"He will flourish," cried the team, their call harmonizing like a church choir. Even from under their protective masks, it was beautiful.

The team carried on busying themselves with their preparations for the show. Every surface would need to be scrubbed and sanitized before the main event. One single contaminant could sour the sweet Rose and the show would be ruined. Charlie would be their salvation; he just didn't know it yet.

# Chapter Forty-One

Bill pulled the car up a dirt track and even from a mile away, he could see the hospital. Artemis House had made no attempt to hide itself. Surely, an organization that kidnapped children and murdered innocent women would be buried deep in the mountains, down hidden pathways, with barbed wire fences and key code access points positioned around a ten-mile perimeter. But that was not what was facing Bill and Mike as the car came to a rolling stop.

From the main road, it simply looked like what it claimed to be. A hospital, like any other. From the outside, it looked completely ordinary. Boringly so. Whatever was being conducted within its walls was well-hidden by its dull appearance. No one driving past would look twice at it. The facility, with its steam towers to the rear and peeling paint encompassing the front, was hidden in plain sight.

"What kind of place is this? The car park is jammed," Bill uttered with annoyance growing in his voice. He had prepped himself on the ride. He was ready for a showdown, not this.

"Typical hospital," Mike grunted.

"This must be all the staff. A place like this can't have visitors. It has to be a hush-hush facility. Surely? Regular hospitals do not go around drugging anyone who gets in their way." Bill clicked his teeth as he pulled the car into the deserted overflow car park. "Overflow? Are you fucking kidding me?"

They exited the car and stood like specks of dust on the sprawling tarmac, taking in the swelling beast before them. Though its shadow was masked under the cloak of darkness, they were both trapped in it. Artemis House was large and intimidating and the smell of death that inhabited all hospitals, lingered in the air and had a strong saccharine chill to it.

Though they were both on guard, they walked through the front doors of the facility without hesitation. The air inside the building became dense and cold, taking a tight grip around their throats as their feet shuffled forward.

The entrance hall opened onto a grandiose reception area situated in the centre of the room, which then led onto around half a dozen snaking corridors but they all looked deserted. The room was impeccably clean, whiter than snow and far colder. Other than the two men standing awkwardly in the quiet, there was not another soul to be found.

"Okay, so where do we start?" Mike asked, troubled by the emptiness. There had been at least a hundred cars outside. Where was everyone?

The safe haven of home now seemed like a distant memory. His normal everyday life. Bickering with Mary and conceding every battle for the sake of his own sanity. Ignoring Charlie and slowly growing more annoyed with him the older he became.

Resenting God for dealing him such a shit hand and turning his back on the church. Hating himself for blindly waiting for a magic wand to appear and wave itself over his troubles. Maybe none of it was normal life, maybe it was only ever a dream.

Maybe he could wake up and find himself inhabiting the body of someone without any of the strife he had been cursed with. A nightmare that had sapped his youth but was finally coming to a close. All he had to do was open his eyes.

He blinked with a deep wish but all he saw were the blinding lights running overhead, their cold shine almost burning his retinas. His youth was indeed gone, all that remained was the dry crust of a wrinkled life. Pain ran through his nerves and he felt the stress of being a husband and father shabbily woven together beneath his skin.

He had worn those labels every day of his life for years and they still itched and scratched as if they were unfamiliar to his touch. Or as if they were tailored for someone else entirely.

His wish for a new life had been denied. His happily-ever-after was a dream. His life, a nightmare. Charlie needed him, now more than ever, and there was nothing he could do to avoid that fact. First, he would save his son and then, he would figure out what the hell he was going to do with his life.

Mike looked back at Bill and saw that his holster was now unbuttoned and his thick fingers danced tentatively over the butt of his gun. On the other side of Bill's belt, he saw the Taser that had escalated everything and felt a shiver squeeze his throat when he thought of what would have happened if in the hellish moment, Bill had reached for the wrong attachment.

An unpleasant feeling swarmed his nerves and he shook on the spot next to the determined, scorned officer. Bill called out, assuring himself that Doctor White was not so ignorant to think that he wouldn't be followed. They had to have been expected but his voice echoed through the empty chill, sliding around corners but catching on nothing. His echo faded and died in an unknown part of the hospital.

*Maybe he assumed I died back at the police station too. And with Mike trapped in his cell, there would be no one to come looking. But he couldn't be that foolish. That blind. Could he? Plus how could he have known Rebecca would have a seizure? He isn't some all-powerful, all-seeing god. He is just a man.*
*And he will die like a man for what he did to her.*

"We need to come up with a plan of attack," Bill said, turning his attention away from the white walls that seemed to be screaming inside his head. He wondered how many ghosts there were in this *hospital* and, with the grip on his throat growing tighter, feared a number too high to count.

"Should we split up?"

"No, no. I don't think that's very wise. The people we are dealing with are dangerous and mad. That is not a combination that fills me with much hope. No, I think there is strength in numbers."

"Okay, good. I wouldn't want to get lost in a place like this." Relief washed over Michael's body, soothing his cold sweats and calming his cracking voice. "Is this Doctor White as mad as you say he is?"

"Without a doubt. Whatever he wants your son for, it can't be anything good."

"We need to find him. We just have to."

"We will, we are not leaving here empty-handed."

"What did Evelyn say when she learned about Mary?" Mike asked, trying to distract himself. Imagining Charlie trapped in a place like this was giving him a sinking feeling.

"I was not the one to break the sad news but it was your son's actions that she chose to focus on. It seems she has a real grudge against him. I'm guessing that she is as fanatical about the church as your wife was?"

"Yes, more so if that's possible. Evelyn was always our priest's favourite. When she moved away, Mary was desperate to fill that gap, to live up to her sister's image. She started slowly working her way up through the ranks but Father Stringer didn't take any real notice of her until Charlie auditioned to be his new bell-ringer.

"It was going to be smooth sailing for her after this holiday but now, everything is ruined. God knows what the people back home will say when they find out everything that's happened."

"It sounds like she was desperate to impress this priest. Could that have contributed to her reaction to Charlie's differences? You said she was wanting to exorcise him. For a mother to try and put her own child through such an endurance is unthinkable. Do you think she would have gone through with it if you hadn't stopped her?" It appeared even when he was riddled with grief, his police instincts were still in full working order.

"I honestly don't know. I didn't recognize her in those short moments. She was a devout believer in faith and righteousness but never to the manic extreme that I saw today," Mike answered with the realization that only hours had passed since everything had become real. It seemed like a lifetime ago when his normal was twisted into this new abnormal. Calm and chaos were now entwined in this horrible, delicate dance.

Bill stayed silent for a moment, reflecting. His mind overloaded. He was running on empty, unsure of which emotion would take the reins as he reached the final hurdle.

"What will happen to us, me and Charlie, after we get him back?"

"Mike, let's just focus on getting him out of here safely. After that, we can turn our attention to the legal side of things."

"Okay," he replied and stood in Bill's shadow as his fate was decided for him. They had reached the end of their corridor and came upon a staircase that signalled that going up would lead to the patient quarters, offices and theatre, while going down would lead only to the furnace.

"Up?" Bill asked and began ascending before Mike could reply. Both men wanted to avoid any intrusive thoughts of what horrors a furnace in a place like this would hold. Mike followed.

Michael Rose, the eternal follower, not to the frenzied degree that Mary was but nonetheless at ease whenever he didn't have to think for himself.

# Chapter Forty-Two

Eve awoke and felt pain radiate throughout her body, which had folded in on itself during her forced sleep. Her head was swimming in a dizzyingly grey lake but the memories of how she came to be locked up in this room, decorated a blistering white, shot back into her as soon as she opened her eyes.

She tried to stand and felt her body erupt into flames. Though she was in tremendous pain from the crash, it was the guilt of abandoning her children that struck the heaviest blow. What kind of mother was she becoming? It was all Charlie's fault. She had never been more certain. He was responsible for all the misery in her life.

Slowly, she started to pace the room but there were no windows and judging by the panelled design, there was no door either. Or at least, one that did not open from inside. The feeling of being isolated only encouraged her beliefs and once again, all thoughts of her children were firmly pushed out. Only her manic delusions remained, growing more erratic with every panicked step on the cushioned floor.

*How dare they put me in a cell when I am only working under HIS direction? They will all pay for this incredulous insult. I will de—*

Her train of thought was completely derailed by a crunching sound that dwarfed her thoughts and an opening appeared less than five feet from where she standing. Doctor White now stood in the open doorway.

"Ah, Mrs Prentice. Firstly, let me apologize for the rough accommodation but I should think this is preferable to one of our display rooms. Nevertheless, it is good of you to join us here."

"Join? I have joined nothing. I have been abducted."

186

"Well yes, that is the truth of it but if you remember correctly, you were intent on driving your car straight through me. My work would have been at an end. I hope you understand I could not allow for such disrespect to take place."

"I don't care about your work. I just care about stopping Charlie from hurting anyone else. He is a beast."

"Then, we share a common bond. Can we not work together?"

"You want to study him like some kind of lab rat. I want to send him back to hell."

"You are a smart woman, Mrs Prentice, but you are clearly blind in this regard. Your nephew is a specimen of great importance. To toss him aside so recklessly would be doing a disservice to our world. He is vital to our survival."

"You're crazy. I will have your license revoked for holding me prisoner. I am on a mission from the great Almighty who deemed Charlie Rose to be a weed, and one that must be cast out from the garden of life. If you stop me, then you too shall feel the fire of hell surround you."

"We are so close and yet, your insistence on making this personal puts us so far away. I see you are ill-suited to your position at the Apollo Preparatory School. A shame, truly."

"How do you know I work there?"

"Information is part of our job here. I thought perhaps there was a chance of your cooperation but I see now that will never be the case."

"Then, you can let me go," Eve said wearily. Her bones were still inflamed and a sore spot on her neck was throbbing. The harder she fought for this conversation to turn her way, the more it felt like there was a hand around her throat.

"Out of the question, I'm afraid. If you will not help willingly, then force will be needed. I can just picture you as bait."

"Bait? For that hideous beast? I don't think so. He is nothing to me."

"Personally, perhaps not. But genetically, the two of you are tethered. As are your children. They are the ones you shall reel in for me."

A primal terror began to stretch across Eve's face, pulling her mouth apart until it trembled. She swallowed an inflamed gulp and choked on her own breath. "You will not touch my children."

"I'm afraid there is very little you can do to stop me. My work here is too important to allow an opportunity like this to slip through my fingers. Charlie has a remarkable condition and his genetic structure is the key to unlocking his potential. Having witnessed his abilities first-hand, I am very excited about what the future may hold for the greater good," he spoke with salivating lips and a quickened breath.

"Do what you want to him but just leave my children out of it." She was now pleading, her motherly instincts back where they should always have been. Her mind teetered between what she must do to prove her faith and what she must do to protect her family.

"You should know by now, I cannot do that. Charlie's mutation is passed down through his mother's genes. Why else do you think I gave the order to have your family taken to the station earlier?"

"That was you?"

"Oh yes, the situation was too delicious. I just had to take advantage of it. How could I turn down the chance to capture a whole blood line? Charlie may be my gold trophy, but I'll happily take silver and bronze as well." A malicious smile curled its way over his mouth. "Once my work with Charlie is complete and I have learned all I can from him, I shall turn my attention toward your children. All three of them."

Eve moved backward, never taking her eyes off the mad doctor. "No. I won't let you take them."

"Let me? You are trapped in here while they are at home. They must have realized your disappearance by now. I wonder what is going through their little heads."

"Stop." The guilt in her voice had come out to play.

"Perhaps they think you abandoned them. At their young ages, any altered genes are likely lying undisturbed. A flare-up might not occur for years to come, without a little assistance that is."

"What assistance?"

"Trauma can work wonders. I imagine never seeing their mother again must have some consequences. Rest assured, we will be keeping a diligent eye on them."

"Never see them again?"

"You're right, that would be too cruel. I shall let you see them one last time, so that you can say goodbye before their experiments begin. To see the fear in their eyes before I rip it out of them. Once I have finished with Charlie, I shall set a new trap, with you right in the centre of it. They are young and fresh. Oh, it will be quite the hunt."

188

"You're insane. You're insane. You're insane." Her throat was now swelling but she pushed the desperate call through her tightening vocal chords, not allowing herself a moment to process the pain.

"Insane. For what? For trying to further our knowledge and capabilities? You talk of wanting to rid the world of impurities but that is all it is with you. Talk. I, on the other hand, have undertaken a calling which will see our beautiful Earth forever prosper. For none shall grow in a garden left to rot."

Eve, who had been carefully still over the past several minutes, suddenly felt fear and doubt rise through her, squashing out the pain but before she could react, Doctor White took one step backward out into the corridor and the door slammed shut.

Once again, she was sealed off from the world with only the confused voice inside her head for company.

# Chapter Forty-Three

Charlie's body had smoothed out once again, the thorns had receded and his skin mellowed back to its milky self but this time, he was not unblemished. The last attack had left an indelible mark. Pure purple cracks ridged across his body, serrating their way beneath the skin, but he was numb to the pain. He had become numb to everything now. Two people were dead because of him. There was no escaping that fact or the shame it brought.

He looked around and he saw the room for what it was. A cell. Another cell, though this one was far smaller. The walls were ghost white and seemed to narrow in on him, closer and closer. Tricking him into believing he was about to be suffocated by the very fabric of the hospital itself.

A small circular vent was embedded into the ceiling directly above him. His wrists were held down with rough leather straps and there was a linked chain resting across his chest, restraining him to a bed. He thrashed and scurried under the restraints, but the drugs still cycling around his insides had sapped his energy.

Every time Charlie breathed, the chain rose and dipped, almost slipping further up his body. Too many breaths and it would slide right over his neck and there it would stay until he could breathe no more. The longer he stayed alive, the longer he would be essentially torturing himself.

A thought was emerging in the back of his mind, far too deep in the shadows for him to realize it was there. It would soon reveal itself but for the moment, it would stay buried.

*Please, someone help me.*

The room may have been as small as his mother's patience but he was lost in its white wilderness. Charlie angled his head and saw a door opposite the bed with a small window in the shape of porthole.

For observation, he guessed. He desperately shook his head, willing for tears to come but he had nothing left to give. He was as dry as the blood on his hands. A group of people now gathered outside the door, excitedly pressing their faces against the glass. It had finally happened. They had put him in a cage.

Men in black suits, pushing and shoving each other out of the way, fawning over the window. The only portal between their nice, respectable world and the one beyond the imagination their small minds could produce. The word had been spread about this particular prey and they were all desperate to see the latest addition to the freak house, but the crowd quickly grew tired of Charlie's motionless frame and shouted hateful encouragement, eager to see him writhe and struggle.

The ones too short or too far at the back grunted in annoyance. Choosing to have their thrill delayed rather than settling on one of the many other doors that adorned the corridor, each with their own porthole that showcased the fascinating and horrifying wonders that Artemis House had unearthed.

Once upon a time, those rooms each played host to the fresh meat, drawing in scores of zealous eyes but their numbers had dwindled. The *creatures* within all but forgotten. Now, all eyes were on Charlie Rose.

Charlie felt their eyes burn past his scars and he heard the murmur of their cackles but before he could resign himself to let out one final heaving breath and accept his fate, the men in black suits were sent scurrying back beneath their rocks. With their appetite whetted, they gladly obliged, knowing full well what came next.

The door blew open and in walked a new man with a surgical mask obscuring his face. The stranger studied him for a moment before sanitizing his hands at a dispenser above the bed. There were no introductions or acknowledgements. To him, Charlie was as inanimate as the bed he lay upon.

It was hard to see someone as human when they had shown you that they were not. He simply strolled in, made a few routine observations and then wheeled Charlie out. He had left the cage but he was far from free.

The bed rolled through the white labyrinth with ease, the man behind him giving only the occasional nudge to navigate a corner, clearly wanting as little contact with the *patient* as possible. He had heard all the news about their newest arrival and how ruthless he could be. The cleansing would bring them all one step closer to their mission but it could never bring back their fallen comrade.

Charlie was ushered past a myriad of doors lining only the left-hand side of the corridor he was being escorted through, all with the same bland panelling. Though he was still disorientated from the drugs, he noted that none of these doors had the little porthole that his one had.

They were not on show for the facility's staff or privileged visitors to gawk at. Anyone in those rooms, though isolated, were shielded from the cruel circus. Charlie didn't know whether to pity them or envy them, so he ended up flailing between the two. Whatever tune those birds were singing, no one would hear it.

Unbeknownst to him, he was rolled past a room where a mother screamed out in a hopeless show of strength. The shrill calls bounced off the walls and returned fire back at her, sending the panic into a spiral that could only go one way. Eve Prentice would soon be deafened by her own grief for the life she had left behind.

Since he was still strapped down, Charlie was unaware that a figure had emerged at the tail end of the corridor they had just entered. The orderly, in a state of silent shock at seeing this person, halted on the spot, unsure of what to do next. Clearly an individual who relied so heavily on the input from others.

Charlie heard the slow shuffle of footsteps approaching them and tried to angle his head up but saw only the strip lights in the ceiling blaring down on him. The orderly, still with his feet glued to the ground and with a mind unable to adapt to this arrival, shrunk under the weight of the approaching figure.

"Hello, Charlie," said the man, placing one hand on the restraint that was holding his feet in place. Caressing the strap with a soft but forceful hand. A practiced hand. An expert hand.

Hearing his name called out produced a strange feeling in him. It sounded almost foreign to his ears but it reignited the glimmer of hope that he thought had been burned out of him. He wasn't the circus freak or the monster he was being made out to be. That role had been miscast. He was still Charlie.

"I'm so glad you could join us here. It's going to be quite the show and you, m'boy, are my star attraction. Trust me."

The strip lights dimmed and the man came into focus as he stood proudly above him. It took only a second before Charlie recognized the face and his stomach fell into a tight knot as the glimmer of hope abandoned him.

"It's okay, Charlie. You don't need to be afraid."

"But h—"

"You will become the key to everything that we do here. That makes you special and you have been gifted a great power but we cannot let it remain untapped. The damage you could do is unthinkable."

Charlie's confusion was dwarfed by a fear that ballooned inside his fragile body.

"Enough people have already died today because of your erratic behaviour. Don't you agree?" It wasn't a question that needed answering. "Now is the time to save lives, m'boy. My team here will extract this gift of yours and use it to make the world a better place. That is all any of us want. Now, come with me."

Charlie went to open his mouth but only short, mousy squeaks could be heard as the trap finally snapped shut, clamping down hard on his shaking throat.

The orderly escorted Charlie down a snaking corridor until they came upon set of polished double doors. The doors opened onto the theatre and the ferocity of its red interior set Charlie's nerves on fire and he remained in a state of silent dread as he was wheeled onto a platform.

The stage.

From this angle, he could see that the audience was beginning to file in. The crowd from outside his room and dozens of others impatiently slotted themselves into position, filling out the rows circling the stage. Circling him.

It reminded Charlie of a nature show his dad had let him watch once upon a time where a group of sharks surrounded their prey before going in for the kill. Was he now the innocent bird resting calmly on the still waters? Was this to be a feeding frenzy too?

All the words that were floating around inside his head dissipated before reaching his tongue, drowned out by his own gulps. His eyes, shooting from one end of the room to the other, were bulging and shrinking as panic swept over them.

Something in the depths of his mind told him to fly away but he couldn't. Soon, the calm surface would be disturbed, broken beyond repair and there was nothing he could to do stop it. To save himself.

The man, who he had once wanted to trust and please, disappeared up a stairway at the back of the room. A few seconds passed before the black mass of his silhouette reappeared, etched against the glass of the viewing box overlooking the main stage.

Tonight, it was crammed full of eager benefactors and facility officials all intent on witnessing this glorious performance. Charlie's instincts told him that the one dead centre would be his doom.

A spotlight running overhead began to lower toward him, honing in on centre stage but the closer it came, the more he could feel the darkness looming around him. It danced and dodged its way across the stage, drawing rapturous gasps from the audience whenever it skirted over the beast. The child in chains. They zeroed in on his every twitch and tremor during the fleeting illumination.

The atmosphere was broken as a voice erupted from the comfort of the observation room. The audience down below fell to a hush on command as the spotlight settled on Charlie, baking him under its beautiful shine.

"Ladies and gentlemen, it's show time."

# Chapter Forty-Four

Bill and Mike walked aimlessly down corridors, unable to find even a whisper of life. Every door they came upon was bolted shut and the halls and corridors seemed to double back on themselves in an endless circle.

"This is hopeless," cried Mike, his mind spiralling farther into the depths of his own frantic thoughts.

"He has to be here somewhere," Bill replied, more to himself than to Mike. He was growing irritable with Mike's constant worries but kept his temper at bay. Conserving all his rage for the monster who had stolen his life from under him.

The corridor they were now making their way down had been marked 'Patients' and a chill set hard in their bones as they looked at the canvas of rooms that stretched down the left side of the corridor. Each room had a myriad of thick steel locks that ran down the length of the wall.

*If this is real life, then check me the hell out of it. What kind of people would work in a place where this is their normal?*

Bill approached the nearest door with caution, his mind trying to weigh down his feet and keep him rooted to the task at hand, but he forced himself forward. He looked inside and saw that mercifully, or not after a moment's pause, the cage was empty.

Inside the cell lay an overturned bed, still half-dangling from a chain that was embedded into the wall above. Splintered wood and shattered bone littered the floor and the walls were coated in an ungodly amount of stale crimson. Trying to shake away the images that the vacant cell was conjuring up left him dizzy and a sickened thought bore its way inside him.

*The little bird in that cage didn't fly away. It had its wings clipped and was most likely driven mad by its own sad desperation. Was dying alone in captivity preferable to whatever that insane doctor had in store?*

Mike watched Bill from behind, not seeing his hands constrict in silent fury, and copied him, walking up to the next door along the corridor with curiosity leading his way, but one look was all it took for him to regret it.

In the middle of the room was a little girl that had her eyes covered with a rag, currently submerged in pool of fresh tears. On the floor were markings where a bed once lay but this patient, inmate, victim, child had been offered no such comfort.

She was gagged and had all four limbs chained to a hook that rested behind her. From the way her body bulged in places and dipped in others, Mike guessed that she was no more than a year older than Charlie and the feeling of panic clawed at him again.

She was draped in discoloured clothes that had been roughly torn and from beneath one of these tears, he could see a circular, black mass embossed with a wire cube that had been burned into her flesh.

"They fucking brand the kids. It's not enough they lock them up, they actually stamp a cage onto their skin!" Mike exclaimed but Bill could only shake his head as he pushed on down the corridor, his words swallowed up by intrusive thoughts.

Allowing himself one final look at the poor child, he saw that she had raised her head and with the rag slipping down her face, she was able to look directly at him. Her eyes (still crying) glowed an empty blue and her uncomfortable, pleading stare was brewing a slow fear inside Mike.

The chains held her in place, the smooth metal slowly serrating its way under her skin, but in her mind, she was as free as a bird. She looked past his horrified face and saw his dreams that now lay dead and his fears that were very much alive. The little girl saw his entire life.

No words passed her cracked, red lips but Mike could hear her inside his head. She was screaming at him, her dry voice begging for help, for water, for her parents, for her life back; but not being in a position to help her at that moment, he moved out of sight of the porthole, leaving the little girl all alone once more. Out of sight, but sadly, not out of mind.

As he turned away, one more thought, painful and detached, came blaring through.

*Save me*

*ring*

*S—ring leader*

*Help. Help.*

*Help!*

*Ring leader*

*RING LEADER!*

"Ringleader?" Mike whispered back to her.

"Huh, what was that?"

"Oh, nothing," Mike answered. If this truly was a circus, then he almost didn't want to meet the man in charge.

"Come on, Mike; it's probably best not to linger down here."

Before Mike could reply, no doubt with another incessant wail of how listless his life was fast becoming, they both heard a sound coming from around the next corner. Bill motioned for him to stand alongside the wall next to him and drew his gun, quickly making sure that the safety was off. Someone was coming and there had been enough mistakes today already.

A shadow on the floor started to stretch and grow as the person drew nearer and ten long seconds later, a face Bill recognized appeared, looking dishevelled but not surprised at their presence.

"Oh, you're the police officer from Almost," Howie said, panting but before he knew what was happening, he was on the ground. The bullet erupted through the air and twisted through blood and bone but his wails were drowned out by the sound of cracking thunder as the gunfire resounded down the spiralling halls.

"Jesus! What the fuck, Bill!" Mike shouted as he slammed his hands over his ears to soften the noise. He was too concerned with his present situation to realize this was exactly how Charlie must have felt during one of his and Mary's many shootouts.

Mike looked to the man clutching his left leg and through the white smoke wisping through the air, he saw the pristine floor become muddied with a thick red as blood began to spurt out of the wound.

"He works for Doctor White. One of his cronies," Bill spoke in a calm and calculated voice, not allowing the emotion to break through.

"But you just can't go around shooting people," Mike rebutted, the sound of thunder now relaxing but unknown to him, a single scream was still pushing its way inside his head. Clawing at him.

"He helped kidnap your son, so I would calm down if I were you. Now," Bill said, turning his attention toward Howie, "you are and I are going to have a little chat."

"You fucking shot me."

"Well, I can't fault your eyesight but your morals do leave a lot to be desired."

"You need to get help."

"You'll be fine. It's a flesh wound at best, just apply some pressure. Here take this," Bill said as he tore a strip of material off his sleeve and wrapped it, tighter than he needed to, around Howie's leg. "Did they not teach you that at medical school? Or was it just how to kidnap kids?"

"Fuck off! What kind of police officer are you?"

"What kind of doctor are you? How many kids do you have trapped down here?" His mouth began foaming with thick anger. His fingers danced over the trigger again, curious as to what another not-so-gentle squeeze would bring him. The desperate need for an adrenaline surge itched away at him, wriggling under his skin.

"It's not that simple."

"Oh, it never is with scumbags like you."

"What do you think would happen to all those kids if this place didn't exist? Society would rip them apart. They're dangerous and in a lot of cases, deadly. Just look at that boy today. He killed one of your men and one of my friends after you were sedated."

"So, you thought you would beat society to the punch. Is that it? Those rooms back there are torture chambers, you sick creep."

Mike, who for the past few minutes had remained passively silent, wanted to speak up, to bring the topic back to Charlie but Bill was acting like a rabid dog. Uncontrollable and lethal. He knew better than to try and get in between a dog and its prey.

"That's not my fault. I was just following orders but after today, I don't know what to believe anymore," Howie tried to argue but every word that crept out of his mouth cowered under Bill's stern demeanour.

"Bullshit. You'll say anything to get out of this," Bill retorted, tearing apart Howie's defences.

"It's the truth. Do you think it's easy to quit a job like this? The amount of secrecy and protection that goes into an organization like this. We walked into this place with our eyes glued shut, not seeing the horrors until it was too late. They get us when we're young too, you know.

"School us on the greater good and the one true faith, so that by time we become adults, this is the only life we know. What choice do we have but to stand by the people who raised us? We're as trapped in this facility as the patients.

"I'll admit some of the staff get a sick joy out of the mission, especially when they witness a flare-up or one of Doctor White's performances, but there are still those of us who care. We're still human."

"You don't know what human is anymore."

"You don't know anything," Howie pleaded, his hands now soaked in his own blood.

"I know that a good, honest, kind-hearted woman is now dead because of your precious doctor."

"Who?" Howie asked, with a note of genuine surprise.

"Rebecca. Back at the police station. You fuckers drugged her, she had a seizure and then died," Bill said, holding back *in my arms*. Not wanting to show any weakness. His finger was still grazing over the trigger. He found that resisting the urge to shoot him again was just as tantalizing as the actual release, more so even. Having this level of control over life and death was euphoric.

"But the drug is just a simple sedative. It gives us time to go about our plans, so it comes in handy but it isn't dangerous. Unless—"

"Unless what?"

"Unless it reacted with other drugs the person was taking. Was she on drugs at the time?"

His finger had moved away from the trigger but he didn't hesitate to turn the gun around and smack Howie round the head with it.

"Drugs? She was on medication for cancer treatment, you little shit."

"Okay, I'm sorry, that's what I meant. I'm sorry it played out like that. Usually, we have time to do background checks on everyone connected to a potential specimen and that would include medical histories. I guess Charlie Rose just slipped under the radar and when we got the call about him earlier today, we had to act fast. I'm sorry your friend was caught in the crossfire, but so was mine."

Bill said nothing in return but a thousand wild thoughts danced through his mind. Grief, anger and rage all coming together to form one unholy partnership.

"How did you know about Charlie?" Mike asked, relieved that the rabid dog appeared to have finally softened back into a simple, trusty bloodhound.

"I don't know. That information is top-secret but normal cases are under observation for a long time, years in some instances, before we procure them. But only the officials are involved in the early stages. The juniors only find out about a prey, uh, a patient, when the siren is rung." Howie sensed the hard stare forming on Bill's sullen face. "It's the truth. I can't tell you what I don't know."

"Okay then, I don't need you to talk. I just need you to take us to Doctor White."

Howie, struggling to stand, looked at him helplessly. "I ca—"

Dealing another blow, this one to the stomach, Bill looked at Howie with his own darkened pupils. "If you're worried about what will happen to you, then don't. What you should be worried about is what I will do to you if you keep obstructing me. Mike's here to get his kid back and I'm here to kill your boss. So, you can either help us or you can stand in our way and see what happens."

"Okay, okay."

"Good; sadly, I don't have an appointment with the great man but I do have an itch that needs seeing to and only he can scratch it for me."

# Chapter Forty-Five

Charlie squirmed on the cold, steel bed, pinned down by the chains that were now slowly cutting into his skin. His juvenile muscles pushing out in protest but failing.

"P-p-lease. Help me," he begged, but the audience were deaf to his wails. They saw him as they chose to see him, as they had been conditioned to see him; he was an animal on display. And no one intervened when an animal at the circus was in distress. Run-down and abused.

He would never be human to the masses that now surrounded him, their shadows growing thicker the longer his agony was prolonged. The chains may have held him down but it was their sickening shroud that kept him in place.

Confined. Trapped.

The lights running overhead started to burn brighter and stronger, crisscrossing in a dazzling display as they were lowered closer and closer toward him. He could feel his skin writhe as it began to bubble under its execution. His body panicked under the heat and tried to fight back against its push but it had been hours since he had any food or drink and he was simply running on empty. Nourishment now felt like a crooked word in his head, unknown and unclean.

The lights finally took their rest at ten feet above the stage and the scorching glow simmered to a dull ache but Charlie, with his eyes now erratic and wild, could still feel their taunting press.

"Ladies and gentlemen, we are greatly honoured to receive you here today and what a show we have for you," Doctor White began, his voice roaring through the speakers.

Thunder gathered slowly throughout the room, a gentle, soothing rumble, as the audience began to applaud the great man, and also themselves for being witness to his work.

"Today, we have our newest recruit. Procured just hours ago and you know what we say, the fresher the rose, the sweeter the smell. And believe me when I say—"

His voice trailed off as he departed the viewing box with a malignant grin painting itself on his face, descended the side stairs and burst into the theatre.

"He shall flourish."

The thunder now exploded as hands were meshed together. All attention was now commanded to the figure grazing through the centre aisle. The masses cheered his every step as he strode up onto the stage. Standing by its rim, he instructed his surgical team to join him. A jubilant chorus sprung forth from the side of the stage as they made their way out into the light, cradled by its warmth.

Turning his back to the audience, Doctor White gathered the small group of juniors around him. "We have a few newcomers in the audience today but that shall not deter us from our performance. If they cannot hold their nerve or their stomach, then it is business as usual," he began, his eyes lingering on centre stage. His prize. "He may give us some trouble when we begin but remember why we are here. The extraction must not be hampered."

His fellow performers nodded in silent unison, taking in every word, breathing in his air, completely oblivious to the whimpering prey less than three feet from where they stood. They squashed down all nerves and fears of stage fright while Doctor White addressed the audience once more, relaying his well-worn speech about the greater good of the facility and how they had been chosen to spread its glorious purpose.

Not a single ounce of doubt was lurking at the back of his throat as he spoke. His hands may have been his tools but it was his voice that had afforded him his position, his power. The voice was the weapon of all cruel men. Different men have different wars but the ones whose seductively hateful words can twist out of their mouth as easy as one, two, three were the ones who fought till the enemy was destroyed. No peace, just victory.

Charlie Rose was the spoils of a war where his success was never in question. It was the one question he would never ask himself. He was far too sure of himself to entertain such a thought. His traps were too clever and his rats too ambitious.

He ran a delicate and dangerous wheel with the rats that had been placed in the neighbouring districts but no shade of worry ever darkened his door. If one rat faltered, it was easy enough to replace, reinforcing the wheel and leaving the weak and the weary to be crushed under the weight of what came next. Only two things were a constant to him; the facility must have its specimens and the wheel must always turn.

Doctor White, standing proud, felt emboldened by how crammed the theatre was. The past three or four performances had garnered only a fraction of today's numbers, and it had been almost an entire year since this many benefactors had attended in person, longer still since the founder had graced them with his presence. Truly, this was a special occasion.

Though Doctor White had been recruited when Artemis House was already established, even in its infancy, it was a formidable beast; he would now be forever remembered as the one who saved it.

*The man who saved the world.*

For all the plans he actioned, there was always someone else pulling the strings. Doctor White would never quit, never stop. The facility must have its specimens and he must have his glory. He was well-aware that the policemen had tracked him down and brought the Rose boy's fool of a father with him, but he saw no cause for alarm.

They had strolled blindly past all the security cameras, actually thinking they had a chance. You couldn't sneak up on a hunter. They would be lost in the labyrinth of corridors. Helpless and, before long, starving.

Despite paying for the privilege of admission, not even the audience knew the exact layout of Artemis House and required the staff to play the role of tour guide. Giving them a wide-eyed tour down circus lane, the museum of horror, before reaching the belly of the beast, the theatre. When did a museum become a mausoleum?

Anyone desperate enough to learn the secrets these walls contained either had to devote their lives to the cause or invest in its survival. Knowledge came at a price.

Mike and Bill may have strolled straight in but nothing could stop his plans, they were already too late. The trap had already closed. No show of strength could open it now. All that was left was to collect the reward for the prize. His prize.

"Let us begin," he declared and the audience let rip once more, drowning out the bait helplessly flailing as the sharks drew nearer.

Soon, they would have first blood and from then on, it would be a feverish, yet calculated attack, shredding the little boy to pieces. Everything that made him Charlie would be ripped apart.

Doctor White and his team all put on surgical gloves before he approached Charlie and rested one hand over his quickened heart, his fingers slotting in between the chains. Charlie looked into his eyes and saw only a black hole staring back at him.

Charlie may have been the one with the thorns and scaled skin, but it was Doctor White, with a crooked smile and cruel tongue, who was the real monster. If only he could turn the tables on him, imprison him in his own cage. Let the adoring masses gawk at the mighty hunter, fallen from grace.

Surely that would be a better sight to behold rather than a shivering child that just wanted to go home. For the first time, he wanted his cursed body to explode again; at least then, he might have stood a fighting chance but that thought slipped out of sight almost as fast as it had come into view. Doctor White may have warranted a battle but he had hurt enough people today already.

The mad, cackling doctor and the trembling twelve-year-old boy had wildly different interpretations on what a show of strength entailed. With his hand still resting on Charlie's chest, almost caressing his heartbeat, Doctor White looked out and addressed the audience:

"The subject is afflicted with a gene which had lain undisturbed for his twelve short years. I think a practical demonstration is the best way for us to achieve our results, further our studies and to show you all just how merciless he can be."

Doctor White lowered himself until his lips were by Charlie's head and whispered softly in his ear, "Reveal yourself, m'boy and you will save yourself a great deal of pain. If I have to coax it out of you, then I will, but I want your body in a near perfect condition before we move on to the next phase."

Everyone he had ever met may have doubted if he actually had a brain between his ears but he had finally learned not to trust the man whose stale breath was bearing down on him, trying to stun him into submission. Charlie trembled at the hiss and Doctor White constricted his hand around his chest. The soft, unwelcome caress was now a painful squeeze as refined nails coiled under the hospital rags and began to rip at his bare flesh.

First blood.

"I w-w-won't," Charlie forced out, refusing to satisfy the wicked man's wishes and received the back of the doctor's hand in return. With a throbbing temple, he saw the maddened look of Doctor White staring back at him.

"Fine, have it your way," he replied and stood upright. "The subject has refused to comply with the natural order of proceedings and so has left us with only one option—forced flaring."

The newcomers in the audience exhaled low mumbles of confusion while the veterans geared themselves up with a joyful anticipation. They had paid for their ticket to this freak show and were intent on getting their money's worth, savouring every last morsel.

"While this method is by no means without risk, it is effective," Doctor White said and was handed an instrument that drew gasps and cheers from the roaring crowd. It was compact and silver, its smooth design reflecting the madness in his eyes but all Charlie could see as Doctor White approached him was three-curved and jagged prongs on the end of it.

"P-p-lease stop," Charlie cried out, his face had streams of thin scarlet oozing down from his forehead.

"That is enough talk now, m'boy. You ruined your only chance to skate through this; now, for your insolence, you can crawl through it," Doctor White replied and with his free hand, tore a hole in Charlie's rags below the ribs. "I will now administer the device and let the extraction begin."

Charlie's world went cold and dark, refusing to acknowledge what was happening but the sound of the drilling as the device began to rotate against his side was too much for him to bear. It reminded him of every awful dentist appointment he had ever had but in that moment, he would have prayed to have a sweaty, oblong man pack his mouth with steel tools as his mouth slowly filled up with blood.

He had bitten his tongue, hard, on every visit but at least those horrors were heavily medicated. On this operating table, however, he was made to feel every cut and poke. Forced to suffer.

Within seconds, blood sprayed out as the device lacerated his skin, twisting inward. His whole body wriggled and contorted to escape its touch but the more he struggled, the worse the pain became and so, all he could do was lie there with a body on fire, screaming for his life.

The louder Charlie cried for help, the more the audience seemed to enjoy it, like a group of boys who find a distressed bird in the wild and throw rocks at it *just to see what happens*. The only difference was that the men who had packed out the theatre were no longer guarded by immature defences and they knew exactly what would happen if the bird's agony continued. It would die, as simple as that but the haunted shrieks would continue long after the defenceless bird was long forgotten.

"Shouldn't we stop, Sir?" One of the surgical team asked, unnerved by how calm Doctor White was behaving.

Doctor White stopped the device, drawing groans from the crowd and studied the wound for a moment before answering, "Stop? How can you possess such ignorance?"

"It's just, surely, there's another way."

"I realize this is your first performance but have you forgotten everything you trained for? We shall extract what we need to tonight, then send him back to his cell so that our distinguished guests can further experience the carnival of horrors.

"*Their* suffering is the key to everything we do here and I hardly need to remind you that some of our audience tonight fund everything that is conducted within these walls, so do something clever with your life and keep your mouth closed."

"But what if the boy dies?"

"Of course, he is going to die. We will repeat the process as many times as necessary until there is nothing of Charlie Rose still alive. We are the faithful, the Chosen. We took a holy vow and this is our right," Doctor White spat back impatiently and after seeing the alarmed look on this understudy's face, he knew what to do.

Reaching for the surgical table, he picked up a scalpel and, with a proud look toward the impatient crowd, masterfully sliced open the neck of the only one stupid enough to challenge him. He had been practicing and perfecting his craft for too long to allow for such a tedious interference.

The crowd fell silent as they watched the understudy fall to the floor, disgracefully pawing at his neck and desperately trying to stem the red flow. The unnamed man died quickly and quietly with a look of confusion and horror frozen onto his face, and a mouth packed with wet, hot blood.

"Our work here is sacred. We cannot stand with anyone who would deny us our rights," Doctor White bellowed to the crowd and while a handful of new members hastened for the exit, horrified by the latest act, the bulk of the crowd stayed rooted to their spot. They had expected no less. It was not a show without some kind of drama. "Now, let us continue."

With his speech complete, he turned his attention back toward Charlie, who for the past couple minutes had been quietly praying for help but now only prayed for a quick death. A voice deep inside told him that both prayers would likely go unanswered but unknown to him (and Doctor White), when the weakly newcomers had fled the theatre, three men had entered.

# Chapter Forty-Six

"Okay, so what now?" Michael asked as he, Bill and Howie shuffled into the theatre, concerned by the score of people who had dashed past them in the corridor, each with their own look of horror and disgust etched onto their faces.

Their entrance had seemingly gone unnoticed by the roaring crowd, too immersed in the latest, unscripted, development unfolding before them. The room looked like a theatre in an old playhouse with a crusty leather finish on the seats and aged bronze architecture running up the walls.

By first impressions, they had bypassed their intended target and walked straight into the middle of a play but looking again, there he was; Doctor Herman White, standing proudly on stage under the sweeping adoration of his audience. If this was indeed a hospital, it was a very peculiar one, Michael noted.

"You're too late."

"What do you mean, too late?" Bill asked, anger behind his words. "He's right there."

"Yes but look for yourselves. The performance has already begun. It cannot be stopped now." They all looked toward the stage and a small group were huddled around the spotlight, skirting its edges. Eagerly waiting for their leader to make his next move.

"We'll just see about that," Bill retorted and was promptly chastised by an audience member, disgruntled at having his trance broken by the bickering men. It seemed that Doctor White's cruel tongue was contagious.

Bill grabbed Howie by the scruff of his collar and pushed him in front. When he tried to resist, Howie felt the cold barrel of the gun nestle into his spine. Reluctantly, he descended the stairs on the far left aisle toward the stage with Bill impatiently following behind him.

Michael brought up the rear cautiously. The path led them directly under the viewing box, granting Bill a shroud in which to carry out his attack. Bill began to salivate at the thought of bringing him down. A pale smile was born when he imagined the look of confusion break over Doctor White's face as his air slowly deflated.

He wanted the doctor's last emotions to be fear and shame but doubted if he could even say those words, let alone feel them. One good shot was all it would take.

From the angle of their hiding place, they had a direct line of sight to the horror scene that was taking place on stage. A body was crumpled on the stage floor and being bathed in his own blood, which was being slowly heated by the spotlight.

The ensemble of men around him were casually disregarding the fallen man as they busied themselves around a patient's bed. When Doctor White moved to the side, Bill, Howie and Michael could see which unfortunate soul was playing the lead role.

*Charlie!*

Michael stood frozen in the shadows as all the air in his lungs was painfully sucked dry. He saw Doctor White place an object on Charlie's side and all the blood in his shell of a body started to boil as the thick air was perforated by an unearthly howl.

His son was screaming for his life. Without knowing what he was doing, he was screaming back, matching his son's desperate call, assuring him that he wasn't alone; but his aid was drowned out by the masses who were now rising from their seats and cheering in celebration of the mutilation happening before their eyes.

The voice inside his head began to grow, seemingly encouraged by the shadows that being placed under the viewing box afforded them.

*Ring leader*
*S—er—is—!*

"What the fuck is this place?" Bill asked, skewering Howie with its sharpness but all he could do in return was bow his head. "We have to stop this."

"You can't. I'm so sorry," Howie said, the sadness in his voice may have been mumbled but it signalled his defeat nonetheless. The facility had broken him. He looked up toward the stage and his eyes glassed over, unmoved, as he saw the child being tortured.

The *oddity* that plagued Charlie's nervous system had so far scurried away from the danger, away from death but there were only so many hiding places within the body of a child and Doctor White's special tool had now found its first thorn, drawing it out toward the light. The branding had begun but the mask was beginning to slip, uncovering the true danger little by little.

The thorn, uncovered and dripping in blood, stood firm but began to slowly dull under the weapon's force. It would only take a matter of minutes before it went from dented to shattered but still, the practiced hand persisted. The show had been stalled for too long now and though he savoured the screams, he longed for the final act. The threat Charlie Rose posed would be neutralized and then they could begin cleansing him of his unholy blood.

Doctor White would undoubtedly enjoy all subsequent performances with his new trophy but there was nothing quite like the first time. Putting the broken body back together again (and again) after it had ripped itself apart was almost as irresistible as the show itself. Almost, but the sheen was never quite the same.

The cleansing ritual was a delicate act, go too far for too long and the prey simply was not left with enough blood for the mutant strain to begin reforming. The more performances they got out of a single specimen, the better; it made up for the worrying lag between procurements and the more blood they could harvest, the better. The only danger was that all the abnormalities had the chance to regroup and flare up again but Doctor White was too skilled to let that concern him.

Some of his past prey had possessed telepathic or telekinetic abilities, some could spit a venomous web. There had been a whole host of exciting additions to the facility over the years and each ritual brought them closer to their mission. A mission that, for the sake of all that was right, had to be completed. A war was coming and they had to be ready. For the greater good.

Only one of Doctor White's previous trophies had withstood seven whole performances before dying alone in their cage. It was as if their soul could take no more and ejected itself from its shell and a soulless trophy had no shine.

His plan was absolute and no amount of push back could deny him his glory. He cranked the tool to full power, drawing another round of dizzying squeals from his prize and smoke began to billow out from the wound, allowing a red mist to descend over his focused eyes.

210

*Extract, cleanse, heal, repeat.*
*Extract, cleanse, heal, repeat.*
*Extract, cleanse, heal, repeat.*

Charlie poured all of his adolescent strength into holding his body back, refusing to give in to what was being demanded of him. He could feel his skin start to blacken, not just streaks but a full body shawl. With his screams now dying out, he looked out into the crowd with strained eyes and saw only their eager faces, drenched in sweat and anticipation, boring into him.

A defeating sigh was building in his stomach and the feeling that he was powerless was ringing loudly in his ears. How could he, a mere mortal, stand against Doctor White, who must think himself a god? For only a god could be so cruel in decreeing when a child may live or die.

This was his Olympus and Charlie, the spoils of war.

# Chapter Forty-Seven

Bill waited until Doctor White turned to face the audience again before drawing in a solemn breath as he raised the gun, pushing it up through the stifled air and signalled for Michael and Howie to bow down.

Michael, who was witnessing the mutilation of his only child, chose to discard Bill's plan entirely, convincing himself that Bill was only here out of some misguided, macho revenge and that Charlie, whatever the outcome, was simply collateral.

"STOP!" Michael shouted, desperate not to be helplessly trapped on the sidelines for once in his life. The foreign voice inside his head was being unearthed, quietly screaming to try and force itself into the light but Bill's gun erupted, a second too late and so, it went unnoticed by Mike.

Doctor White angled his head to the noise, the intrusion and was able to dodge the bullet as it ricocheted past him. It struck a wall offstage with a dull thud, killing only the cheers of the baited audience.

"You idiot!" Bill barked, fumbling with the gun in his shaking hand. It went off accidentally, striking the lip of the stage and hurtling splinters toward the front row, showering them with its glossy oak finish.

He immediately fired another shot, but the gun jammed and a backlight sprang to life, illuminating the shadows where the three men had staged their coup. All heads now turned to face down the opposers and dozens of hateful glares bore down on them from the audience.

"I see we have some unexpected guests," Doctor White hissed, quelling the rage in his voice at being interrupted yet again. He clicked his fingers and some of his more loyal patrons subdued the three men. "Do join us on stage. You're just in time for the best part of the show."

Two of the surgical staff remained by Charlie's withering body as Doctor White strutted over toward the men as they were escorted on stage. They were all thrown down in front of him, but it was Howie who squirmed the most as they were bathed in the doctor's grim shadow.

"Oh Howie, I had such high hopes for you."

"Please, Doctor White. I didn't mean to betray you, but he shot me," Howie replied and showed his flesh wound.

"Shut up, it's him that has betrayed everyone," Bill began and spat at the doctor's feet. "You call yourself a doctor but all you do is cause harm to people. You're sick. And you lot out there watching this horror show are sicker."

"Is that truly how you feel, Officer—I forget your name. I always do with the unimportant."

"Woodley, and yes. You people are the ones in need of a doctor. One who is a damn sight more competent than you."

"Well, if I ever meet this man who matches up to your expectations, then—"

"The only person you're going to meet is your maker, you fucking lunatic."

"Then by all means, shoot away," Doctor White insisted, spreading his arms out and displaying his torso as a prime target.

Bill grazed his fingers against the gun but could only mimic its ferocity. Realizing he was beaten, he slowly lowered it before it was snatched out of his hands by a member of Doctor White's ensemble.

After a moment of silence, Doctor White's Adam's apple dipped and lolled as it let out a slow chuckle, causing the audience to follow suit and although Bill was fuelled with hate and adrenaline, he turned red in the face of their taunts.

"As I suspected on our first meeting. All mouth with no brains."

"You son of a bitch!"

"Yes, well as much fun as this is, I have work to do. The show must go on." Doctor White gave the nod to one of his men and he struck Bill down with a glancing blow to the back of the head. The sergeant hit the stage hard and was unconscious within seconds.

"Stop it!" Michael cried.

"Oh Mr Rose, how rude of me, you are so paltry and listless, I completely forgot about you."

"You are going to let Charlie go now!" Michael demanded. If his eyes had veered over toward his flailing son, his voice would surely have cracked and he would have been brandished with his own chorus line of laughter.

"You foolish man. You understand nothing about our work here. You and little cowboy friend there think me the devil because of my actions but never stop to ask yourselves why my work is so vital. Why it is necessary. Your son has a gift and he is going nowhere."

"You should be thanking me for intercepting him when I did. Without that valuable tip off, he may have skated through life undetected until it was too late to be of any use."

"You're insane. You are the devil," Michael said, gently shaking his head, not wanting to believe the madness. The scream inside his head was growing.

"No, I am not a devil. I am a god. I'm a miracle worker and since you are already on your knees, I suggest you start praising me."

Once the audience had calmed their roaring laughter, Doctor White instructed his men to keep hold of Bill, Michael and Howie as he returned his attention back toward the star of the show.

Charlie, who had been gently whimpering throughout the unexpected intermission, felt the cold steel touch and burn through his flesh once again, turning his hairs rigid but his muscles weak. He opened his mouth to squeal, but ended up choking on all the screams that now lay dead in his throat.

Charlie turned his head to the side and saw his father being forced to his knees every time he tried to rise up. He saw his dad take a smack to the side of the face and the two of them locked eyes with each other. In that moment, Charlie chose not to think about all the times his father had betrayed his innocence and chastised his spirit, but rather zeroed in on the base fact that he had come here to rescue him from this circus.

*Oh Charlie, I'm so fucking sorry for it all. We should have stayed home where it was safe and predictable. And boring. I'm gonna stop this mad clown of a doctor and get you out of here. It's going to be alri—*

"I think there has been enough of these tiresome intrusions," a voice announced from the viewing box, the time-worn tone of it standing strong in comparison to the withered body of its host. "Doctor White, you have indulged yourself too much with this catch. You have left me with no choice but to join you on stage."

The speech came blaring through the speakers situated around the corners, snaking its way through the aisles. It hissed in the ears of all who heard it and while it emboldened the audience, Doctor White grew uncomfortably still.

A door opened and the lights were turned low as the figure descended the stairs at the back of the theatre. He made his way toward the stage shrouded by the comfort of the shadows, inviting murmurs from the masses as to who the new addition was.

While they all knew the venom of his voice, only the faithful few would have recognized the face of the man making his way slowly into the light. He had never interfered with the actual performances, preferring to remain hidden as he went about his work. Artemis House thrived on secrecy and the founder's anonymity was paramount to its survival.

Charlie was still pinned to the bed but he heard the shuffle of old bones as the man who had approached him in the corridor earlier drew nearer. The voice in Mike's head, now a writhing screech, came into view as the founder of Artemis House stepped into the searing light of the stage.

*Ring is lea—*
*Str—der.*
*Stringer is leader!*
*Stringer is leader!*
*Stringer is leader!*

# Chapter Forty-Eight

"Impossible!"

"I see that your mind is as closed now as it was when I last saw you. A pity."

"That was only two days ago," Mike forced out, still in disbelief. A thousand questions running through his frantic mind. His head was beginning to burn but he put that down to being gently cooked under the spotlight and disregarded it. A painful confusion dominated his thoughts.

"Yes, I have missed you too." Father Stringer chuckled before turning his attention to Charlie. "You especially, m'boy."

"Don't you touch him. Don't you dare!"

"You are not really in a position to stop me, Michael. Do try and think things through before wasting everyone's time with your pitiful sounds."

"I don't understand. Why are you here?"

"My dear fool, this is my establishment. My temple where I am free to serve the Almighty unimpeded by the confines of society. The modern world has placed too many restrictions on those of a pure faith and so, I built this place to act as a haven for like-minded people," Father Stringer replied, gesturing toward the crowd.

Their excitement swelling with every spoken word. "Here, we are readying ourselves for the coming war in which we must prevail. And it is specimens like your son that will ensure our victory."

"You capture kids, humiliate and torture them, all for some deranged fantasy with your imaginary friend in the clouds. You need help. You all do," Mike said, now with the confidence that there was no true god; for no higher power could have had a hand in making a man like Father Stringer.

His face had twisted from the simple preacher who admonished latecomers and ranted about immoral movies to the lunatic responsible for this circus of horrors.

"It is words like those that shall see your sinful world dismantled, reduced to nothing. For once we step into the light, Michael, I cannot ask my followers to return to the shadows. My work up till now may have been concentrated there, but once we have secured our victory, we will be the shining light that will guide humanity in the new world."

"Children like Charlie are a threat to everything, you and us alike, but under our care, they have a chance to do something meaningful," Doctor White interjected, trying to prove his usefulness under the glare of his mentor. He locked eyes with Charlie, who now quivered with an intense fear and allowed a shade of menace to slip through. "Here, their gift can truly flourish. Here, they have a purpose. They will serve the Almighty—"

"By force?" Mike asked with a quick glance at Charlie's restraints.

"By any means necessary," Father Stringer said, taking the reins back from Doctor White and dealt him a look that rendered him silent once more. This may have been his performance but it was Father Stringer who would outshine them all.

"We cannot let them forsake the gift they have been granted. The Almighty has blessed them but only the faithful are capable of harnessing their true potential. Every child that gives their life to the mission is immortalized in a way you cannot even begin to understand."

Words had always been Father Stringer's weapon and the entire audience was hushed as the two men duelled. Every time Mike tried to rise up and stare straight into Stringer's cold and empty eyes, a hand on his shoulder forced him back down to his knees.

Mike was holding his own quite well, bolstered with a strength he didn't know he possessed, but not even years of batting away Mary's faith had prepared him to go up against the extent of Father Stringer's delusions.

"The only thing I understand is that you are despicable. You look at Charlie and see only a thing to be abused for your own sick needs. He is just a child and you are the true monster."

At this, Father Stringer's eyes narrowed before turning a bitter red. To the audience, the scene on stage resembled a mouse cowering under the glare of a snake set to strike. They all took in a sharp breath and craved the climax.

"You are a weak man, Michael and only the strong and pure may feel the comfort of the Almighty's embrace. You were not even the leader in your own home, but it is your obvious desperation for an easy life that makes me grateful that you are not one of His followers," Father Stringer spat.

He angled his head toward the audience before continuing, "We are all on one mission and those who try to turn us away from what we know is good and true want us to be consumed by their selfish ideals. They renounce the Almighty to find their own path, but do not allow yourselves to be seduced by their sinful ways.

"Just because you are the lead in your own story doesn't mean you have any control over it. Life happens, until it doesn't. People come and go, until they don't. You breathe a hundred, thousand, million breaths day after day until all the days simply run out. And you just stop. You are so alive, until you're not.

"The Almighty has a plan for us all, your only choice is whether to serve him or be cast out," Father Stringer declared. His words were like fire and everyone in the theatre could feel the heat of them, faithful and sinners alike.

"You're insane. Why couldn't you just leave us alone?" Mike had tried resisting, fighting, but now, he was pleading.

"My work here is sanctified. Everything I do is for HIM. My role back home afforded me the opportunity to scout out those who have the makings of greatness. Did you really think my interest in your family was because I was just so desperate to have you grate your teeth through every sacred sermon? Or that I was overjoyed at seeing Mary fa—?"

"Don't you mention her name!"

"Ah yes, I was informed of her demise before I set off on my journey here. A sad affair but seeing how it acted as a catalyst for young Charlie, it was a necessary sacrifice. She wanted to serve the Almighty and she has done that in abundance."

Mike said nothing in retaliation but his insides were screaming. His voice, and that of another.

"I could feel just how special Charlie was years ago; all I had to do was wait until the time was right."

"You mean you planned all of this?"

"Of course I did. I was not about to let his power slip through my fingers. I could have procured him when he was younger but the results would not nearly have been as promising and so, I waited until he was ready for me to intervene. I made my arrangements, ensured that your sister-in-law was employed in our educational facility so that your family had a legitimate reason for visiting the area and knowing that wherever his first flare-up occurred, whether here or back home, there would be people on hand to strike. Everything was in place; all I had to do was wait."

"But th—"

"When I got the call earlier that it had finally happened, that six years' worth of planning was finally going to pay off, I raced straight here, delighted with what it meant for the mission."

"You manipulated everything. Everyone."

"Your words are dull and your whole existence is tiresome. You are a gardener but yet you are blind, Michael. Preserving beauty is not enough, it has to be bent to the will of the Almighty. For none shall grow in a garden left to rot."

Father Stringer, bored with his opponent, turned away from Mike and concentrated his attention on the boy who was going to bring his vision into the light.

"Right, m'boy, I think your debut performance has been stalled long enough now. On with the show." He gave a look to Doctor White that told him everything he needed to know. His chastisement would come later and the doctor was thankful to be spared the public humiliation.

As much as he cherished the founder, this crowd was here because of him and his hunt. If they were to see him ridiculed, reduced to nothing but a hollow man, then his power over them would be at an end.

For years, Doctor White had acted with impunity while Father Stringer remained shrouded, protected by his double life. He was the one out there in the hunting grounds, risking everything to advance their position. How could his ego not grow with every successful procurement?

The doctor's word was so readily accepted now that he had fooled himself into thinking it was law, that he was the higher being everyone worshipped. He had risen too far to fall now. To crash back down to Earth and become just another face in the crowd, the nobody he used to be.

Doctor White, determined to take back control of the audience's adoration and attention, continued with the extraction and Charlie's whole body trembled under the glare of the man who was now desperate to rip him open just to hear the applause it would inspire.

Charlie felt his flesh tear and burn around the device being plunged into him, but his insides still refused to give into the deranged demands. Charlie looked to his dad for help but he was still being held down by one of Doctor White's, or rather Father Stringer's, men. The loyal follower who stood by and allowed atrocities to take place before their very eyes.

Mike, watching his son being mutilated in the name of the God that his mother had been so desperate to appease, felt tears flood out of him. All the hatred and confusion that had built in him during his confrontation with Father Stringer now turned inward, opening a gateway for something dark to take hold.

His mind turned sour and his thoughts became rapid, violent and for a reason that was still unknown to him, not his own. The scream that had been imbedded in him less than an hour ago was now shrieking a horrible tune. His head was on fire and his skull began to crack under the weight of the blaring noise.

Through the smoke in his head, he saw a vulnerable child reaching out for help and some shadowed man refusing their hand, opting instead to walk away and condemn them to a life of prolonged misery. When the smoke cleared, he saw the man for who he was, the monster who would abandon an innocent child in a place like this; himself.

The girl, despite everything that had happened against her during her stay in Artemis House, had chosen to trust this stranger. She had looked deep into Michael Rose and, seeing his history play out in full before her eyes, had tried to alert him about Father Stringer's true self but he had been too distracted by the troubles of his own life to heed her warning.

Mike had turned his back on her and now, he would pay the consequences for his ignorance. Two images now implanted themselves into his mind. The first was Charlie as he was back home, happy and so full of life while the second was the little girl from the cage whose spirit and humanity had been crushed out of her.

While he had seen the desperation in her eyes as he looked at her bound body, willing him to set her free, he had not seen the lonely fire that had burned all the hope out of her broken shell. She, with her own unique *gift,* had been beaten, abused and branded by wicked men but it was Michael's inaction that had corrupted her. Too consumed with his own needs, he had allowed this evil to persist and a child, in desperate need of a saviour, was left abandoned once more.

The primal, rushing screams now curdled the blood swimming around his skull until it poured out of his eyes, ears, nose and mouth. Michael Rose, now adorning a thick red mask, collapsed and was dead before he hit the stage floor.

220

The nice, respectable image he had neatly packed into their car just yesterday had now been muddied beyond recognition. His wet, discoloured eyes still locked with those of his son.

# Chapter Forty-Nine

Father Stringer stepped back and was already sure of what, or more precisely who, was responsible for Mike's death. No one looked upon *her* and lived to see another day. The teenage girl in a dead alley had undergone four cleansing rituals before she had really started to shine, the last of which had only enhanced her capabilities. Making her one of the deadliest preys to ever grace Artemis House.

Though it would have been easy to neutralize her threat, every room of the hospital was fitted with miniature gas canisters concealed within the air vents in the ceiling, Doctor White had made the argument to continue with her *treatments*. So long as she remained alive, she could still prove useful.

The uproar from the audience at seeing Mike drop down dead was enough to rouse Bill from his painful rest.

"What the fuck!" He exclaimed when his head stopped spinning. His coarse voice punched outward as all heads turned to the second dead body on the stage. Bill saw Mike's ruined body, a stranger now commanding all the reverence from those around him and Doctor White's face tense up, but above all else, he saw Charlie look absolutely destroyed.

Above the stage, an ornamental clock began to chime.

1—

"It is alright, everything is under control. These men are intruders, obstructers and so, their fate is of no consequence to us. They would deny you these performances and put our mission at risk. Do not let them sour your minds," Doctor White announced.

His voice was calm but every word had to slip past a tongue that was slowly choking on itself. The show had been delayed too long and the looming shadow that was his power was beginning to falter. All that remained behind the mask of his own ego was a man and he would sooner die than reveal his true, plain self.

While everyone looked to Father Stringer for guidance, except Bill who looked on Doctor White's jittery figure with nothing but disgust, Charlie was still focused on his dad's lifeless body. Refusing to shake the thoughts and urges away that were now hammering him from within. A tear escaped his eye before he turned away from his dad, his last hope.

6—7—8—

A memory was unearthed and Charlie was transported back to the bell tower, lost in the grey between visions and reality. Consumed by his own erratic thoughts. Faceless, nameless shadows circled him, preparing their attack and he was caught dead centre.

One hand, smooth from the surgical gloves, gripped his ankle while another, skeletal, took a hold of his shoulder. When he looked up, he saw Doctor White and Father Stringer bearing down on him, their tight clutch bruising his already discoloured skin. They were trying to keep him under control, their control but he struggled against their combined force and ended up choking on his writhing tongue.

9—10—11—

Charlie Rose felt his mind teeter on the edge, swinging violently between calm and chaos. A nightmare come alive.

12.

It landed with an urgent thud in the pit of a primal anger that was now desperate to be unleashed. His soul, seduced by this infestation, was stripped of everything that made him vulnerable, everything that made him Charlie but he was too far in the depths now to do anything other than welcome the intrusion.

His inside shadow was slowly wrapping its grip around him, pulling him down into the dark waters. He had spent what felt like an age flailing; now, it was time to succumb to the anger and drown.

He felt his body swarm with flies, millions bubbling just beneath the surface, sapping his juvenile spirit dry and all intent on escaping. He howled like the beast he had never wanted to be as his body buckled and exploded for the final time.

His skin turned to an aching purple and rippled as all the thorns inside him burst out, breaking through his fragile stem. His muscles bulged and cracked and the chains holding him in place slipped off with ease, as if they were made of silk. The pain of his body being ripped apart dwarfed in comparison to the joy of his true form feeling the free air.

The two men holding him down were flung backward, discarded as if they were nothing. Charlie's soul was laid bare, exposed to the now silent mass and his thoughts were swallowed up by a dark, red mist. His mind was beginning to languish in a darkened cave.

Every eye in the room was still on him, not with burning anticipation, not anymore, but rather a shit-scared realization that the bird was out. The animal was unleashed.

He clattered off the bed and rose up on his new weight. The ground shook under him. His teeth, now fashioned into razor sharp fangs, serrated along his tongue as he tried to speak and only inaudible grunts could be heard by those closest.

Doctor White, quietly retreating behind a couple of his stunned surgical team members, let his eyes scan quickly over this new development and a feeling of sick wonder stole over him. Old habits die hard and even now, he was preparing his next move.

The idea of fleeing, of saving everyone in the theatre (not just the audience and staff but also the private investors who had paid for his pleasure) never entered his mind. Even in the face of Charlie's glistening jaws and blood-streaked body, the hunter would not turn and run. To admit defeat would be the true end of him.

Father Stringer dissected Charlie's every move forward, learning in tandem with his subject just how formidable it now was. It truly was a remarkable opportunity. With Charlie's power harnessed, the war would be over before it began. Victory had never looked so sweet.

All they had to do was subdue the contaminant but once freed, a bird is not so easily put back in its cage. The audience, not knowing whether to cheer or scream, sat in the uncomfortable air, desperate for guidance. They had been promised a show and Doctor White did not disappoint.

Their attention was fixed on the beast and a single look in their direction was all they needed for the cocky, untouchable air that carried them through life to fade. They would receive no protection from their glorious leader or his second-in-command; they were too enamoured by the creature to think about their safety and so, the only thing stopping them from joining the growing pile of corpses on stage was how fast they could run.

Artemis House relied on the steady flurry of the curiously inhumane among high society to keep its mission on track but when faced with certain death, people valued their lives far beyond the ideals of a couple of men who were willing to unleash hell upon them just to keep themselves standing tall.

They all fled for the exit at the back of the room, clawing at one another. Their animal impulses were given free rein as they pushed, shoved and stomped on the unlucky ones who fell. They all shared the same disillusioned sense of humanity and also the same collective thought during the mad dash to the door; it was every man for himself, by whatever means necessary.

"The show has not finished," Doctor White barked but his voice died under the sound of the stampede.

He always took offense to people who left a show before it had concluded. You couldn't put on a show if there was no one around to watch you. He took great pleasure in hunting them down afterward and erasing all their memories of him and the facility.

The facility lived by its secrecy and they had abused the trust placed in them. It was a sadistic task but to Doctor White, it was thrilling. Having the power over someone, manipulating their lives in such an intimate way always ballooned his ego to new heights.

Artemis House would be nothing but a dream to them afterward, with inmates like Charlie Rose lurking in the shadows of their minds, forever stalking, haunting. The hunted would become the hunter. A nightmare that would never die.

"We shall continue. NOW."

Doctor White turned to an understudy, cowering between him and the beast, and instructed him to proceed as normal but as the stage rumbled with every flex of the beast's newly malformed muscles, he witnessed all of his fellow performers abandoning their posts and running away, inflating the already manic crowd.

Charlie looked on as the same people who had fought over each other outside his cell, desperate for a first look at the caged beast, were now being trampled as they were frantic to get away from him. The irony of their stupidity allowed a grin to twist his fractured mouth.

Just like there were two sides to every coin, there were also two sides to every cage, within and without, and the masses had made the mistake of allowing themselves to believe their own lives were superior, that they would always throw heads but a dark cloud was brewing within Charlie's own head.

The rich and elite were preconditioned to believe they were untouchable but as the dozens of audience members scrabbled over the door handle without a conscious thought other than *me first,* they failed to realize that while one pushed one way, another was pulling the opposite way.

Now, they were the ones trapped within, and as Charlie leaped from the stage and soared up the aisles toward the herd, they would soon learn what it felt like to be on the tail end of things. To be the unfortunate one.

The monster launched itself at the back of the herd and took down one of its more cautious members with one effortless swipe. A single wail slipped out of the unlucky man as he crashed to the ground and then stunned himself into a painful silence. The tension inside him building, desperate to release his screams but not daring to make a sound.

Howie, who up till now had remained silent in a desperate hope to blend into the background of the stage and have his betrayal forgotten, continued to kneel, only now it was terror holding him in place. With his tongue cowered at the back of his throat, he looked on as the little boy attacked the crowd.

They were all seconds away from death and there was nothing he could do to help. To stop the atrocity. He was just a man and Charlie, now, truly was the monster he had already judged him to be.

The beast snarled over the fallen man, its thick saliva raining down onto the prey's trembling body, mixing with his sweat and as it shifted its weight, a thorn pierced one of his ankles. The thorn tore through flesh and bone as easy as a knife falling through butter and blood poured out of the hole in the unfortunate man's leg. The pain was enough to vent his screams until his tongue curled up.

The demon sent from hell itself heard the distressing wails from under him and removed the weight from his body. The cry had pierced through some wall in his head and a voice (a squeaky, stuttering voice) was knocking on the other side, saying stop. Pleading to stop.

He may have had the thorns, fangs and scaled skin but he was still just a boy. It was Father Stringer and Doctor White who were the real devils, with Artemis House playing the part of hell on earth.

The walls crumbled and released poor, innocent Charlie from his cage. He grabbed the pendulum with both hands and steered it effortlessly away from the chaos he thought he wanted. It would have been so easy to take revenge on these men who had used and abused him, but that's not what he wanted. He had hurt enough people today already. All he wanted was freedom. He was a bird and all he wanted to do was fly.

Charlie stood and looked out at the panicked, privileged herd (still unable to work out how to open a door) and sped right past them, not even stopping for one final look at his tormentors still on centre stage. They did not deserve his attention. His heaving body tore through the doors with ease and he ran away down a corridor, leaving the true animals trapped in their frenzied confusion.

# Chapter Fifty

Father Stringer, not wanting to be associated with the shambolic turn of events any longer, swiftly left the stage and made his way toward the stairs that led to the observation room. The same stairs that were freely available to the audience members scrambling around helplessly, but their herd mentality had decided their fate for them.

The distinguished, honoured benefactors that had watched from above as the horror show unfolded were nowhere in sight when he entered the booth.

*Deserters.*

Thirty years' worth of planning was now at risk of going up in smoke all because of one impurity. But once *they* enter, there is no leaving.

*Charlie Rose cannot be the exception.*

Father Stringer collected some vital papers from a desk next to the viewing window, now showing the crowd sweating through manic chatter, too afraid to move an inch, and he departed through a door to the rear of the room with a plan still being birthed in his mind. The shameful uncertainty he adorned, reminded him of why he had so easily adapted to working from within the shadows.

"What the hell have you done?" Bill demanded of Doctor White but with his head still throbbing, his voice was now no more than a whimper.

"This is not how it was supposed to go. If it wasn't for your intrusion, then everything would have been carried out as planned. We were minutes away from branding him and so that flare-up would have been conducted under proper direction and safely cleansed. Everything that happens now is down to you." He aimed the last barb in Howie's direction, wanting him to feel the burden. To see what his betrayal had cost them all.

Howie, with a look of distress settling behind his eyes, wanted to turn and run away but the makeshift bandage had slipped sometime during the unexpected interval and he was losing blood, fast. As he tried to stand, pain shot through him as intensely as when the bullet first struck.

"I don't know where you got your screwed-up sense of morality but normal people do not *cleanse* children. Or murder innocent women," Bill spat out, not realizing the slow drip of Michael Rose's blood flowing toward him. The stage was washed out by a mixture of blood, sweat and tears, and now resembled the ruined canvas of a hysterical artist.

"You know nothing of normal people. You confine yourself to a dead-end town and accept the dreary day to day, never daring to change it or yourself. Too scared to jump in case you go too high."

"What do you know about anything?"

"More than you."

"Okay then, tell me this. Why did you kill Rebecca? She was the only thing I had in my life and you took it away." Bill could feel himself about to crack but Doctor White's one-word reply was enough to keep his emotions in check. He would not let this madman see him cry.

"Insurance."

"What the hell does that mean?"

"The sedative that was given to her was different to yours. She had a very special cocktail of my own devising. Would you like to know the secret ingredient?"

"Just talk." It had been too long a day and his tone was too far in the throes of impatience to pull back.

"Rat poison."

It wasn't just the casualness that interrupted Bill's train of thought, but also the cold confusion that he now felt. The sick grin that was growing on Doctor White's blunt face made Bill almost turn and vomit. Almost, but he held firm. He had to know the truth.

"I could have simply waited her out and let the cancer take her, but I couldn't run the risk of a deathbed confession."

"You knew she had cancer?"

"Of course I did. We gave it to her."

His train of thought was hurtling toward him but he was desperate for answers and his feet were frozen solid. He couldn't move. Not until he had justice for Rebecca.

"You really don't know anything, do you?" Doctor White chuckled, revelling in Bill's confusion.

"I don't understand!" Bill exclaimed as his body was torn between panicked bewilderment and seething rage.

"If you play with fire, you're going to get burned. Well, that is what happened to your delightful friend. On one of her visits here, she crossed paths with a remarkable young chap who had a fairly standard gift by our reckoning. Boring for us, but deadly for her. She cared too much about the *patients* and ended up being really quite careless." Now, he was laughing.

"You're not making any sense. What would Rebecca have been doing in a place like this?"

"Working for us," Doctor White responded and the confused look now set into Bill's stony appearance. "She had been on our payroll for quite some time now. One of the things that this grand facility depends on is secrecy and we rely on people like Rebecca to act as our eyes and ears in the outside world.

"Father Stringer had already alerted us to the fact that his *protégé* was going to be in the area and ordered us to anticipate a procurement, just in case of a flare-up. Little did Mike know that when he called your pitiful station about his wife's death that he was unleashing the full might of Artemis House upon his family."

"You're making this shit up. You have to be. Becca was the kindest person around. She would never go along with your cruelty. That wasn't in her nature."

"What do you know of nature? Shall I spell out to you in terms even you will understand? Mike called your station and as soon as he gave the name 'Rose', your darling Becca knew she had to act. She notified us here and I relayed the information to Father Stringer.

"All our plans centred on the beast of a boy and Rebecca played her role beautifully. Truly a wolf in sheep's clothing, but not even a glowing performance was enough to save her. Given how rare a find this was and what it meant for our future, I felt it best to terminate her. It was simpler that way. Safer. I was not going to allow her to tarnish my trophy."

Bill looked at Doctor White with the same level of confusion, convincing himself that they were having two separate conversations. His one about the lovely Rebecca who knew how to laugh at his unfunny jokes and keep him firmly planted in the ground whenever a professional win took his head into the clouds, whereas Doctor White was detailing a seditious, cold-hearted woman. A puppet for the child-catcher that would dance to his tune when called upon.

"It's not true. That's not who she was."

"Perhaps I simply knew her better than you did, Billy boy."

His train of thought had not just been derailed but completely obliterated. On the outside, he may have escaped in one piece but his mind now lay shattered on the tracks. Every piece had a memory of Rebecca, a tiny essence of her impact on his life (her smile, her soft touch, her legs to heaven) but now, they were all stained. Disfigured.

Doctor White had stolen her from him and now sprouted ugly, hateful untruths about her. All his precious memories of her bent out of shape until she was someone he failed to recognize.

He had known her for almost fourteen years. It was impossible to begin to believe a word the madman was saying but the more his thoughts lingered over the doctor's cruel tongue, the more he was forcing himself to accept it. He hated this man in front of him for what he had done to Rebecca but he hated himself more for now thinking such wicked things about her.

Bill opened the gates and let anger flood in, washing away the small stain of doubt that had been troubling him. Traditional justice would never be enough for the likes of Doctor White. Out of the corner of one eye, he spotted something sparkle under the spotlight. It was just a glint but he knew instantly what it was.

The gun. His gun. The junior who had confiscated it must have dropped it in their panicked dash to the exit. He was never one for believing in religion but in that moment, he would have prayed to any god who presented him with this final solution.

He collapsed to his knees and started to crawl toward it, knowing how pathetic it must look to the great hunter behind him but he couldn't let the doctor see it too.

"If you are done wallowing, I have work to do. A rose to harvest. He'll never make it out of the labyrinth alone," Doctor White said and ushered himself past the crumbled mess with the same proud air that he wore like a second skin.

Bill lunged for his gun and was able to get two fingers around it while Doctor White thought he was still some helpless puppy making a scene just because he could.

*Blinded by his ego. Thank you, karma. Now, let's end this!*

He turned and grabbed the doctor by one of his ankles, trying to get a good purchase and pull him down. Bill knew Doctor White was not the type of man to ever beg for his life but he could still lose it all the same. He wanted to see the light, that filthy, discoloured light leave his eyes and smell the rich fear on his breath as he realized he was about to die.

Fear wasn't going to be optional with the plan this time around. Doctor White thrived off the fear he caused in others, their panicked sweats adding an unhealthy shine to his armour, but now, it was his time to fear the reaper.

"What do you think you are doing, you pathetic, little dog?" He asked as his clawed ankles gave way and he collapsed practically on top of Bill.

"What someone should have done a long time ago," Bill answered with a forced throat, aiming the barrel directly into the doctor's chest. His shaking fingers took hold of the trigger and squeezed as tightly as they could; he was practically strangling it.

Jammed. Again.

The doctor's chuckle returned but without the herd's echo to strengthen it up, it died a quick death. Doctor White seized his chance and, looking Bill directly into his stern, determined eyes, slammed his head down into his face. Hard. Blood erupted from Bill's nose and cheek but still, he held firm. Refusing to release the squirming man.

"You will die for everything you've done. For what you did to Rebecca."

"You saw that little bitch every day for years and had no clue that she had a life outside of your menial station. She needed some fun in her life and she wasn't getting any from you. She made that very clear."

"Shut up, you son of a bitch or I'll—"

"You'll what? I'll tell you exactly what you are going to do. Nothing. Because that is what you are. You're like a dog chasing a car. You'll give up before the catch because you haven't got a clue what to do with it. When it's in your sights, you're running on adrenaline and nothing else but when you start to slow down, you realize you are still the same unimportant person you always will be."

Bill panted heavily through the mouthfuls of blood. His face was throbbing and all it took was a little pushback for his grip to be broken. Doctor White stood up, Bill swallowed up by his shadow and strutted over to centre stage.

"You're wrong."

"You came here because of Rebecca but now, you know the truth, so what are you going to do? She betrayed you and everyone around her. You lost an officer today, yes? He died, thinking Rebecca was one of the good ones but in actuality, she was as rotten as they come. You shouldn't be blaming me for putting that bitch down, you should be thanking me."

Bill rolled over and pushed himself up. His face ached but his mind was clear. He took two steps toward the doctor, now smiling, and raised the gun. He said a silent prayer and let out one long breath as he pressed the trigger, twice. The bullets thundered through the air and struck Doctor White precisely where his heart most surely wasn't. His final punishing laugh was killed in his throat and as he fell to the ground, his crooked grin slid clean off his face.

Charlie may have been the star attraction but ultimately, this was his show. His body, lying in centre stage, would slowly bake under the spotlight until his second skin had been burned off, shedding all his glory and revealing, in the end, he was a man like everyone else. Just one whose brain had been monstrously mis-wired.

The hunter had fallen in his own trap and it had finally snapped shut on Doctor Herman White.

# Chapter Fifty-One

Charlie ran through the sterile maze, becoming more frantic with every dead-end he found. The sounds of the stunned herd were slowly dying in the background but he was no nearer to freedom than when he had been chained to the bed. All he could smell was his own animal scent (heavy and pungent) becoming stronger the more frightened he became.

His body was growing tired, his thorns were standing firm but the purple streaks on his skin were starting to lighten. Weakening. He knew they would never fade completely though. It was his war paint, running the length of his body. He had escaped the clutches of the enemy and these were his battle scars to prove it. His very own labyrinth.

The price of a freedom he may never feel.

The hole in his stomach from where he had been partially branded was still seeping with blood. He needed to stem it and his dashing escape was only making it worse but rather than seeking help in this hospital from hell, he ploughed on through the maze. Through the pain.

He had read enough fairy-tale books to know a basic rule of survival; don't get lost and he started using the constant red drips as a trail, so he would never fall down the same rabbit hole twice. He may have escaped the hunter's trap but there was still a whole forest to navigate before he would feel the soft, intimate air of the outside world.

Charlie stopped for a breath in a random corridor that somehow seemed familiar, a corridor littered with portholes. His legs buckled under the stress of his new weight and he felt his mind turn to static. Voices, desperate and afraid but at the same time angry and determined, pushed through the fuzz.

He shook as fast as he could, turning his brain in on itself to try and squeeze out the voices but they just kept on grating. It was more than the *patients* in this corridor alone calling out to him; it was every corridor, every cell and every tortured soul. The whole damned population of Artemis House was crying out at once, screeching one word in unison.

*CHARLIE!*

He remembered what one intrusive voice had done to his dad and did not want to imagine a whole hospital full of noises fighting for the space to stretch out in his fragile mind. Among the cries of anguish was the sound of something different. Someone different.

He took a chance and found he was able to focus on that singular sound. He honed in on it, a beacon of light in this dark circus that guided his feet to the appropriate door three corridors away. Mercifully, it was a room without a porthole. His own world had enough horrors without being forced to suffer through another's crooked vision.

He came to rest outside this saviour door but rather than dulling the pain inside his head, it twisted, swelling with every word now hissing through his ears until the sound became recognizable. The voice may not have been strange anymore but it was anything but soothing.

Something inside him told him the only way to kill the voice that was now slithering around inside his head was to confront the snake head on. Charlie grabbed the handle with both hands, one to turn and one to steady his shaking wrist and opened the door just a crack before the static settled.

Without seeing her constricted face, he knew who was on the other side of the door. Who this cell belonged to. The hissing was coming through as clear as anything now and the dreaded pit in his stomach swelled like a balloon. His throat closed up and as he stood in the now open doorway, he felt like he might burst. One sharp glare was all it would take.

Eve Prentice turned and saw a withered spectre standing in the doorway. At first glance, she saw only the hunched figure, a shadow painted against the white wall backdrop but her serpentine eyes focused instead on the open door. She was free.

After however long of being maliciously confined, she could taste freedom through the coarse air. There was just one obstacle in her way and when it advanced just an inch into the room, she saw who was now blocking her escape. She saw her nephew in all his disfigured glory.

"Stay back! Don't you dare come any closer, you beast," she barked at Charlie, who shivered under her cold gaze.

"P-p-please, help me," Charlie began in agony. The sharpness of his teeth receded and his voice slowly returned to him but the short journey from his throat to his lips made it feel like his mouth was crawling over broken glass. Looking at the hateful way his aunt was staring him down, he felt as though he was back in the humiliating grip of the theatre.

"This is all your fault. Why couldn't you have just stayed in your hole and left my family alone? We were perfect before you came back into our lives." Though her words may have cut deep, she had said them in a voice that was wearing thin. Being locked in the cell with only the sound of her mad delusions echoing back at her had only heightened her insecurities.

"Please, it's Father Str-r-inger. He's here."

"Don't you mention that name! He is a holy man and would never tolerate such extreme actions. He would never allow for me, his most loyal follower, to be imprisoned."

"But he is r-r-responsible for everything that's happening here. This is his h-h-hospit-tal."

"SILENCE!" Eve demanded, refusing to believe the conclusions she had already come to herself. Father Stringer being connected to Doctor White was the only thing that her shattering mind could make sense of but that didn't make it any easier to accept. What did it mean for her and her faith? Was she still being tested? Was she ever?

Her mind was frantically dissecting every word and action of Father Stringer she was ever witness to. He was a man who was able to rip people from the edge of their self-destructive morals and steer them toward the guiding light of the Almighty.

Apollo Prep was a highly selective school, only accepting the best, whether they be staff or student, but Father Stringer was a man who had the influence to pull strings and place her within the strict institution. He was a man who invited worship, not because of his position, but because of his power.

Eve Prentice now saw what had been expertly hidden behind her faith all these years; that she was nothing more to him than one of his puppets and that fact alone filled her with pure anger. The only thing in the room that she could take her frustrations out on, other than herself, was the one who had destroyed her happy, purposeful life. The weed sent to bring her garden to ruin.

To save herself, her children, she must do what was necessary. To Charlie. Once he was removed, the Almighty would protect her family from anyone who would try and tear them apart. Only with the beast gone would everything make sense again.

Charlie was still standing in the doorway, silent and cold. Her words may have been like ice pushing through his shaking stem but that was nothing new and in his adolescent mind, all he saw was his aunt, his family and a small wish was born; that this fairy-tale may yet have a happy ending after all.

"It's time to end this, little one." She paced toward him, her eyes on fire and he quickly learned why his uncle Brian had acted the part of a peacemaker around her. A mouse does not stand up to a snake and live to tell the tale. He may have been naïve but he was not blind. Though she may wish to distance herself from her own persecutors, her glow was all too similar to theirs and Charlie's wish for a happy ending was killed in seconds.

"You are a contamination and I shall be the one to expel you from this mortal life," Eve said with as much force in her throat as she could muster. Her face was plastered with a mixture of hate and horror. She wanted to reach out, for her hands to find his gulping throat but beneath her stern skin was a woman who was suddenly deeply afraid.

For too long, she had been the commander-in-chief in her family, whipping her privates into loyal submission and revelling in every victory but as she faced down the thorned beast, she realized she was worn out by all the battles. She was the last Smythe standing and her legs were beginning to shake.

"A-a-aunt Eve, I'm your f-f-f-family."

*Root and stem! Root and stem!*
*I will do it, Lord. I will do it.*
*I have to do it.*
*Root and stem.*

"I am not a violent person but just look at you. You are no one's family. You could never belong in a normal world. You never have. The world is designed in a pure image and you are the opposite of everything that is right. Impure and inhuman. The only place fit for your kind is the fiery pit you crawled out of."

Charlie looked up at his aunt through dry, sad eyes and knew she would never accept him. Eve lunged both hands for the monster's throat and was able to almost close her fists around it.

*Yes. Grant me the staying power to see your work complete and my garden shall be forever green.*

*I'm doing it.*

*ROOT AND STE—*

A squeal reverberated around the room and down the twisting corridor but with her mind lost to her own fantasies, she failed to realize the pained shrieks were coming from within her own raging body.

Charlie Rose was hugging his aunt and every thorn on the front side of his body had pierced her thick skin. Driving in so deep that they were skin to skin. His touch now a deadly embrace. After a few moments, her consciousness was released, her hands uncoiled from around his throat and she stumbled backward. Looking down, she saw that her body was littered with puncture marks the size of golf balls and blood was quickly being drained out of her.

Although she may have feared doing what had to be done, she had never doubted why she must cut Charlie down and so, it never occurred to her that, even with his new beastly appearance, there was a chance she could fail. She was doing the sacred work of the Almighty. And she was a devout believer.

Failure should never have been an option. Eve was desperate for more and more recognition for her holy work but just like how Doctor White and his entourage were blinded by their inflated pride, she had been blinded by her righteous greed.

Eve collapsed to the floor and the last thing she saw before her eyes lost their red mist and became dull and heavy was Charlie solemnly closing the door to the cell, sealing her off from the world beyond. The walls stayed a visceral white but now, they gave off a cold shine and a greyness was taking over everything.

Would the Almighty grant her a space in the eternal garden when her own had been brought to ruin by that cursed weed? A weed she had failed to remove.

Evelyn Prentice, dying a painful death, was desperate to be proven right about her beliefs but as her body twitched and then stopped for the last time, she was left with a sickening uncertainty. She had abandoned her children in this fruitless pursuit and now, she would never know if it had been worth it. Who would protect them now?

Back in Almost, Brian was fielding frantic questions from his confused and terrified kids with answers he didn't have. He would do his best but with him as clueless as they were, sometimes the best just wasn't good enough.

Their children would forever torture themselves with the thousand reasons of what could have been so important that leaving was Eve's only option. To them, one second she was there, a strong, loving, fiercely devoted mother and the next, she was none of those things. She was simply gone.

# Chapter Fifty-Two

Charlie stood outside the room and wanted to scream until his lungs exploded, but he could only choke on his own absent squeals, his body teeming with a hatred that was completely foreign to him and directly aimed at his own twitching shell.

He had stolen the lives of three people and the guilt and shame took hold of him with an unrelenting grip. He was no longer the innocent twelve-year-old boy that he had been twenty-four hours ago; he had changed. Transformed into the monstrosity everyone feared him to be and he hated himself for it.

Despite his mind reeling from exhausted terror, he found it all too easy to decide on what would come next. He cursed his wretched, deformed body and wanted to rid himself of this burden.

A voice inside his head, determined and tinged with a flat tone, told him to carry on walking down the corridor and so he did, never looking back toward the cage that was now a coffin. That door may not have had a porthole but it now contained a horror like all the rest.

His feet carried him through the corridors as if he had made this journey a thousand times before, never doubting which way to turn when faced with a myriad of avenues. He soon ended up in the reception area and just ahead of him, he could see the double doors that led outside. Freedom was a mere ten feet away.

Charlie, draining the last of his childlike innocence, burst through the doors and felt a cool midnight breeze sweep across his face. He was free to run, free to fly, free to do whatever he wanted but as he looked out toward the car park under the empty, blackened sky, he felt trapped all over again.

How could he ever live a normal life when out there was a swarm of people with their secret cravings concealed well beneath the surface of their ordinary lives? How could he ever live a normal life when he could never be normal?

Each car that circled him in thick darkness belonged to someone who had cheered at his pain, revelled in his misery and applauded his torture. The world inside his head may have been fractured but it was this cold sprawling mass that made him shiver.

He now knew why Doctor White had been so intent on branding him. He was their property. He was weak, tired and a child. Where could he run that they would not follow? Artemis House had wicked, masterful hunters at their disposal.

There was nowhere he could hide, live, exist where they would not track him down. Going home was never going to be an option; that would just be delivering himself into Father Stringer's dark clutches. They had his scent now and they would never stop trying to reclaim what they truly believed to be theirs. Their belief had replaced their morality and he knew he would never be safe. Never be free.

He would never see Legacy Comics again. Or the clubhouse, though something told him that he would be forgotten all the same.

Charlie crouched down and hid, from himself, like he did in the police station. Only this time, there would be no reprieve, his body would not switch back to its safe, predictable, boring self. He may look like something straight out of a horror show but his heart was still very much that of a twelve-year-old boy. It didn't matter that he could now spread his wings, he knew he would never fly. All he could do was fall.

They had taken him and put him in a cage but there was still one thing that he could take back from them. One thing in his life that he had any control over. His death.

With a final flourish, he gripped the largest thorn he could find, saw it glistening under the emerging Christmas moon and twisted hard until it snapped clean off, scratching his hand in the process but the pain was muted. He rose his hand out in front of him as far as he could reach and with a calm yet firm grip, he swung it back toward his stomach, plunging the thorn deep inside.

The thorn skewered his adolescent stem and splintered into a dozen pieces. Charlie collapsed to his knees, his hands slapping hard against the chilled tarmac. This last act brought no pain. Like his screams and tears, he was truly empty. Everything about him had been sucked dry by the monstrosity that was Artemis House.

His broken body only shuddered as he saw the blood, rose red, flow freely out. A little at first, just enough to bury the facility's branding on his side under a thick blanket, and then a little bit more until he was knee-deep in a lake of his making. His breaths grew shorter and his mind phased in and out of consciousness as a seemingly never-ending stream surged around him.

He was growing weaker by the second. All he had to was lie down and be swallowed up by the crimson river. All the people who had scorned and sneered at him throughout his life now had a heavy hand on him, pulling him under its clotted current but he made no attempt to fight them off. All the fight and hope had been purged out of him. This was his fate and he would gladly welcome it. His mother would be so proud.

People had always judged him at first sight, whether it was Mrs Finch from across the street, Nick and Denny in the clubhouse or even his own parents in the comfort of his own home. Other people's prejudices was the real shadow he would never be able to shake off.

His body may have changed but his eyes had stayed their silvery-blue self. People would look at him and see only a monster staring back, mistaking his cries for help as the mad, raving howls of a beast gone wild. He had zero chances of escaping that heart-breaking fact.

That truth hit him harder than any backhand ever could and left him colder than any bracing wind. This is who he was, scarred and bruised. This is who he had always been but he refused to be a spectacle for other people's amusement any longer. The show was over.

He'd rather die quickly and prematurely than face a lifetime of merciless and callous judgement. He didn't need the thorns or scales to know that. All they did, apart from tear his life apart, was show him the true nature of people.

To *them*, Charlie Rose would always be a beast.

A monster.

An outcast.

# Epilogue

The herd was still frantically hovering close to the theatre entrance, too terrified to step one foot beyond that hallway in case they became lost in the wilderness. Now, if they heard the thundered step of the monster returning to finish what it started, then they could easily dash back inside, but with the doors coming away from the hinges, all they would be able to do was pray. How long would their fear hold them in place? Never daring to risk their safety for the sake of their freedom. The rest of their lives?

While they all cowered at every imagined sound echoing through the white forest, Bill had ventured farther than the length of his own shadow. Howie wanted to escape but the fear of betraying his masters once again was too strong for him to ignore and so, he stayed still in the hope that he would simply fade into the fabric of the theatre walls.

Though Bill had seen Charlie attack the group of amoral men when he leaped from the stage, he also saw quite clearly how he had simply chosen to walk away. If Charlie really was the monster he appeared to be, then he would easily have wiped them all out and still had plenty of time to make his escape. He wasn't a deranged beast after all; he was just a child. One that was more afraid than anyone else in this house of horrors.

Bill came upon the beginning of the blood trail and discovered that all the resentment he had had for Charlie was now replaced with a concern that he wanted to believe had always been there, just discreetly filed away to the back of his mind.

A deeper dive into his own subconscious would tell him he was absolutely wrong, that he had been as easily corrupted by fear and anger as everyone else. For that fact alone, he owed it to the boy to follow the trail of blood wherever it may take him.

Bill descended a set of stairs, twisted around corridors and blindly walked past the final resting place of Eve Prentice, not stopping to consider why the drops at this particular point were heavier and more scattered than the rest of the trail. With Doctor White dead and the herd still lingering by the theatre, corralled by their own fear, he told himself the danger was over.

Father Stringer had appeared while he was unconscious but Bill just assumed he was another of Artemis House's deluded staff; one that had buckled and ran when the tide had turned against them. Bill never would discover his true identity.

All he had to do now was find Charlie. It took twenty minutes before he reached the reception area, still as deserted as when he had arrived a lifetime ago. The drops of blood were starting to thin but he allowed himself a smile when he saw them continue right up to the doors that led outside.

*You did it, Charlie. Good for you, kid. You freed yourself.*

Bill headed outside and felt his insides instantly turn on him with vomit starting to swill with a watery unease. Less than ten feet from the door, the trail stopped dead and illuminated under the pale glow of moonlight was the body of Charlie Rose.

Bill knelt down beside the child he had failed to protect. He knew he was gone but he reached out all the same, his hands finding a small patch of skin that was mercifully spared from his thorns but nonetheless streaked in a dying purple. Charlie's body was as cold as the midnight air, all the warmth that flowed through the small boy had emptied. Now, he was nothing more than a broken shell lying in a pool of blood.

Bill opened his mouth to vent his piercing screams, but they were all swallowed up by the iced wind pushing its way into his trembling mouth. It was painful but it was no less than he deserved.

All he wanted was to pick Charlie up and take him away from this cursed hospital (back into the land of reality where children weren't the playthings of men with more money than mercy), but he couldn't wrap his arms around the body without his skin being ripped apart by the thorns. Death had done little to dent their ends.

His soul protested, but he knew he had to leave Charlie behind. There was no other way, and as he stood up and began to walk toward his car, he looked back at the boy and whispered an apology before he, too, turned his back on him.

He dropped down into his car and as he sped away, his mind twisted with everything that had happened today. He had failed Charlie when he was alive but there was still something he could do to try and make things better, though something told him that it would never be enough.

The image of Charlie Rose would be seared onto his brain, haunting his every painfully silent moment. Never granting him peace. Peace was a reward he had no right to claim and so, he would gladly welcome the constant reminder of how he had let everyone around him down. He had failed too many people today. Mendez, Becca, Mike.

*Charlie.*

Living with collateral damage was just part of the job. It always had been. It was a thought that would wriggle itself inside his mind, boring out holes (small at first, hardly noticeable, but over time, deepening into great fissures) but this time, it was different. Charlie was by no means a small hole. If he had started as a great chasm, just what would he become?

He asked himself what would happen now to the children like Charlie. The ones with the special *gifts*. Anything had to be better than what he had witnessed in Artemis House.

*Surely.*
*Definitely.*
*Maybe.*

Bill arrived back at the police station just after one in the morning and was met by the same scene of carnage that he had left behind hours ago; a scene he had desperately tried to forget. His eyes met Becca's collapsed body and every word Doctor White tried to spit about her now fell flat. He pushed out all encroaching thoughts, upholding her glowing image and forbidding her memory to be tarnished with such darkness.

He could not imagine coming into work day after day, walking by the place where Rebecca had laughed, where she had teased him, and finally where she had died and carrying on as normal. He would do right by Charlie, knowing full well it was only a desperate attempt to wash his conscience clean and see that Artemis House was brought to ruin.

Preferably burned to the ground with Doctor White's decaying corpse still splayed out on centre stage and then round up the herd whose ugly cheers were still ringing in his ears but then, his time in the police force would be at its bitter, uncomfortable end.

To continue to *serve and protect* was just laughable and he would not desecrate the memories of all those suffering children by turning this whole sorry affair into some cheap joke. Sergeant Bill Woodley, who had served eighteen years faithfully, dutifully, had reached the end of his rope.

It took a further six hours of harangued phone calls with superiors and officials before he was taken seriously about the circus he had witnessed. It was early Christmas morning and no one was expecting to be awakened by a tale of institutional murder.

No one believed a place like Artemis House could exist with its tortured practices because ordinary people didn't go about experimenting on children for the sake of their faith.

His voice had been tired before he made the first call to DI Burrows and as he finally pushed through on what felt like his hundredth call, he was able to demand action be taken. He was about ready to drop until the New Year, but his second demand was that he be allowed to join the raid.

He was exhausted, grieving and wounded, but he owed it to Charlie and all the other children still trapped there to see that justice was done in their names. To prove to them all and himself a little, that there was still such a thing as right and wrong. Even if that meant facing the consequences of his own actions.

He had made a lot of mistakes today, but one thing he was confident on was that killing Doctor White was not one of them. He may have acted out of revenge, but some people were just too dangerous to be allowed to live. Did that make him any better than the mad doctor or the scores of people who got off on the sight of child mutilation?

He didn't know; all he knew was that anyone who could operate unimpeded in a torture chamber was more than capable of buying their way out of any legal entanglement. Doctor White may have been a power-mad dictator but that just made it all the easier for him to slip through the net and carry on his cycle of abuse.

The longer he lived, the more children would be at risk. He didn't want another Charlie on his conscience; frankly, one was too many but he had made his bed and now, he would have to lie in it, night after night, painfully awake, staring at the empty blackness of the sky. No stars, just shadows.

At just after nine in the morning, when all the cavalry was roused from the comfort of their pits and substantially briefed, though there were still some within the ranks who doubted the tall tale, Bill led the advance against Artemis House but what greeted them was not the circus that he had left just hours ago.

Daylight had crept over the hospital in his absence and now, everything was different. Thick, blackened smoke was rising behind the building but his focus was concentrated on the hospital itself.

A fleet of seven cars had pulled into the parking lot and each car had more than enough space to breathe. As soon as the engine was killed, Bill sprang from the vehicle and charged over to the entrance.

The spot where Charlie had fallen was now as bare as the parking lot that greeted them. Bill began to get a sinking feeling, but he forced his face to remain its neutral self. The ground had also been extensively cleaned as the river of blood was nowhere in sight.

"He was right here. The Rose boy died right where we're standing."

"You're sure?"

"Of course I'm sure." His face may have been featureless but his voice, still wearing thin, was sharp. "Someone's moved him."

"Don't worry, Bill. We'll get to the bottom of this."

They all headed inside and the white intensity had subsided but the walls were now touched by an eerie shine.

"Which way to this theatre?" DI Burrows asked as her eyes scanned a dozen different avenues.

"I-I-I don't know," Bill admitted. The trail of blood was gone. Bill caught a few murmurs from the lower ranks and chose to shy away from their contempt rather than face it.

It would take a further eight hours and an extra three teams drafted in from disgruntled, neighbouring counties to scour over every inch of the hospital. In total, close to a hundred people descended upon the house of horrors but the result of that extensive, exhaustive operation was nothing.

They swept through the hospital, the ghost town as it now appeared, always in groups of at least five to ensure no one got lost or left behind and found not a single sign of the place having ever been inhabited.

They discovered every cell door was open, including the very one that Charlie had closed himself, but there was not a soul to be found within the immaculately clean rooms; though a subtle green mist was circulating around the vents in the ceilings.

The halls were barren and Bill, eventually, found the theatre but it was as deserted as the rest of the hospital. Centre stage was also washed of all remnants of life and the body of Doctor White could not be unearthed.

The teams withdrew, with everyone chastising Bill for this wild goose chase. If he had been right, it would have been the discovery of the century but now, they all just looked completely foolish for entertaining such a wild theory. If he hadn't already decided to hang up his uniform, it would probably have been forcibly taken from him.

Everyone assumed that losing Rebecca was too much for him to take but after having their Christmases wasted, there was very little sympathy for him. In the time it had taken him to somewhat convince the people at Central of the reality of Artemis House and gather the troops, someone, or more likely a team of people, had been busy.

As hard as he tried to think of the mysterious man who had escaped through the observation room, he came up empty. The hospital had always been soulless but now that sinking feeling disturbed Bill even more. The facility survived on its secrecy and now, the only knowledge of it resided with a man who was set to be ridiculed by all who knew him. A man who was at the end of his rope.

He sat in the back of a car as they all departed for the well-earned comforts of home; he refused to believe that he had imagined the events of the previous day. The hospital may have been empty on his return but just hours ago, it had been a beast of a building with unthinkable terrors contained within. That he was sure of.

Bill was so consumed with shame and self-doubt that he was still oblivious to the smoke that was rising behind Artemis House. The furnace had been the only room in the entire hospital with a lock on its door and the team who came upon it were too weary and annoyed to think it was significant.

*Of course, there would be a lock on this door. That's just common sense. It means nothing.*

Fire brewed in the belly of the beast and the forest was now ash, taking all its secrets with it. The nightmare of Charlie Rose had begun in a bell chamber, and now, it ended in a smoke chamber. Maybe now, he could fly. He had been so close to getting away. He had been almost free.

Almost.